The Inventors
and
the Lost Island

The Inventors
and
the Lost Island

A. M. MORGEN

LITTLE, BROWN AND COMPANY
New York Boston

Copyright © 2019 by Glasstown Entertainment
Map illustrations by Diana Sousa
Map image copyright © Oleg Golovnev/Shutterstock.com

Cover art copyright © 2019 by Iacopo Bruno. Cover design by Karina Granda.
Cover copyright © 2019 by Hachette Book Group, Inc.

Little, Brown and Company
Hachette Book Group
1290 Avenue of the Americas, New York, NY 10104
Visit us at LBYR.com

First Edition: April 2019

Little, Brown and Company is a division of Hachette Book Group, Inc. The Little, Brown name and logo are trademarks of Hachette Book Group, Inc.

Library of Congress Cataloging-in-Publication Data
Names: Morgen, A. M.
Title: The inventors and the lost island / A. M. Morgen ; map illustrations by Diana Sousa.
Description: First edition. | New York ; Boston : Little, Brown and Company, 2019. |
Summary: George and Ada embark on a journey to the Galápagos to restore George's family name and save the world from Don Nadie, head of the nefarious Society of Nobodies.
Identifiers: LCCN 2018022799 | ISBN 9780316471534 (hardcover) |
ISBN 9780316471527 (ebook) | ISBN 9780316471558 (library edition ebook)
Subjects: | CYAC: Adventure and adventurers—Fiction. | Buried treasure—Fiction. |
Lovelace, Ada King, Countess of, 1815–1852—Fiction. | Inventors—Fiction. | Scientists—Fiction. | Orphans—Fiction. | Galapagos Islands—History—19th century—Fiction.
Classification: LCC PZ7.1.M66983 Inm 2019 | DDC [Fic]—dc23
LC record available at https://lccn.loc.gov/2018022799

ISBNs: 978-0-316-47153-4 (hardcover), 978-0-316-47152-7 (ebook)

Printed in the United States of America

LSC-C

10 9 8 7 6 5 4 3 2 1

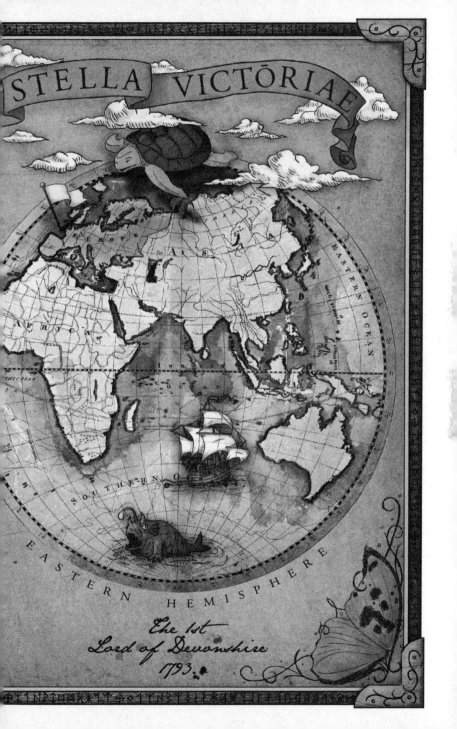

Chapter One

Nothing good ever came of a house with no front door.

That was what George, the 3rd Lord of Devonshire, was thinking to himself as he strode out the back entrance of his house at No. 8 Dorset Square. All around him, the late-afternoon sun slanted through the trees and made the glass windowpanes of the doorless No. 10 blaze with golden light. His former neighbors, the Mallard sisters, had moved out rather suddenly a week ago, after receiving a generous offer from an unknown buyer. The mansion had been leveled to the ground before the sisters had finished loading their trunks into a moving wagon. Already, the brick walls of a brand-new house had risen in its place.

A brand-new house with absolutely no front door.

George breathed in deeply. The air was crisp and fresh. Graceful starlings flitted through the dimming sky before settling down in the trees for the evening. But No. 10 stuck out like an unsightly blemish in the otherwise perfect neighborhood.

George, who had been the unluckiest boy in all of London, knew that odd things should not be ignored, because they might be dangerous. Even Ada Byron, his genius neighbor and new best friend, had agreed that such a strange house meant trouble, though they had conflicting theories about why.

George was convinced that the owner of No. 10 was a rival truffle farmer who was after him—or, more specifically, after his truffle business. The leaky attic of No. 8 had proven to be the perfect environment for growing the valuable fungi, so it seemed reasonable that the new owners of No. 10 were truffle farmers looking to reproduce the unique environment of George's attic by building a greenhouse and seeding their own operation with George's precious truffles. A greenhouse had no use for a front door.

Ada's theory, however, frightened George more than the thought of truffle thieves. Her theory was that the house's owner belonged to the Society of Nobodies, the criminal organization that had stolen Ada's inventions and chased them across Europe in pursuit of George's treasure map. Ada suspected that No. 10 did have a front door but that it was hidden by complicated mechanisms meant to discourage intruders.

That was why George was setting a trap at his house for the owner of No. 10. Ada was setting her own specially designed trap across the street at her house, No. 5. How else would they know who was right?

Whistling casually, George retrieved a tall ladder from his garden shed and hoisted it onto his shoulder. He held it carefully to avoid the sticky barnacle glue that he'd borrowed from Ada and smeared on the rungs the night before. In plain sight of No. 10, George leaned the ladder against the side wall of his house as if he were going to do some home repairs. To further entice potential truffle thieves, he began chatting loudly to Mrs. Daly, his manservant Frobisher's pet rat who resided in the walls of No. 8, about the incredible truffle crop he was about to harvest. The thieves lying in wait inside No. 10 wouldn't be able to resist climbing the ladder to sneak into his attic now, he thought smugly.

To his shock, Mrs. Daly answered in a muffled voice. "Hmmhoo, Oorge."

3

George then realized it wasn't the rat's voice he heard. It was Ada's voice, floating through the front door from the speaking tube she had recently installed between their houses. George rushed inside to the trumpet-shaped porcelain mouthpiece sticking out of the wall, next to the front door. "Hello? Ada? Is that you?"

"Are you finished setting your trap?" Ada's voice sounded hollow and tinny.

George grinned. "Yes. Come over and I'll prove you wrong."

"Don't hold your breath. I'm always right," she chirped.

The speaking tube went silent. A shiver raced up George's spine. If Ada was right, a formidable enemy lurked behind the windows of No. 10.

The Society of Nobodies was a gang of vicious thieves Ada had once called the Organization. They had used stolen science to make weapons that could crack a pirate ship in half and machines that could fly through the air or swim underwater. George and Ada, along with their friends Oscar and Ruthie, had barely survived their last encounter with the Society. If the Society was next door, then...well, George couldn't even fathom what it might mean for their safety.

Someone tapped on his shoulder, and he screamed.

"Sorry," said the messenger who'd stepped in through the front door while George's back was turned. "Didn't mean to interrupt your . . . conversation with the wall. I'm here for the—"

"Special delivery for the King?" asked George breezily, as if he hadn't been caught talking into a wall. By now, he knew better than to try to explain Ada's inventions to strangers. They only became more confused. "Yes, I have it right here. One moment."

He darted up to the attic and returned with a smooth, polished wooden box. The engraved words on top, DEVONSHIRE TRUFFLES, seemed to wink in the light of the setting sun. "Please make sure this package arrives at Windsor Castle safely."

"Of course, sir," said the messenger, his eyes bulging— either because he was impressed by the lovely box or because he was trying not to gag from the smell of the truffles inside. To some people, truffles smelled heavenly. To others, they stank. The messenger bowed, then tucked the very fancy box and its very odorous contents into his leather bag.

George ambled to the library to record his latest royal order. He lifted the tip of his quill to record the King's purchase in his accounts ledger—

And was immediately interrupted by a jarring *THUMP* that shook the walls of his house. George's inkpot rattled on the desk. Ada's giant mechanical frog made quite a racket whenever she landed it on his roof. Seconds later, her footsteps rang out on the stairs, followed shortly by the sound of her flutelike voice echoing in the foyer. "George?"

"In the library!" he called out.

Ada appeared in the entryway and paused, smiling. George heard the *clack clack* of several hard-boiled eggs knocking against one another inside the pockets of her yellow dress.

Instead of hello, she said: "Did you get a new clock, Lord Devonshire?"

George frowned. "Not yet. It takes time to refurnish a house."

Ada cupped her hand to her ear. "That is so strange. I could have sworn I heard a clock chiming *wronnnng, wronnnng* as I was coming down the stairs."

"Ha-ha. Very funny. You're the one who's going to be wrong," George said smugly. "I couldn't help but notice, though, that your trap isn't set up yet."

Ada tilted her head to one side, an amused smile lifting

her cheeks. One of her loose curls fell across her face. "My trap's been set for hours."

George scrunched his brow in confusion. He pushed back the curtain to see Ada's house from the window. "I don't see anything unusual except your maid still sitting on the front steps."

Ada laughed. "That's not the maid. That's the trap! Remember the automaton you bought me?"

"Of course! From the Jaquet-Droz workshop in Geneva." George had first seen the organ-playing automaton while they were looking for the Star of Victory in Geneva. She resembled a human woman, but like everything sold in his grandfather's favorite workshop, she was a piece of clockwork made up of gears and mechanisms. With his truffle money, George had bought the machine as a birthday present for Ada. "You named her Hippolyta, or was it Cleopatra?"

"Neither. I named her Hypatia after my favorite mathematician. But I call her Patty now. Don't you recognize her?" she said, nodding out the window.

"That's her!" George squinted in surprise at the figure sitting as motionless as a statue in front of No. 5. Her face was white porcelain and framed with tight blond curls.

7

George had first noticed the automaton because of her unique pendant in the shape of a butterfly, which looked exactly like a drawing on his grandfather's map. Though he couldn't see it from so far away, he could picture its silver wings. It was another mysterious clue that George would probably never decipher. Had his grandfather copied it on purpose? The 1st Lord of Devonshire loved puzzles.

"She's the most wonderful present I've ever had," Ada gushed. "She's an amazing machine. Her arms are controlled by the gears in her back, so I can program them to perform any sequence of movements. There's no end to what she can do—repairs, navigation, maybe even surgery one day. And she'll be perfect to control my new water cannon."

"She's your trap?" George asked.

Ada raised a gleeful eyebrow. "I made it look as if she had been delivered earlier but no one was home to accept the package. I've rigged her arm to throw a lasso around anyone who walks up the steps toward her."

"That's quite clever. She's excellent bait," George remarked grudgingly. She was the perfect thing to lure the Society. Anyone else walking by wouldn't give Patty a second glance, but the Society of Nobodies loved complicated machines. Turning to Ada, he said, "It's a shame you won't have a chance to see Patty in action, since the owner of No. 10 isn't the Society."

Ada sniffed in disagreement. "I hope you're right. Really, I do. I'd rather it not be the Society after what they put us through in Venice and how ruthless they were about your grandfather's map. But if you were being logical, you'd see that my theory makes more sense. The Society wanted your grandfather's map. They didn't get what they wanted. Therefore—"

"Therefore, they have no reason to come after me anymore," George interjected quickly. "Let's go up to the roof and wait. I made us some sandwiches, and there's a pot of stew on the stove," he added to change the topic to something that didn't make his stomach sour with nerves. The thought of Roy, the redheaded brute from the Society, living next door after trying to kill him was enough to ruin his appetite completely.

While George stoppered his ink bottle and wiped the nib of his feather pen clean, Ada ran her hands along the empty shelves in the library, collecting dust on the edge of her palm. "Are you sure I can't store some of my instruments here? With all the work I'm doing for C.R.U.M.P.E.T.S., my room is full to bursting," she said.

George busily tidied his desk. "This is a library, not a pantry. I have truffles in my attic. I don't want crumpets on my bookshelves. Besides, if we keep any more pastries in the house, Mrs. Daly will invite all her rat friends over for a feast, and Frobisher will insist that we keep them. Oscar may like living in a menagerie, but I don't."

Ada's face fell at the mention of Oscar's name. An undertow of sadness tugged at George's chest, too. He often had to remind himself that his friends Oscar and Ruthie no longer lived a few miles away at the royal menagerie in the Kensington Palace gardens. Once, it had seemed like the journey of a lifetime for George to leave his house and cross the street. But now that Oscar and Ruthie were sailing the seven seas with Oscar's father, Captain Bibble, his friends felt as far from Dorset Square as the stars in the sky.

Ada brushed her brown curls out of her face, discreetly wiping away a tear at the same time. "You and Oscar are always thinking about food. I didn't say crumpets. I said C.R.U.M.P.E.T.S. The Council for Radical Undertakings in Mathematics, Physics, Engineering, Technology, and Science."

"The council for . . . ?" George asked. He knew the next

word wasn't *radishes*, but he couldn't remember what it was. Ada was right. He was always thinking about food.

Ada sighed. "It's a brand-new scientific gathering happening in London. I received an invitation to submit an invention for consideration. If I get accepted, I'll finally be able to prove to my mother that my inventions are worth something. She thinks I'm wasting my time making sloppily built toys instead of devoting my mind to *serious* scientific pursuits."

Ada pulled the invitation from her pocket and put it under George's nose with a flourish. It was printed on creamy white paper and stamped with a gold wax seal in one corner. The date was less than two months away. The location was London. A specific address would be revealed to those who accepted the invitation.

The invitation certainly looked impressive to George, but he wasn't sure Ada's mother would feel the same. Though Ada's inventions were the most wonderful things that George had ever seen, Lady Byron had forbidden Ada to make any more flying machines after her mechanical bird had crashed into the Adriatic Sea. She even insisted that the frog, which had jumped back and forth between No. 5 and No. 8 a million times with no problems, must have a safety harness and an extra braking mechanism. If Ada needed some space away from her mother to build her invention for C.R.U.M.P.E.T.S., then it was George's duty as a friend to help. "Of course there's room for you to store your instruments here," he said, smiling at Ada. "But first, will you join me for dinner?"

In the kitchen, George placed two bowls of truffle stew on a serving tray next to a neatly stacked pile of cucumber sandwiches. Frobisher usually prepared their meals, but the man-servant had left for a well-deserved and much-needed vacation at a curative health spa in Vienna. After spending many years at sea as a pirate called Jon the Gardener, Frobisher had developed a terrible case of land sickness when he gave up piracy, and he needed help recovering his land legs. When Frobisher returned from the spa, a brand-new identity would be waiting for him so that his former life as a pirate would be completely erased. All legally arranged by Ada, of course.

They carried their sandwiches and stew up the narrow stairs to the attic, snuffing out all the lights on the way, then climbed out onto the roof to wait for their prey in the shadow of Ada's jumping machine. The contraption vaguely resembled the bottom half of a giant frog or equally large grasshopper, with two long legs that were bent nearly double at the knee joints. Coiled tightly between the legs, the machine's two massive springs were waiting to vault over Dorset Square when they were released, calculated to alight precisely on the matching landing pad on Ada's roof across the street. Though he told himself that the Society had not moved in next door, George threw a tarpaulin over the frog to hide it from view. Just in case.

Darkness fell around them like a blanket. As the stars began to twinkle through the breaks in the clouds gathering overhead, George felt a familiar jumble of excitement and fear prickling in his gut. Something could happen at any moment. Ada adjusted the telescope aimed at her front steps, and George secured the top of his sticky ladder to the gutter, but otherwise it could have been any night spent with a friend. They ate their food and wrapped themselves in quilts to keep warm while they minded their traps like two fishermen waiting for fish to bite.

A few carriages rumbled by, sleepy starlings tittered in the trees, some stray cats yowled in a far-off alley. Soon George's eyelids became heavy. His chin nodded toward his chest. The sound of the wind rustling through the leaves was a beautiful lullaby. With any luck, he'd sleep peacefully all night under the stars and in the morning his ladder would be empty and Patty would be on Ada's front porch, safe and sound.

Suddenly, Ada was shaking his arm. "Wake up! They're here!"

George jolted awake. Ada glared at No. 5, her eyes burning bright as the gas lamps dotting Dorset Square. "It's not a truffle farmer. It's the Society. One of them got Patty's arm. He's heading for No. 10. Hurry."

A shiver of dread shook through George like an earthquake. He looked across Dorset Square. Patty had fallen onto her side. The dark shape of a man raced through the trees away from Ada's trap. But the figure was like something out of a nightmare—he streaked over the grass on thin legs as tall as fenceposts. Patty's disembodied arm dangled behind him like a worm twisting on a fishing line.

In ten long strides, the man crossed Dorset Square and disappeared around the side of No. 10.

"After him!" Ada cried. She was already climbing down from the roof into the attic.

George raced after her, and soon they emerged onto the lawn and skidded to a halt, eyes searching for any sign of the shadowy figure.

"Did you see how tall he was? I didn't calibrate Patty's strength properly to account for someone of that extreme height. Patty's horizontal grip is stronger than her shoulder joint. Her arm sheared off with the rope when the man ran away. He must have gone inside," Ada whispered breathlessly, then vaulted toward No. 10.

George grasped Ada's skirt to pull her back. "Wait—shouldn't we get something to defend ourselves with?"

"There's no time. Our new neighbor is the Society. We can stop them once and for all. Here. Now. Patty's arm is the evidence we need to charge them with trespassing." Ada peeked around the edge of the house. "The coast is clear. I'm going."

She lifted her skirts and raced across the muddy strip of dirt that separated George's house from No. 10. George knew Ada well enough to know that nothing he could say would stop her from charging into danger.

So he took a deep breath and plunged after her.

Chapter Two

"A re you sure he went this way?"

Ada shushed him, then crept closer to No. 10. George followed at her heels. The shadows between No. 8 and No. 10 seemed to stretch and grab at their feet.

After searching for a few seconds, Ada whispered, "Eureka," pointing at a sheet of corrugated tin nailed against the side of No. 10 that faced George's house. The tin sheet was swinging slightly like a pendulum. Ada gestured at George to help her push it to one side and prop it open with a loose brick. Doing so revealed a large rectangular opening a few feet above the ground. The bricks had not yet been laid to close it off completely.

Peeking inside the black opening, George saw a narrow

hallway that stretched into the dark house. There was no sign of the man who'd run off with Patty's arm.

"I didn't notice this before. That metal sheet must have been blocking the only way inside," George muttered, trying to keep the fear from his voice.

"Help me up," Ada said. Her smooth-bottomed shoes were slipping against the brick as she tried to climb up to the opening. George offered his knee as a foothold, and once Ada was inside, she pulled him up after her.

George's skin exploded with goose bumps as soon as he stepped inside. The walls on either side of him were still in the process of being plastered. Dust coated the floor. With a jolt of fear, George realized he and Ada were leaving footprints behind them, but the tall man had left none.

"Do you see Patty's arm? Let's just grab that and go—"

"Not yet," Ada replied. At the end of a short hallway, the walls opened suddenly into one enormous room, which was about the size of George's entire house. The weak orange light from the street lamps outside did not reach the ceilings, which vaulted nearly to the roof. A narrow balcony ran the length of the entire room above their heads, but there were no stairs to reach it.

"One room? What sort of house is only one room?" Ada wondered aloud.

"I don't know. Maybe it's supposed to be a ballroom. Or a library. Or both."

With a shiver, George had the sudden feeling that he'd been here before. Though he couldn't quite place it, the room was familiar. He stopped. Squares of white marble were being installed in the floor, gleaming in the gloom as if lit from within. The tiles were similar in color to the marble in George's foyer. No—they were the same exact color, a shade called Unicorn Horn. George had spent years polishing the marble in his home—he'd recognize it anywhere.

The strange shiver crawled over his skin again as he surveyed the rest of the room. Every wall was lined with wooden shelves painted white. The decorative molding on the shelves was the same intricate pattern of oak leaves carved on the cornices of George's foyer.

"Ada..."

"There's Patty's arm. Oh dear, it's cracked. I'll need to reinforce her joints with iron bolts, I think." Ada rushed toward a pile of crates covered in a sheet. She picked up Patty's white porcelain arm from where it lay near the base of the boxes. The rope was draped over it like a dead snake. She stomped in frustration. "There's no sign of anyone here. I think he escaped."

Meanwhile, George was drawn to a set of bookshelves on the far side of the room. A row of narrow drawers for maps topped a set of tall shelves for atlases. He was not an expert on shelves, but their size, dimensions, and general appearance were so similar to those in his own library that he had to blink to assure himself that he wasn't dreaming. It was as if these shelves, in a completely different house, were made to hold his grandfather's collection of books.

George peered at a small crescent-shaped indentation near the front of the middle shelf on the third row from the left. Though his grandfather had restored it from the ground up, No. 8 was the 1st Lord of Devonshire's childhood home, so he had preserved it exactly as *his* father had originally designed it. And because George's grandfather had also loved puzzles, many rooms were filled with secret compartments and places to hide his treasures. If George was wrong about this shelf, then nothing would happen. But if he was right...

He pushed his finger into the indentation. A small strip of decorative molding popped off the front of the shelf to reveal a narrow compartment. "Zooks!" George said softly, staggering back with the piece of carved wood in his hand.

Ada whipped her head around. "George, what are you doing?"

"Proving a theory," he replied breathlessly.

George pressed the carved side of the wooden molding in his hand against the molding on the next-highest shelf. The carved pieces of wood fit together like a key into a lock. With a sharp click, the back panel of the shelf released to reveal yet another empty secret compartment above the one he'd already revealed.

Ada gaped. "How did you do that?"

"This is exactly the same as the library in my house," George said. His grandfather loved puzzles with many steps and surprises that built upon each other like links in a chain. The solution to one puzzle was the key to the next and so on and so on. George looked around the room, unsure whether he should be delighted or disturbed.

Ada strode toward him, then suddenly stopped, dead in her tracks, in the middle of the room. Her whole body stiffened and her eyes grew wide as they fixed on a point beyond George down the hallway through which they had entered.

George's heart thumped. "What is it, Ada?"

She looked at him. "We should leave, George."

"But—" George retorted. "This looks exactly like my house, Ada!"

Ada hooked Patty's arm underneath George's elbow and pulled him down the dark hallway, dragging him back toward the temporary side entrance, while George persisted, "Why is there no front door? Where's the kitchen? Where's the staircase to get upstairs?"

All of a sudden, though, he stopped. At the end of the hallway he saw what Ada had seen through the jagged opening half-covered by the tin panel.

On the outside wall of his own house, someone had drawn a faint chalk outline of a door.

"But…"

He blinked again. An X was drawn inside the chalk outline on No. 8. The mark was almost invisible in the midnight darkness. But it was unmistakably there. It lined up perfectly with the temporary entrance to No. 10, which lined up perfectly with the hallway, which lined up perfectly with the hallway inside his own house, just steps away. No. 10 and No. 8 were close enough to span with a board.

The plan of the house clicked into place as neatly as the missing piece of a puzzle.

This strange house didn't need a front door or a kitchen or a staircase because it would have those things as soon as it was connected to George's. No. 10 wasn't its own house at all.

It was the new wing of No. 8.

Chapter Three

George's heart didn't stop pounding until they toppled through the doorway of Ada's workshop.

Only then did George finally feel that he could breathe again. Ada's room was even more cluttered than usual, but the extra piles of scribbled-in notebooks and scattered machine parts made George feel safer. As if they were a barrier between him and the outside world. With every breath, his fear of what they'd seen in No. 10 dissolved until only anger and bravery burned in his chest.

"How dare they!" George yelled at nobody in particular. "First, the Society tried to steal my map—and now they're trying to steal my house!"

Calmer now, Ada lit an oil lamp, then cleared a space

on her workbench for Patty's arm. They had carried the mechanical girl up from the front steps, and now she was sitting next to the workbench, patiently waiting for her missing limb to be reattached.

"George—"

"I saw the look on your face. You saw it, too—the Society bought No. 10 and intends to attach it to my house!" George paced between towers of books and piles of paper.

"Don't jump to conclusions," Ada admonished.

"But you said—" He stared back at Ada, but her expression was resolute. "Fine. You want me to be rational and examine the evidence. Here's the evidence: My mysterious next-door neighbor is building a house with no front door. Its inside matches the inside of my house. Its hallway matches up with my hallway. Its floor matches my floor. Someone has drawn the outline of a door on the side of my house exactly across from the only way into No. 10! Someone from the Society carried Patty's arm into that house. Ergo and wherefore, I can conclude that the Society is going to invade my home at any moment."

"*Invade* is a strong word, don't you think? I agree the chalk was suspicious, but unless it's explosive chalk, no damage has been done. An empty building is hardly a crime. Let's take a moment and think this through."

George slowed his pacing by a fraction. Panicking wouldn't help. As usual, Ada was the voice of reason. The last time they'd seen the Society, its dastardly members were heading off to pursue their old enemy, Il Naso, in Spain. If the Society was now in Dorset Square, there was no telling what its plans might be.

"What should I do? I should go to the authorities, shouldn't I? Should I write to the Mallard sisters and find out who purchased their land? Or I could go down to the registry office and check the deed myself. Should we go right now?"

"Hmmm," Ada said, lowering her magnifying goggles over her eyes.

George wrung his hands. "You're quite right. It's Sunday. The registry office won't be open. Do you know where the Mallard sisters are?" Perhaps the women who had lived in No. 10 Dorset Square knew something that George could use against the Society members who had purchased their house.

"Errrm," Ada mumbled.

"Please, Ada. This is very serious and—oh heavens! I beg your pardon!" George rushed to turn away as Ada pulled down Patty's dress, revealing her smooth porcelain shoulder.

Ada snorted with laughter. "She's not a real person, George. She doesn't need privacy."

In George's haste to shield his eyes, he stepped too far into the clutter in the middle of the room and tripped over a stack of books, knocking them all to the floor. "I'm sorry. I'll pick these up."

Ada dropped Patty's arm, which landed with a thud on the workbench. She dove onto the ground, scrambling for the scattered books. "No, no. I'll take care of it."

They both reached for the same slim, dark blue book. George grabbed the binding. At the same time, Ada plucked a yellowed slip of paper from between its pages, quickly folded it in half, and slipped it into her pocket. Curious, George turned the book over to read the title on the cover. *Useful Needlework*.

"This is my book," George said in surprise. In fact, it was one of only two books that he currently owned. All the rest had been sold to pay off his father's debts after his grandfather died. *Useful Needlework* had survived because it had been hidden in one of the secret compartments, exactly like the one he'd found in No. 10. In every respect, *Useful Needlework* looked exactly the way one would expect a book entitled *Useful Needlework* to look.

That is, not very useful at all.

Ada rocked back on her heels to stand up. She rubbed her cheek nervously as she adjusted the lamp on her workbench. "I was going to return that to you soon."

"Why did you take it in the first place, though?" As soon as he asked, the answer popped into his head. Another one of his grandfather's books, *The History of the Rhône*, had helped them find the Star of Victory in Geneva. Ada must have taken *Useful Needlework* to hunt for clues that might tell them why the Society wanted his map. "You were hunting for more clues!"

"Well—"

George's heart began to thump. "What did you find?"

Ada frowned. "I found a few things," she said cautiously.

George's spirits lifted. "Really? Like what? Anything more about the island from the scrap of the map?"

"No islands, but I learned some useful needlework. I've been doing the Brighton stitch all wrong. The vertical stitch should always be on top of the horizontal one."

"Very funny." George lowered his voice. Ada's mother

wasn't home, but one of her nosy servants might be listening on the other side of the door. "Did you find something about the map or not?"

Instead of answering, Ada leaned closer into her work. A corner of yellow paper sticking out of her pocket flashed in the lamplight.

"Maybe you'd like to share what's on that piece of paper you're pretending you didn't just take out of the book?"

Ada tucked the paper deeper into her pocket, then turned back to Patty. A sour feeling bubbled in George's stomach. Ada was avoiding answering his questions. She had promised not to lie to him—which meant that right now, she was avoiding saying the truth. Ada knew something. Something terrible.

"What is it? What did you find?"

Ada sighed. "It's nothing. Just an old letter, that's all."

"Nothing?" George felt a flush of heat creeping up his neck. "Nothing" was the worst thing Ada could have said, because Ada always had something. "You promised not to lie to me. After everything we went through in Venice, I thought we trusted each other."

"I haven't lied to you, *technically*," she snapped. There was a trace of hurt in her voice.

George pressed her harder. "Then why won't you show me that piece of paper? What is it?"

"Don't you imagine that your grandfather had a life outside of making treasure maps? Not everything we find has to be a clue. Maybe he hid something, and he didn't mean for you to find it. Maybe he didn't intend for you to examine every pen stroke of every word of every piece of paper he ever touched in his entire life." She turned the wrench to tighten Patty's bolts to emphasize her point. Patty's blond curls swung. "Maybe it was just a coincidence I found it. It was hidden very well inside a false page," countered Ada.

George swallowed. "False page?"

Ada turned around, finally, and met his gaze. Her eyes burned bright as a coal fire. "Drop it. You don't want to know."

"It *is* important. What is it?"

Ada gripped the edge of her workbench. "Aren't you happy, George?" she asked, her voice suddenly softer and gentler. She waved her hand at the window toward No. 8. "Isn't your business doing well? Don't you have everything you want?"

George was surprised that his nose began to itch as though he might cry. He shook away the feeling and instead thumped his knuckles loudly against *Useful Needlework*'s cover. "Don't change the subject. You know how much the map means to me. I'm a Devonshire. It was my grandfather's map, and his book, too. If it contains some secret, and if it's related to the Society or that house next door—I have a right to know."

Ada pressed her fingertips to her forehead and closed her eyes. "It's just that... once you know something, you can't unknow it. It's part of you forever. And it changes you. It hurts you. Believe me, I know. I know what it's like when people... disappoint you. Especially people you love. I just want to protect you."

Protect? George swayed on his feet. "Miss Byron, if you believe I'm in some kind of danger, I deserve to know. I don't need your protection. I need the truth."

Ada blew air into her cheeks and threw her hands in the air. "Fine! What do I know? I'm only your best friend in the whole world." She marched over to George and put the piece of yellowed paper into his palm. "Don't say I didn't warn you."

George unfolded the brittle parchment.

It was a letter worn with age, its middle deeply creased from being opened and closed many times. The bottom right corner was singed brown. George's skin prickled with nerves as his eyes scanned the words.

Dear George,

Should I call you Lord of Devonshire? I think not. Alas, clearly you think yourself deserving of the title. You have stolen everything from me: my house, my possessions, my family. My dearest treasure.

Every time you think of me, I hope you burn with disgrace. No legacy is so rich as honesty; therefore, your legacy will be shameful poverty, as it was always meant to be. My prison is made of iron and stone; yours is all around you.

I curse your true name, 1st Lord of Devonshire.

For now, do not fear. I'll keep your secret—until I can have my revenge.

Signed, truthfully,

There was no signature. Nobody had signed it.

At first, George thought the note was addressed to him, but it was addressed to his grandfather, with whom he shared a name. *Secret. Burn with disgrace. You have stolen everything from me.* The words made bile rise in his throat.

Whoever had written them was very, very angry at his grandfather.

George closed the letter carefully, then slipped it inside *Useful Needlework* and gently closed the cover.

"Are you all right, George?" Ada asked softly.

George smiled. His mind had exploded into a whirlwind as he read the nasty words in the letter, but now it had settled down into perfect serenity. "Of course I'm all right. Why wouldn't I be all right?"

Ada blinked rapidly. "Are you sure? Aren't you—I mean, didn't you read the letter? It's addressed to your grandfather...."

George rapped his knuckle against the book's cover. "It's all part of the puzzle my grandfather left behind. Perhaps he was working on it when he suddenly passed away and didn't have the chance to hide it properly. You see, he never made anything simple. *Simple doesn't build character,* as he always said."

Ada crossed her arms. "Why would he write a letter like that to himself? If you add this piece of evidence to what we know about the map and what is happening across the street, a reasonable person might conclude that your grandfather stole something very valuable. Look, I have a theory of my own." She tried to wrest *Useful Needlework* away from him, but he dodged her. Sighing, she said, "That letter specifically mentioned he stole a *house* and a *treasure*. And then it mentioned *revenge*. The Society has already tried to take your treasure map, and we just saw that the owner of No. 10 is intending to attach it to yours. Which means that the Society is probably working for whomever those things originally belonged to—"

"Don't be absurd! My grandfather never stole anything in his life. He certainly didn't steal a house or possessions or any *dearest* treasure," George said ruefully.

Ada sighed. "I knew you'd act like this. Why do you think I didn't want to tell you about this letter? If you hadn't knocked over *Useful Needlework*, you never would have known. Let's just pretend you don't have the worst luck in the world and forget all about it."

George's mouth twitched. "This letter has nothing to do with our new neighbor or my luck, you'll see. There's another explanation. I'll go to the registry office tomorrow and prove it."

Ada stepped over the mess on her floor, and soon her cool hand fluttered against his cheek. "You're in shock."

George backed out of her room into the hallway, narrowly avoiding tripping again. "I'm not in shock. I feel fine. Stop looking at me like that."

"Your face is pale, and you're cool to the touch. The same thing happened to me when I found out my father was really, truly dead. Come back in and sit down. You could faint at any moment."

George took a deep breath to steady his voice. "Stop it. I'm not going to faint. I'm brave now, don't you remember? And I'm sorry that your father lied to you and abandoned you, but this is an entirely different situation. I know who my grandfather was, and nothing you or anyone else says will ever change that. He was a hero, plain and simple. He was the 1st Lord of Devonshire. His legacy is not *shameful poverty*."

Ada frowned. "Now, George," she said sternly. "I know you loved your grandfather, but you might have to accept—"

"Accept what? Accept that everything I know about my grandfather is a lie? That he was a common thief, no better than the Society?" George squeezed the book in his hand until his knuckles were white. "I'll admit that strange things are happening, but they've got nothing to do with the sort of person my grandfather was."

"George, I'm only trying to help—"

"You think you know everything, Ada Byron, but you don't. You made up stories about your own family because you couldn't accept that your father was a scoundrel and a leech and he treated you terribly. That's just not true of my grandfather. My stories aren't made up."

Ada's lip quivered. Regret filled his chest—he'd only meant that Ada's father was wrong and that she deserved a far better one than a scoundrel like him. "Ada..."

But it was too late. Two pearl-shaped tears appeared in the corners of Ada's eyes. She wiped them away furiously as George watched, stunned that his words had hurt her. Suddenly, the pain in her face transformed to anger. "Of course you don't believe that anything could tarnish the precious Devonshire name. You're as stubborn as an ox and just as thickheaded. Get out of my house. And don't come looking for my help when you return to your senses."

Before he could stop her, Ada stepped back into her bedroom and slammed the door behind her, leaving George with nowhere to go but home.

Chapter Four

The sky opened and pelted George with raindrops as he slumped across Dorset Square to his house. If it was possible, the gap between No. 8 and No. 10 seemed to have narrowed. Could the Society invent a house that moved? George wiped his feet on his doormat, imagining No. 10 crawling across the grass on hundreds of tiny mechanical legs like a centipede. He glanced back at Ada's window, but she had closed her curtains.

You don't know everything, Ada Byron, George thought grumpily. His father had told him that he had porridge for brains on many occasions, but George was no longer the scared boy his father had once known. He was a hero now. He had found the Star of Victory. He was an adventurer who flew through the skies in a mechanical bird. He was a business owner with royal clients. He could solve his grandfather's puzzles.

It was true that he'd done those things with Ada's help, but that didn't mean he couldn't do other things without her. At the very least, he could try.

George stomped to his desk in the library, where Ada had found him earlier that evening. He slammed the slip of yellow paper onto the polished wood in front of him, determined to prove Ada wrong. She'd missed something about the letter. It was a code or a cipher. He lit a candle and got to studying it. It had 108 words, four things his grandfather was supposed to have stolen, eight letters in the word *treasure*. But none of the numbers made any sense. He could think of a thousand rational explanations for how that letter had come to be hidden in one of his grandfather's books—and nine hundred and ninety-nine of those explanations did not involve his grandfather stealing a house or a family or a treasure and lying about it to his grandson.

The Star of Victory, his grandfather's lost treasure, was perched on the corner of his desk, sparkling in the candlelight. George picked it up using only the tips of his fingers so as not to smudge the gleaming surface, which he polished every day. The Star had been created from two gems that fit together: an egg-shaped blue sapphire set inside a spray of silver, blade-shaped rods. In fact, what George had learned was that the Star itself was *not* the treasure, but rather another clue in a larger mystery.

When he looked through the Star at the tiny piece of the map he still had, the ink on the page seemed to stretch and lift, rising up into the air like a mountain or an island. The Star was a lens that was supposed to help him decode something hidden in his grandfather's map.

But he still didn't know what.

That was the wonderful part of his grandfather's puzzles. One prize led to another, like a trail of discovery. For example, when George originally set out to find the Star of Victory, he had not only returned home with the Star, but also with happiness and fortune and friends.

He had doubted his grandfather once before when they were searching for the Star of Victory, and it had been a mistake. He wasn't going to doubt him ever again.

His grandfather was not a bad person.

He had never stolen this house or anything from someone else.

The house belonged to the 1st Lord of Devonshire, fair and square. And now it belonged to George.

Tap. Tap. Outside, something was striking a sharp, rhythmic beat. *Tap. Tap.* It sounded like a woodpecker or Ada's mechanical bird. George jumped to his feet and rushed to the window, hoping to find his friend's face beaming back at him. Across the square, Ada's curtains were still shut tight—but there was a flickering glow reflecting off the cobblestones in front of No. 10.

George bumped his forehead against the windowpane in shock. Somewhere inside the house next door, a candle was burning.

George looked at the portrait of his grandfather that hung over his desk. The stern, loving gaze gave George courage. He pulled on his inherited sailing jacket and marched over to No. 10.

The sky was dark and the ground was slick from the rain. His gut kicked. His heart seemed to beat the words *turn around, turn around, turn around.* But the mysterious house drew George in like iron to a magnet.

He approached the side opening they had discovered earlier. The sheet of tin was still propped open, and after George pulled himself up through the opening in the wall, he tiptoed down the short hallway into the strange, open room for the second time that night. Someone had placed candles on the windowsills and a lantern on the unfinished fireplace mantel. Its halo of light illuminated a painting hanging above the fireplace that hadn't been there earlier.

George drew closer. The painting was a portrait of a young boy and girl holding hands on a windswept seashore. The children must have been brother and sister, because they bore a striking resemblance to each other: smooth black hair, arched brows, and skeptical expressions adorned both pale faces, which were quite round but tapered to a pointed chin. The boy's buckled shoes and knee-length pants were decades out of fashion, but the paint was as crisp and vibrant as the rich colors Oscar mixed on his palette. The blues were particularly brilliant, none more so than a spot of blue in the girl's hand near the center of the painting.

George stepped into the circle of the lantern's light to see what she was holding—and gasped. It was a gem that was as blue as the sky, as bright as the sun, and as radiant as the stars.

The girl in the painting was holding the Star of Victory. The very same treasure that sat on his desk in No. 8.

"See anything familiar?" a voice boomed from behind George.

George spun around. He pressed himself against the fireplace to hide. In the far corner of the room, beneath the second-floor balcony, a man was hovering in midair in the darkness. The man took a step forward and George realized he was not hovering—he was just impossibly tall, with a long black cloak that hid his ankles and feet. His neatly trimmed white hair nearly scraped the ceiling, and his dark cloak made his body seem to melt into the shadows.

George knew he should say something brave, but all he managed was "You—you stole Patty's arm."

The man took another step toward George on his tremendously long legs, crossing the vast room in two strides. Before George could dodge him, the tall man whipped a long, black walking stick from beneath his black coat and banged it into George's knees, splaying him out on the cold marble floor like a rag doll.

"You haven't answered my question, George," the tall man said. "Do you see anything familiar in that painting?"

George staggered to his feet, confused tears stinging his eyes. The man knew his name. How did the man know his name? "I see the Star of Victory," he mumbled.

"I can't hear you all the way down there. Speak up, boy," the tall man said, cupping his hand to his ear.

George cleared his throat. His confusion was heating up into a blazing fire of irritation. This was the man who was trying to take his house. "You heard me. If you know who I am, then you already know that's the Star of Victory. It was my grandfather's treasure, and I found it."

The tall man threw his head back and laughed. His silver hair gleamed in the lantern light. "Ha! It's a sentimental trinket. Nothing more. If you think that *treasure* is what it appears to be, then you're going to be sorely disappointed when you learn the truth," he said, drawing out the word greedily.

George's cheeks burned. "Why would I believe a word you say?"

The tall man looked deeply offended by the question. "Because I'm the smartest man you'll ever meet. And the tallest and the most powerful. I've been out of prison less then a month, and look what I've been able to accomplish. Who else could build something this quickly? I didn't even have to go inside your house to line everything up perfectly to connect it. Aren't you impressed?"

Though George's mind spun, his anger focused his thoughts onto the single task of defending his home. "I don't care how smart or tall you are. I'm the 3rd Lord of Devonshire, heir to my grandfather's estate. The Star of Victory is mine. No. 8 is mine. You're just jealous of what I have."

"Jealous?" The tall man gripped his walking stick tightly. The veins on his forehead bulged, while his face flashed a dark shade of red. "The house is *not* yours. It didn't belong to your grandfather. Nothing belongs to him. He stole it all."

"Oh, and I suppose you think it belongs to you instead because you happen to have a painting of a famous treasure that now belongs to me?" George countered. "How very convenient for you to show up out of the blue and take it all for yourself. What gives you the right to say that? Who are *you*?"

The tall man's lips arched into a wicked smile. "I go by many names. Das Niemand. Signore Nessuno. There are some who call me Don Jefe. Since you asked, I prefer to be called Don Nadie. It reminds me of my favorite poem, *Don Juan*. But in all languages, I am a Nobody."

An icy jolt of terror stiffened George's spine. His worst fear was coming true. He was alone. Defenseless. His enemy was going to steal not only his family legacy, but his life as well. "You're part of the Society of Nobodies. They sent you here to kill me."

A low chuckle bubbled up from the man's throat. "They

don't send *me* anywhere. I send *them*." The man made a casual wave of his hand. "I sent them to your house. I sent them to Miss Ada Byron's house. I've sent them to other scientists' houses. To Geneva. To Venice. Even to Spain to follow a certain policeman to reclaim a map that's rightfully mine. Don't look so scared. If I wanted to kill you, I would have done it already."

George swallowed the fear tickling his tongue. "You can't have my house. And you can't have my map."

Don Nadie leaned far over, until he was so close to George that he could reach out and strike him if he chose. His dark eyes glinted in the candlelight. "And what are you going to do about it?"

"I—I'll get the map first," George mustered, trying to sound brave even though he felt anything but.

The man called Don Nadie sighed; then another wicked smile curled across his face. "If you must."

George thought that now would be a very good time for Ada to come swooping in to provide a distraction so that he could leave. He cast a desperate glance at the windows, but saw only the reflection of a candle sitting on the sill. Next to the candle were stacks of cream-colored paper and golden sticks of sealing wax. George's eyes caught on a familiar name printed at the top of the paper. "C.R.U.M.P.E.T.S.? Why do you have..."

But before George could finish his question, his own mind supplied the answer. Memories of their beach battle against the Nobodies flashed in front of his eyes. The Society had a legion of horrible machines. Airships that hid within clouds. Mechanical bats that sliced through wood. Metal fish with sword-sharp fins that could hold a battalion of soldiers inside their bellies. Inventions, Ada said, that the Society had stolen from the world's greatest scientists.... "You sent these invitations out? You organized C.R.U.M.P.E.T.S.?"

Looming above George, Don Nadie howled with laughter. "I will be a spider and let my prey come to me, just as you did. You walked right into my web, and you are stuck there, even though you don't realize it. Just like those scientists coming to C.R.U.M.P.E.T.S."

He darted his walking stick over George's shoulder, but instead of striking him, he pressed a button hidden on the fireplace behind him. With a sickening *clang*, iron bars slid over the windows. Before George could scream, Don Nadie pressed the button again, letting the bars up. "An impressive trap, is it not? I'll use their inventions to create

45

the greatest weapons the world has ever seen. Nothing will be able to stop me from reclaiming what's rightfully mine."

"You're..." *Absurd.* An unpleasant memory popped into his head—he'd called Ada absurd when she first told him about the Society of Nobodies, on the very first day they met, when she thought it was called the Organization. Her words came back to him clearly now, as if she'd just spoken them into his ear. *The Organization will eat at the foundations of society like termites until the whole kingdom crumbles to dust.*

George cast another desperate glance out the window, hoping to see Ada on the other side of the glass. He wished he could fight this man, but he was too tall and George would only get tripped by his walking stick again. George's words would have to be braver than his actions. "We stopped you once. We'll stop you again. My friend Ada knows all about C.R.U.M.P.E.T.S."

The man called Don Nadie sighed. "Don't you know that a silly statement like that can get someone hurt? Because if you do anything to warn those scientists, there will be certain....consequences."

George gulped. "Consequences?"

"Yes. Consequences involving your cherished manservant who, I happen to know, is on his way to the same health spa in Vienna where your friend's mother, Lady Byron, frequently indulges in curative retreats. It would be such a shame if the spa were to burn down with all the guests inside. Miss Byron would be so upset if anything happened to her mother."

George's stomach somersaulted. It was bad enough that this man was after his house. His house was not alive. But threatening Frobisher and Ada's mother, both of whom were very much alive, stoppered his throat.

The tall man must have seen these thoughts on George's face. He gave a small nod and said, "Having your loved ones taken away from you is terrible, isn't it?"

Fury and fear tumbling inside him, George knew he had to do something. He clenched his fists and lowered his head, ready to barrel through the tall man's legs at full speed. But then, quite unexpectedly, Don Nadie stepped aside.

"You can go home now," Don Nadie said casually.

George's palms began to sweat. "I—I can?"

"Of course. You'll need a good night's sleep."

George smoothed his hair from his forehead. "I don't understand. Is this part of one of my grandfather's puzzles? Why would you do all this and just let me go?"

At the mention of his grandfather's puzzles, the tall

man's eyes flew to the portrait and lingered there, staring as if he were expecting the painted girl and boy to speak to him. The corners of his mouth twitched, almost softened into a smile—then all at once, his face hardened. "Your grandfather didn't make puzzles, George. He played games. There's a difference. Now it's my turn to play games."

The tall man lifted his walking stick again. George winced. But instead of bringing it down on him, Don Nadie put the end of the stick into the cold, dark fireplace and squeezed the handle. It made a strange crackling buzz as a glass cylinder set into the stick began to rotate faster than a spinning wheel. A blue spark shot from the stick's tip and immediately set the kindling in the fireplace ablaze with a rushing *whoomp*. George felt the heat of the fire against his skin even as his blood ran cold.

"As soon as I retrieve that map, my days as a Nobody will finally end. I will be a Somebody again, and no one will be able to stop me. Least of all you," Don Nadie sneered. "Now run."

George sprinted out of No. 10 into the cool, misty night as fast as his legs could carry him. The tapping of the tall man's walking stick didn't follow him. Somehow, that was worse than if Don Nadie had broken his word and chased George outside.

Their earlier fight forgotten, George bolted to Ada's house and banged on the door until his fist ached. He needed to know that she was safe. Finally, the butler yanked open the door and furiously turned him away. Ada was not home, he snapped. She had left shortly after George, and she hadn't returned.

And so George went back to No. 8, opening the door to find a grayish, fading darkness waiting for him. He climbed out onto the roof to watch Ada's house with the telescope she'd left behind. He took the Star of Victory with him, hoping somehow it would protect him from the villain at No. 10.

Because that was what the tall man was, George thought as he fidgeted in the cold night air. A liar and a villain.

As the morning sun rose over the rooftops of London, George fell into a fitful sleep and dreamed that the tall man had turned into a giant, fearsome spider. His legs grew and grew, curling into eight limbs that wrapped around George to shut out the light.

Chapter Five

Several hours later, George woke up in a panic. When he realized that his encounter in No. 10 Dorset Square was not a nightmare, he almost fell off the roof. Why had he fallen asleep? Something terrible could have happened to Ada. The tall man next door was in charge of the Society. He had set up C.R.U.M.P.E.T.S. as a trap for the greatest scientific minds in Europe. What if she had figured out what was going on and they had decided to do away with the girl genius once and for all?

A plan formed in his head. First, he needed to find Ada and make sure she was safe. Once he found her, he would go to the registry office to find out the identity of the man who owned the house next door. Don Nadie, Don Jefe, Signore

Nessuno, Das Niemand—those couldn't have been his given name. George couldn't report Nobody to the police.

George put the Star of Victory in his pocket for safe-keeping as he climbed down from the roof into the house. He had just finished pulling on his boots downstairs when a heavy knock came at the front door.

"Open in the name of the King," called out a deep voice from the other side.

"The King?" George mumbled to himself. Then, in a much louder voice—"Is this about the truffles? If he wants more, he'll have to wait."

A flurry of voices on the other side of the door confirmed George's suspicion. The King's truffles had been delivered only yesterday, and already the King must want more. George huffed in annoyance. *I haven't got time for truffles right now!* he thought to himself, throwing the door open impatiently.

Four royal officers in red coats stood on the doorstep. Their faces were still as statues.

"How may I be of service?"

One of the officers stepped forward to peer around George's head. "Good morning, young man. We have an arrest warrant issued by the King of England."

Arrest warrant? George's tongue felt as thick as a brick in his dry mouth. "An arrest warrant for whom? Perhaps you've come to the wrong house," he said, throwing a hopeful glance at No. 10.

The officer thrust the warrant in George's face. "George, the 3rd Lord of Devonshire, at No. 8 Dorset Square."

George's knees buckled. He clutched the door to stay upright. Black clouds crept into the perimeter of his vision, and his brain exploded with the buzzing of a swarm of flies. "George, the—the *3rd* Lord of Devonshire?" he stammered. "There's been a mistake, surely."

"No mistake. He's accused of high treason for the attempted assassination of the King using poisoned truffles."

Cold terror gripped George's chest. "That sounds very serious," he said faintly. "Come in, won't you? I'll go find the 3rd Lord for you. I'm sure he's here somewhere."

Trembling in every limb, George shuffled aside to admit the officers, all of whom wore long swords at their waists. He walked up the front staircase as calmly and slowly as on any other day. Because of his past bad luck, George was used to dealing with unpleasant surprises, but this was something completely different. With each careful step, he tried to make sense of the situation.

The tall man had told him he should go home and get a good night's sleep.

He must have known the officers were coming.

He must have sent them.

The walls seemed to spin and stretch around George, encircling him like a web. As soon as he reached the landing, he could not hold back the panic any longer. He launched himself up the stairs, no thought in his mind save one.

Run.

George's pulse pounded in his ears like a drumbeat. *Run. Run. Run.* Luckily, being chased by the Society of Nobodies all over Europe had greatly improved his athletic ability. He was able to stay out of the reach of the soldiers, who were weighted down by their heavy, starched uniforms and significant weaponry.

About halfway up the second flight of stairs, George remembered that Ada's mechanical frog was still on the roof, where she had left it before their expedition to No. 10. He bounded up the rickety staircase to the attic, emerging into the dark, damp, musty room.

"Surrender in the name of the King!" a gruff voice called from below.

Huffing, George climbed out of the attic window onto the roof. Ada's frog sat on its landing platform, still hidden underneath a tarpaulin. George pulled the tarpaulin away and clambered up the metal rungs on the side of the machine. He buckled himself into the harness on the driver's seat, which Lady Byron had insisted must be fastened before the machine could be turned on. He'd ridden in the jumping machine a few times, but Ada was always tinkering with its designs. Ada never labeled any of the controls on her inventions, but he remembered that she'd pulled on a lever to release the springs.

But what did all the other buttons and knobs do? George's fingers hesitated over the control panel, his heart thumping louder than the sound of the men streaming into the attic.

A red-coated guard angled his head and shoulders out of the window. "You there. What are you doing in that contraption? Step away from it! Surrender now," he barked at George.

George pulled the lever.

The frog's springs released with a loud *boing*, catapulting into the air with George inside. The *whoosh* of wind blew his blond hair into his face, but it did not muffle his scream. Below, the rooftop of No. 8 grew smaller and smaller as the frog hurtled higher and higher. The guard was on the roof, a tiny red figure shaking his fist at the sky.

But as the frog descended, George realized in horror that he was not heading for the rooftop of No. 5 as he had intended—because instead of leaping *over* Dorset Square, he was leaping *away* from it. He must have needed to flip whatever switch would reverse the frog's direction. The frog landed on the rooftop of a building overlooking Baker Street with an impact that made George's teeth rattle. As the frog's legs shuddered beneath him, the harness squeezed tighter, pushing the air out of George's lungs.

George shifted the lever forward. He meant to stop the frog to allow himself to climb out and hide, but the springs released again with a clank, hurtling George over Baker Street onto the rooftop of a brand-new mansion overlooking Regent's Park.

"Ada, how do you stop this thing?" George shouted, though she was not around to hear him. He unbuckled himself from the boa constrictor harness but had only managed to get one arm out when the frog jumped again.

George's screams were snatched away by the wind whistling past his ears. People in the street below were screaming, too. He barely avoided being flung away and impaled on the iron fence surrounding Regent's Park by hanging on to the harness for dear life. His palms burned as they slipped over the rough fabric of the harness. When the frog landed on the soft green grass inside Regent's Park, just barely missing a woman pushing a baby carriage, George buckled himself in again. He'd rather have the air squeezed out of his lungs than shatter every rib when he hit the ground. He had to stop the machine before it squashed someone.

But as soon as the buckles were fastened, the frog jumped again. And again. It crashed down with one leg in the muddy bank of an ornamental pond. The other leg was submerged in the water. Geese and swans took flight to escape being trampled. Frantically, George picked out a smaller switch in the center of the panel that looked useful. He flicked it down.

With a shudder, the frog began to jump again, but this time in a series of smaller, faster leaps, much closer to the ground. Within seconds, George had crossed an incredible distance. Men, women, and children screamed and fled as he galloped through Regent's Park. Dogs broke loose from their leashes and chased the frog, howling and baying.

"Stop it!" George cried as he mashed down every button on the control panel at once.

The machine belched out a black puff of smoke. One spring came loose with a horrible, wrenching *clang*. The legs continued to pump up and down, sending the frog spinning in a dizzying dance through a maze of clipped hedgerows. Leaves and twigs showered down on George's head.

With an unsteady leap, the frog rammed through the hedgerows, stumbling into the center of a garden filled with people. George could barely make out the lettered banner above them proclaiming: THE 20TH ANNUAL GREATER LONDON FLORICULTURAL FÊTE AND EXHIBITION OF FLOWERS AND FLOWERING PLANTS. When they saw the frog burst through the rosebushes, everyone's faces contorted in expressions of shock before they fled from the lurching metal monster. Completely outside George's control, the frog launched itself toward dozens of trestle tables loaded with vases full of brightly colored flowers.

"I'm sorry!" George shouted. The frog sputtered and coughed out another cloud of black smoke from its belly. *It must be running out of fuel*, George thought. *Not fast enough, though.* He was starting to feel queasy, but there was no time for that.

He felt underneath the control panel. There had to be a button or lever or something to turn the machine off. His fingers found a ring at the end of a cord. He yanked. A grappling hook shot out of the front of the machine. Its sharp silver hooks shattered a vase of peach-colored roses.

A woman turned back from the scattering crowd and began beating on the machine with her silk parasol.

"Enough!" George pushed his hair from his eyes. There was more than one way to slay a beast, he thought. He loosened the harness straps so that he could lean all the way forward to yank open the cover of the instrument panel, which rebounded and slammed back onto his hand. Sawtoothed gears and mechanisms whirred at blinding speeds.

He grabbed the parasol from the woman, who was now beating at George's legs. "May I?" He jammed the handle of the parasol as hard as he could into the spinning gears. With a dreadful squeal, the gears ground to a halt, and the frog died in a final puff of black smoke. It teetered and tottered, then toppled over onto a table piled high with tulips. George leapt out of the seat and collapsed onto the grass—

Just in time to see a police officer from the Bow Street Runners come galloping into the gardens.

"Step away from the contraption," ordered the police officer. He had no weapon, but the row of silver buttons on his black coat glinted menacingly.

George's head was spinning. His stomach heaved. One glance around him told him all he needed to know: the garden was completely destroyed. Tables were broken, ladies' hats lay abandoned among the ruined remains of prizewinning blossoms, and there was a single baby shoe orphaned on the lawn. If he was innocent before, he certainly wasn't now.

"Officer, I wasn't—I didn't—my neighbor is after me—this isn't my fault. I was trying to *stop* it."

Before George knew what was happening, another police officer arrived with a pair of heavy iron handcuffs and roughly shackled George's wrists. With a police officer firmly holding each of his arms and his hands shackled together, George was marched through Regent's Park like a common criminal. Flower fanatics and casual picnickers glared in his direction. A few hissed at him as he passed. George had never felt so low in his life.

If the tall man had wanted to humiliate him, he had succeeded.

When they arrived at the police station, George scoured every corner of the room with his eyes, expecting the tall man to be waiting for him. It was almost a relief to see that Don Nadie was not there. Maybe this was all a misunderstanding. Maybe he could sort it out with someone reasonable. At the very least, he thought, the situation could not get any worse.

But the longer George sat, the more his relief dwindled away until it vanished completely. He had once been the unluckiest boy in London.

He knew from experience that things could always get worse.

Chapter Six

While George was being chained to a hard wooden bench in the front room of the police station, the guards who had invaded his home arrived, huffing and puffing. The red-coated guards began arguing with the black-coated police officers over which of George's crimes was the more serious: poisoning the King with murderous truffles or destroying the flower show. The small front room filled with more and more men in coats until there was hardly room to breathe.

"I did not poison the King," George interjected weakly, but no one listened to him. He looked down at his shackled wrists. He felt strangely calm again, despite the chaos of the police station around him.

It felt like falling, George realized. Not long ago, he'd jumped out of Ada's airship over the ocean into empty space, a wall of water rushing to meet him. There was nothing to do but wait for the impact. This time, there was only one hope of rescue when he was done falling: Ada. If she didn't intervene, he'd be hanged for sure. And if he wasn't hanged, he'd be sent to prison. And if he wasn't sent to prison, he'd be put in the workhouse.

At least Frobisher was far enough away that he wouldn't be dragged into this mess with him. Poor Frobisher. He had reformed himself after years of piracy, but his freedom was as fragile as George's. If the police found out he was really Jon the Gardener, infamous pirate, he'd be hanged right next to George. Maybe worse, if the tall man at No. 10 got to him.

A cloud of despair swirled in George, darker than the fumes from the frog. He closed his eyes against it, trying to dispel the terrible lump of dread in his chest. Images of his friends burst into his mind to give him comfort. Oscar at the bow of a pirate ship. Ruthie standing on Oscar's shoulders. Ada kneeling in the middle of her room, surrounded by whirring gears and ticking machines.

Then a hush fell over the police station.

George's eyes flew open. A portly man in a brown wool tailcoat with a starched linen collar stood in the doorway, staring at him. The red-coated guards snapped to attention, their arguments forgotten.

Hope blossomed in George's chest. The man was a gentleman, George could tell. Ada must have sent him. The man spoke to the guards, then the police officers, then he squeezed through the crowd to the bench where George was chained.

Sure enough, the man put his hand comfortingly on George's shoulder. "Someone get this child a glass of cold water at once. Can't you see he's parched?"

One of the guards leapt to comply. "Yes, Vice-Chancellor Shadwell."

"Thank you," George breathed.

Vice-Chancellor Shadwell directed the police officers to unlock George's handcuffs. "Lord Devonshire, I apologize for the way you've been treated. It's a good thing I got here when I did to remind these officers that suspects are innocent until proven guilty. Allow me to introduce myself. I am Vice-Chancellor Lancelot Shadwell."

Although they clearly already knew each other's names, gentlemanly custom required that George introduce himself with a polite bow. "George, 3rd Lord of Devonshire." George rubbed his sore wrists where they'd been chafed by the handcuffs. He felt his whole body relax now that he knew Ada had sent someone to rescue him. "There's been some terrible misunderstanding. Perhaps you can help me clear it up."

"I couldn't have said it better myself. You've been accused of some serious crimes. I won't rest until we get to the bottom of this." Vice-Chancellor Shadwell brushed the dust and dirt off George's shoulders and sleeves in a fatherly way, then led George into a small side room. The walls were painted the color of a muddy puddle on a cloudy day. The vice-chancellor shut the door behind them. "Please, have a seat."

George sat down on one side of a worn wooden table, and the vice-chancellor sat on the other. A small cup of cool water was brought in. The vice-chancellor smiled while George gulped the water down gratefully. He wasn't a large man, but he was solidly built, with broad shoulders, like a rock in the middle of a turbulent ocean. For a fleeting moment, George wondered what it would be like to be Vice-Chancellor Shadwell's son. He probably didn't keep secrets from his children or leave confusing letters hidden in old books.

Vice-Chancellor Shadwell rested his hands on the table. His eyes were intense beneath bushy brows. "I know you didn't mean to poison the King," he said. "I don't know much about the truffle business, but I imagine that it must be difficult for even a well-established mushroom seller to ensure the safety of his products. So many mushrooms look alike. Instead of a nice Portobello mushroom, you pick a deadly Destroying Angel. An innocent mistake, I'm sure."

George shook his head. "Impossible, sir. The truffles I sell are grown in very safe conditions. I can assure you that no poisonous mushrooms were grown under my roof—er, in my gardens."

"And yet the fact remains," said the vice-chancellor, "that the King became seriously ill immediately after eating a truffled duck egg for breakfast. Can you explain that?"

"It must have been the egg. Ducks are very grubby birds," George said. He took another sip of water.

The vice-chancellor leaned back in his chair and folded his broad arms. "We examined the duck after we killed it. Its corpse showed no signs of illness or disease."

George nearly choked. "Oh dear. Give the duck's family my condolences."

Vice-Chancellor Shadwell's eyebrows rose in shock.

"Interesting. You have more remorse for a duck than for the sovereign ruler of your country?"

George tugged on his collar. The air around him seemed to have grown warmer. He was beginning to doubt that this man had been sent by Ada. "No, no. Of course I'm sorry for what happened to the King. It's a terrible tragedy that he was poisoned."

"So you admit that he was poisoned!" Vice-Chancellor Shadwell declared.

A bead of sweat trickled down George's neck. "Well, I don't know. I guess he must have been."

The vice-chancellor's face grew dark. The features that had seemed kind moments ago were now hard and unforgiving. He leaned over the table. "Don't you want to know if he's going to recover? Or are you so uncaring that you can't even inquire after the King's health?"

"Is he going to be all right?" George asked, but his own voice sounded far away. He was beginning to feel somewhat ill himself.

"It's too soon to tell. If his doctors knew what he'd been poisoned with, it would greatly improve his chances of surviving. What did you poison him with, Lord Devonshire?"

A flare of resentment surged within George. This

man was trying to trick him into confessing to a crime he hadn't committed. "Nothing! I've never hurt anyone in my life. I'm innocent."

"Tell me, Lord Devonshire. Does an innocent man flee when guards knock on his door? Does he destroy one of London's most cherished floral competitions? Does he refuse to cooperate with authorities when they try to help him?"

"I didn't mean to wreck the flower show," George said desperately. "It was an accident. Everything happened so fast. If I could go back and do it again, I would never have run. I wasn't thinking clearly. I was scared."

The vice-chancellor's eyes softened again beneath his angry brows. "You were scared of going to prison?"

"Yes," George said.

"For poisoning the King?"

"Yes."

No sooner had the word slipped from George's tongue than the vice-chancellor stood and banged on the door. "Guards, bring back the shackles."

"Wait! What's happening? No! I didn't poison the King."

Panic raced up and down George's spine. His chair

toppled backward as he shot up and ran to the vice-chancellor's side, grasping the man's sleeve in desperation. "It's Nobody's fault. He's framing me."

The vice-chancellor paused for a moment. His face wrinkled with confusion. "Nobody's fault?"

"Please, you misunderstood me. I meant it's somebody's fault, but not mine. His name is—"

But the words dried up in his mouth, scorched away by the memory of the tall man's threat against Frobisher and Ada's mother if George attempted to stop him. Though Frobisher was suffering from the loss of his sea legs, he was far from helpless. There was a chance he could defend himself against an attack. Lady Byron, on the other hand . . .

"I'm innocent," George repeated feebly. "I swear."

The vice-chancellor brushed George's hand off his sleeve as if it were a speck of dirt. He lowered his face to George's own and, in barely more than a whisper, said, "You've already confessed. I shouldn't be surprised. Crime does run in your family, Lord Devonshire."

George's stomach turned into a rock. Vice-Chancellor Shadwell was talking about the 2nd Lord of Devonshire, George's father, a notorious gambler. George had spent two years trying to ward off the debt collectors his father had brought upon them by squandering their family fortune. Clearing his throat, George summoned his grandfather's words. "My father…he didn't act like a Devonshire, sir. I'm not like him."

"I'm not talking about your father."

Before George could voice his confusion, the vice-chancellor produced three pamphlets, placing them on the table for George to read. Each pamphlet was a decades-old, faded edition of the popular *Proceedings of the Old Bailey*, a public summary of court cases decided by the judges at the central London court. George had never cared for the *Proceedings* and their gory tales of real-life crime and punishment, but they were sold on every street corner alongside newspapers, and for over a hundred years, Londoners had devoured the latest murders and robberies published within those cheap pages. A corner inside each pamphlet was turned down so George could quickly find the entries Vice-Chancellor Shadwell wanted him to see. Someone had underlined his grandfather's name in each of them:

17 September 1781   Yesterday Robert Freeman, alias Frisky Bob, and <u>George Devonshire</u> were

committed to the Gatehouse, Westminster, by Justice Cotton, for picking a gentleman's pocket of 15 guineas, a silver snuff box, and two gold rings of considerable value.

22 March 1782   Yesterday George Devonshire, the son of the respected shipbuilder Thomas Devonshire, was accused of being one of the persons who robb'd and gagg'd Captain Romaine on his ship, *La Isla*, bound for the port of Guayaquil, causing a wreck of devastating proportions, for which he now hangs in chains at the Gatehouse, being concerned with a large gang of thieves in several felonies, burglaries, and acts of piracy.

2 May 1782   Saturday last George Devonshire, one of the robbers under condemnation in Newgate, made such a disturbance in the Chapel during the divine service by quarreling with the prisoners, that the Keeper was oblig'd to take him out of the Chapel and put him into the hole call'd Little Ease.

George went utterly cold. The name *George Devonshire* was pulsing over and over in his brain. "But…this isn't right. This can't be right. The 1st Lord of Devonshire was a hero."

Vice-Chancellor Shadwell tutted, then turned and called, "Guards!"

The red-coated guards screwed the heavy iron handcuffs onto George's wrists once again.

Shaking his head in disdain, the vice-chancellor escorted George out of the room. "This boy has confessed to the attempted murder of the King of England. As vice-chancellor of England, I deny his right to a trial and declare him guilty. By special order of Princess Victoria, heir to the throne, he is condemned to a fate worse than death: He will be taken to Newgate Prison and kept shackled in the dungeon with only the rats to keep him company. He shall have no visitors, no freedom, and no chance for appeal."

George fought back the tears that welled up in his eyes. His arms ached with the weight of the iron cuffs. "Please, don't do this! It wasn't my truffles, I swear. Find Ada Byron. She'll figure out who really did it. She'll prove I'm innocent. I know she will."

"Ada Byron?"

George nodded eagerly. "Yes, yes! She lives at No. 5 Dorset Squa—"

"I'm sorry, son." Shadwell gripped George's shoulder. "You must not have read the newspaper this morning. Ada Byron is dead."

Chapter Seven

It was not unusual for George to have terrible days. Before he met Ada, when he'd believed that he was cursed with bad luck, each day of his life felt more terrible than the one before. His tenth birthday, when he'd found his grandfather keeled over next to his father's grave, was supremely dreadful. But that day paled in comparison to the horrific awfulness of this day.

Ada's life had ended, and George's life had ended, too. Though the crime reports that the vice-chancellor had shown him lingered at the back of his mind, Ada's demise screamed in his ears. The tall man must have taken her—killed her. If only George had stayed awake last night, maybe he could have protected her. This was all his fault.

A sob tore out of his chest.

Police officers tossed him into a prison carriage bound for Newgate Prison. The carriage was already packed with other prisoners, members of a gang of shoplifters and pickpockets. Curiously, most of them were girls not much older than George, though the dim light at the back of the carriage carved deep shadows into their faces. They narrowed their sunken eyes at him, looming above him like an army of ghosts. Vaguely, he registered the taunts and jabs they made at his expense, barely whispered under their breath.

"Now, girls, go easy on the poor lad. He's having a bad day. Enjoy your stay at Newgate, *Lord* Devonshire," Vice-Chancellor Shadwell said as a royal guard shut and bolted the carriage door. All the light disappeared, and the carriage became as dark as a tomb. As dark as Ada's tomb would be.

A surge of hot rage swept through George. He flung himself to the door. "Let me out! Let me out NOW! I didn't do it!"

Behind him, the girls jeered.

"Give me another chance, too."

"I'm innocent. Honest, I am."

"Ask me mum, she'll tell you. I'm a good girl!"

A heavy fist thumped on the side of the carriage. It lurched forward, rumbling its way south through London toward Newgate Street.

George collapsed on the hard wooden bench. He'd lost everything to the Society. Don Nadie had won. The last twelve hours of his life felt like battling a strange monster in the dark; every time he fought back, another tentacle would slither out from the shadows to strike. Now, even if he proved his innocence, Ada would still be gone. He imagined Oscar's and Ruthie's faces when they learned the news, which sent a fresh wave of misery through him. He buried his face in his hands and began to weep.

"Cheer up, we're all in the suds now," the girl seated across from him called out. "No use blubbering."

"What a sniveler. I'll give him somefink to cry about," said another girl.

"Aw, shut yer potato trap, Maggie," a squeaky high voice said. "You's the one with the thick fingers that's got us in this mess."

"'Twasn't my fingers what done it. Was the new girl got us nabbed with her gummy mittens."

George thought of Ada's slender fingers and how

they'd never again make a machine or peel a hard-boiled egg. Fresh tears dripped down the tip of his nose. "I never got the chance to say goodbye," he exclaimed to no one in particular. "She's dead. My best friend is dead, and the last time I saw her, we were arguing."

One of the girls slid next to him on the bench. It was odd that she wasn't wearing handcuffs. Her knobby elbow poked encouragingly into George's side. "Your friend must have been a right trusty trout, then."

"I have no idea what that means," George replied, his face still buried in his hands. "I'd like to mourn in peace, please."

"Suit yourself. But you shouldn't waste no tears on the dead. Ain't no use thinking nothing about the dear departed."

"You didn't know her. She wouldn't mind if I think about her," George said roughly. He turned away to look through the bars at the streets flashing by. Ada wouldn't have wanted him to sit here blubbering, that much was true. She would have wanted him to *do* something. To make her life mean something. George clenched his fists. She would have wanted him to make the Society pay for what they'd done to her.

The girl's soft, warm hands covered his wrists where the handcuffs shackled him. She leaned closer, whispering in his ear in a very different voice. "If your friend were here right now, do you know what she'd say to you?"

George froze. He knew that voice, but it was impossible that he was hearing it. He looked up into the fierce, dark eyes of a ghost. "It's you! You've come back for revenge!"

Ada's ghost sighed. "No, that's *not* what she would say. She would say, 'Hold on to something, Lord Devonshire. This might get a little bumpy.'"

George patted the ghost's knees, then her hands, then her shoulder, then her face. She wasn't a ghost at all. She was solid and real and...alive.

"Miss Byron!" George exclaimed, embracing her fiercely before pulling away again. "I don't understand. What are you doing here?"

"Rescuing you, obviously," Ada replied. She turned to the girls at the back of the carriage. "Now, Maggie!"

The girl called Maggie grabbed an iron crowbar that had been hidden under her seat. With a practiced jab, she inserted it into a small slot in the floor of the carriage opposite the doors, then thrust it down with all her weight. There was a loud *pop* as the carriage broke free of its hitch.

The rest of the girls rushed at the carriage doors, which flew open as the iron hinges disintegrated into clouds of rust-colored dust. At the same time, George's wrists started to feel uncomfortably hot. He looked down to see that his handcuffs had begun to dissolve in the same way as the door's hinges. His skin itched terribly, and red blisters formed where it touched the smoking metal.

Ada grabbed his aching hands and pulled him to his feet, then slammed his ironclad wrists against the side of the carriage. In a gust of red powder, his handcuffs crumbled into pieces.

"Acid," Ada explained cheerfully.

"Acid," George repeated, ready to weep again with gratitude and also from the tenderness of his raw, itchy skin.

"Yes. Time to go, everyone!" she shouted.

But Ada needn't have said anything. The other girls were already launching themselves out of the busted-open doors with cries of glee as the unhitched carriage careened wildly through the streets. They dispersed, torn and raggedy skirts fluttering behind them, weaving through a gathering crowd of onlookers like strands of multicolored thread.

"But—" George began to protest. His teeth chattered and his vision blurred with the fierce rattling of the carriage over cobblestones below.

"Don't think. Just jump," Ada said.

So George jumped. His feet hit the hard cobblestones with a jolt of pain that raced through his ankles and into his shins. Ada pulled him up, and a second later they were running, escaping into the twisted alleys that wound through the heart of London.

Chapter Eight

After they had run all the way to the Thames River, Ada finally slowed down and led George behind a row of scraggly bushes. Panting, George slung his arm around Ada to assure himself once again that she was alive. Huddled together, they listened to the river splash against the stony shore and waited as a pack of police officers ran past, then disappeared down another street.

"What happened, Ada?" George whispered. "I thought you were dead. The vice-chancellor of England told me he read your obituary in the paper."

Ada smiled. "I am dead—legally, anyway. Not physically dead, as you can see."

George laughed in delight, but the laugh turned into a

groan. "I might as well be dead, too. Do you know what they said I've done? Everyone thinks I tried to murder the King with my truffles. But I didn't—I swear on Frobisher's life I didn't. I'm innocent. You believe me, don't you, Ada?"

The occasional police officer strode past their hiding place as George told Ada what had happened the previous night after he'd gone back to No. 10 Dorset Square. He shared every detail with her: his trip to No. 10, the portrait over the fireplace that contained the Star of Victory, the tall man revealing that he knew George's grandfather and that he had organized C.R.U.M.P.E.T.S. and confessing that he was the one who had sent the Society of Nobodies after George and Ada, and now, Il Naso in Spain. Sheepishly, George finished by explaining what had happened to the mechanical frog after the royal guards showed up to arrest him.

Grimacing, Ada said, "I'll build another."

"Now that you've rescued me, how are we going to clear my name so that we can stop the Society?" George asked hopefully.

Ada took off her white linen apron and tied it around George's head and jaw to disguise him. On her own head, she put a lace-trimmed mobcap that hid most of her hair.

With a smile, she said, "From what I've heard, the evidence is very convincing. Convincing enough to land you a one-way ticket to Newgate Prison."

All of George's emotions flooded out like a hurricane. "How can you be smiling at this moment? You were headed to prison, too! For joining a gang of shoplifters? Really? What nice company you've been keeping in your afterlife."

"Keep your voice down," Ada said. She popped her head over a bush, then ducked back down. "We have a long walk ahead of us, and it won't do any good to be shouting about prisons and gangs the entire way."

He tore the apron off his head and raked his fingers through his hair. "Keep my voice down? In case you've forgotten, I've been accused of attempting to murder the *King*."

The same fiery hate he'd felt as he cowered before the tall man reared up in his chest. George tried to swallow it down, remembering what his grandfather had once told him: *You must never hate anyone, because if you hate someone, that means you are afraid of them.*

Whatever happened, George didn't want to be afraid of the villain in No. 10. George was brave now. A hero.

"The tall man is behind all of this. *He* poisoned the King. Don Nadie, Nobody, whatever his name is, should be rotting in Newgate right now for what he's done. And then he should spend the rest of eternity in—"

"Oh dear," Ada interrupted. "I see that I'll have to spell it all out for you. Firstly, no one poisoned the King. I was at the palace having breakfast with my friend Princess Victoria, and nothing out of the ordinary happened. The King has a terrible diet and is prone to indigestion on a daily basis. If I had to offer a theory, I would say that someone easily might have suggested to the royal doctor that *perhaps*, this time, the King's indigestion was caused by something more serious than eating twenty-five chocolate tortes for breakfast. The power of suggestion is very— George, there's a spider on your shoulder."

"A spider?" George frantically brushed his shoulders. "Where? Where is it? Get it off!"

Ada snorted with laughter. She opened her arms wide as if she wanted to speak to the whole world. "There is no spider! Don't you see? *Suggestion*."

George's cheeks flamed red-hot. He straightened his jacket. "It's not funny! A poor, innocent duck is dead because of what that man did."

"I am sorry about the duck," Ada said sadly. Her face darkened. "Though if Don Nadie is planting a suggestion that you attempted to assassinate the King, that's what everyone will really think if the King dies."

"Do you think he's framing me for a murder he hasn't yet committed?" George's heart pounded with fear. "We have to stop him before he does any more damage. He even planted fake crime reports about my grandfather in the Old Bailey Proceedings."

George withdrew the reports Vice-Chancellor Shadwell had given him from his pocket. Ada examined them over his shoulder. "These don't look fake."

"But...they can't be real. Trust me," George said firmly. They couldn't be real. If they were real, his grandfather *had* kept secrets from him. And although Ada and Oscar had shown him that anything was possible, that one particular thing was not. The 1st Lord of Devonshire was not a liar or a criminal. That was not his legacy.

Ada handed the reports back to George. "You won't want to hear this, either, but I dare say Don Nadie might be the person who wrote that nasty letter to your grandfather."

George's mind flashed back to the letter. "Ada—*nobody*

signed it," he exhaled. Some of the pieces were starting to fit together, just like the secret puzzles that made up his grandfather's bookshelves. He pulled the Star of Victory out of his pocket and stared into the cracked jewel, as if he could find the answer hidden inside the swirling blues of the sapphire. "At least Don Nadie can't hurt my grandfather. But he might hurt a lot of other people. He's going to attack C.R.U.M.P.E.T.S., and he threatened your mother's and Frobisher's lives if we warn any of the scientists. I tried to tell the vice-chancellor about him, but who is going to believe me now?"

Ada let her head sink into her hands. "My mother already thinks my inventions are dangerous. I can't believe that my invitation to C.R.U.M.P.E.T.S. might be the thing that gets *her* killed. She'd never forgive me."

"Don't worry, Ada." George playfully nudged her shoulder with his, trying to cheer her up. "Maybe she'll never find out. Besides, how much harm could Don Nadie do with a bunch of musty old scientists, anyway?"

"Oh, the possibilities are endless. There's the entire presentation on electromagnetism, and Michael Faraday will demonstrate his latest experiments on electromagnetic liquids and the optical properties of electricity. Could you imagine? If we could make the spark of life visible, if we could harness the energy of the earth, then there's no end to what kind of terrible weapons he could make!" Ada huffed. "Whoever this Don Nadie is, he's far more cunning than anyone we've seen from the Society so far."

"Well, he already has the spark of something in his walking stick," George grumbled. "He said that as soon as he retrieves that map, he'll be a *somebody* again. What could the map to the Star of Victory have to do with this?"

Ada shook her head. "I don't know. But whatever your grandfather is hiding is far more valuable or dangerous than we thought. Don Nadie has a personal interest in the Devonshires."

George swallowed hard. He remembered what his grandfather had once told him about the map: that if discovered, its hidden secret would guarantee the owner victory in any battle. His mind whirred with possibilities like one of Ada's machines. What miraculous thing could be disguised in the map's ink? And what would happen if Don Nadie found it first?

He thought of the crime reports. He thought of the vile letter, too, so full of hate and anger, concealed in his grandfather's book for years.

Why would anyone hate his grandfather?

Memories—real memories, not strange clues tucked away in books or musty newspaper reports—flitted into his head, one after another. His grandfather with a cup of steaming tea, the tip of his pen hovering over an acrostic puzzle or a map. The wooden toys he'd carved for George with his own hands, demonstrating with endless patience how to make a jig doll dance or throw a bandalore so that its string would wind up again around the wooden disc. Smiles—the countless, beaming smiles of everyone his grandfather passed on the street when they walked to the baker's to pick up gingerbread at Christmastime. Everyone loved the 1st Lord of Devonshire. George most of all.

The 1st Lord of Devonshire was good. He was a hero. And the tall man was a villain.

It made sense that a villain would hate a hero.

And because his grandfather was dead, it was up to George to stop the villain, who was very much alive.

"Don Nadie wants the map. Getting it is part of his plan, so if we find Il Naso first, maybe we can stop his plan in its tracks," he said. "How are we going to do that?"

Ada's face hardened into a fierce look that George knew too well. "We can't find the answers we seek in

London. Let's get the map from Il Naso in Spain before the Society does."

A gust of wind whipped through George's hair. After his nightmarish morning, he could at last draw in a deep breath. On the marshy breeze, he smelled the possibility of adventure. (He also smelled sewage drifting in from the Thames.) The weight of his impending doom was lifted off his chest. Beyond all reason, a smile tugged at the corner of his lips. He was finally going to solve the puzzle of the map. His grandfather was no longer of this earth, but piece by piece, he was assembling a tapestry for George to guide him forward and give him strength.

Simple doesn't build character, he'd said.

Except—

They were missing something. Or someone.

"The Society is already chasing Il Naso. We're sure to meet them along the way, and we can't face them by ourselves."

Ada crossed her arms, smug. "Are you saying we need help, Lord Devonshire?"

George smirked. "It wouldn't *hurt* to have a couple of pirates on our side. And an orangutan. After all, it was Oscar who saved us from the Society last time."

When George had first met Oscar, he didn't see how they could ever be friends: they seemed like complete opposites. But soon George had grown fond of Oscar's cheerfulness and had become impressed by his many talents. When they'd been trapped with no hope of escape, Oscar had set off an explosion to save them using only a simple rock and his flint stone. The memories of golden flames danced in George's head. He couldn't bear the thought of embarking on an adventure without his friend with the paint-stained fingers.

Ada clapped; then her clapping turned into a whoop of joy. "Orangutans are quite useful, too! Plus, Captain Bibble and his crew hate the Society as much as we do. We'll form a fleet!"

"That's the spirit! But..." George paused. "A fleet? A fleet of what? Captain Bibble only has one boat."

"Come on. I have something incredible to show you," Ada said, beaming. "We have a whale to catch."

Once they were sure no police officers were coming, they hurried along the river for a while, until they were farther east in London than George had ever been. The air was thick with smoke, and particles of smog seemed to cast a dull haze over the skyline. With every block, houses and shops crowded closer and closer together. This was a dirtier, shabbier city than the comfortable neighborhood near Regent's Park that George knew.

They continued walking along the river until they reached the London Docks. The square pool of water was crowded with ships of every size, all moored along the edge with their sails stowed and their cargo holds open. Their bare masts stuck up like strange trees draped with vines of rigging rope.

Ada weaved and dodged her way through the docks, where workers in flat caps and patched woolen trousers wrangled gigantic crates. George lagged farther and farther behind, letting all the sights and sounds soak into him as if he were a sponge. If they weren't successful in their quest to get the map, this might be the last time George set foot in the land of his birth.

Workers swarmed like ants around the ships, loading one, unloading another. Cranes swung huge pallets overhead. Crates and barrels were stacked everywhere, their contents hidden and stamped with names even George didn't recognize. He could only guess what was inside from the various smells: the green-grass scent of tea leaves, the sickly-sweet stink of tobacco, and the woodsy perfume of fresh-cut timber planks.

"Look out!" a dockworker cried as a huge crate swayed on ropes directly overhead.

Ada led George to the end of a long, quiet dock, where a sailing ship patiently bobbed in the water. Waiting for them, apparently. Together, they walked up the gangplank. "A sailing ship? That's very traditional of you, Miss Byron."

Ada pressed her lips between her teeth in a guilty grin. "Just one more surprise, I'm afraid," she said, then reached up and pulled on a lever sticking out of the ship's mast.

With a loud *whoosh* and *thump*, the mast dropped into the depths of the ship and out of sight. George stumbled backward in amazement. A loud clicking noise made him spin around. Below him, gleaming metal fins sprouted from the portholes where cannons should be, while bit by bit, a long tail emerged from the stern. He watched in awe as wooden planks flipped to reveal undersides of burnished metal, only tearing his eyes away as Ada tugged him belowdecks through a small hatch. George pressed his face against the nearest porthole.

In less than a minute, the sailing ship had transformed into a mechanical whale.

George laughed with delight, even when the beast began to sink lower, lower, lower, his last whispers of doubt drowned out by the rushing roar of a new adventure as the whale plunged beneath the brown surface of the Thames.

First they'd recruit Oscar and his father to help them fight the Society. Then nothing would stop George until Nobody slinked back into whatever nasty hole he'd crawled out of.

Chapter Nine

All of Ada's inventions were like paintings done by the same artist. George pictured them in his head: her mechanical birds, the small one that had first invaded No. 8, and the much larger one that he'd crashed into the sea; her frog, which George had also destroyed; and now, her whale. They were all eerily graceful yet jerky, impossibly complicated yet rough. Her machines also always had a ridiculous number of levers and buttons and knobs, many of which looked like everyday objects plucked from their ordinariness: wooden spoons, clothespins, and cabinet knobs. So even though George had never been inside this whale, he felt instantly that he was somewhere familiar.

"Oscar's last letter came a few days ago. He said they

were fishing just west of Spain's southern coast, so I'll set a course."

Ada sat down at the control panel in the whale's head, which looked as though it had recently been the bow of the sailing ship. Two upholstered armchairs had been bolted to the floor, one directly in front of the ship's massive wooden steering wheel. Ada flipped levers and switches. In response, a golden needle on the dial in front of her spun wildly. George thought the instrument looked awfully similar to a compass he'd recently misplaced, but his complaints were lost in the rumble that tore through the whale as its engine whirred to life. Feeling the floor wobble beneath his feet, George walked unsteadily to the copilot's seat next to her and plopped down.

"When did you build this?" he asked. He craned his neck upward, where brass joints ran along the seams of the wooden planks from floor to ceiling. To protect from leaks, he guessed. It reminded him of a rib cage made of metal.

"I've been working on it here and there," she said, smiling.

George knew Ada well enough by now to know that she often accomplished impossible feats before breakfast.

But this whale was something else entirely. Building a ship usually took a hundred men an entire year to finish. "You've outdone yourself. It's so big...and complicated. It's much larger than the mechanical fish we stole from the Society."

"You mean the fish made from the design the Society stole from me first?" Ada raised her eyebrow. "This *is* it! Since it was based on my plans, disassembling it was fairly easy. I made it bigger and better. With a few minor improvements to the ballast system, I was able to expand the hull so that we could go on longer journeys without being so cramped."

In the dull light of the whale's cabin, George noticed the dark shadows under Ada's eyes. Working was always more important than sleeping to her. "What longer journeys were you planning to take? Wait, don't tell me—I want to be able to claim ignorance if your mother interrogates me."

Ada's smile faltered.

What if Lady Byron was so furious about his dragging Ada into a disastrous situation that she forbade George ever to see Ada again? The thought was too awful to say out loud. Instead, he practically shouted, "The whale is marvelous!"

Ada's smile returned. "Do you really think so?"

He nodded. Ada's inventions were so brilliant that George hardly understood them, let alone how to compliment them. He looked out the thick glass porthole directly to his left, where the last sliver of sky was shrinking and swirls of greenish-brown water were rising. They continued to sink into the river until the whale submerged completely with a loud *blub*. "So far, it's been excellent at sinking!"

Panels in the sides of the whale flexed as Ada steered the machine away from the docks. "Not quite the praise I was hoping for, but I'll take it. Would you mind manning the periscope to navigate above the water? Getting out of the docks and into the river might be a little tricky."

A slim green-and-silver instrument popped down from a hatch above him. It was used to see the world above water while they were underwater. George felt a rush of warmth when he saw that the sight piece had stopped right at his eye level—Ada must have designed it to fit his exact height. George pressed his eye against the periscope to see a blurry circle of sky.

When his vision adjusted to the lens, he spotted a nest of ships that stood between the mechanical whale and the open river. "You need to veer to the left. There's an American tobacco ship right ahead and a few more beyond, then we're clear."

"A tobacco ship?" she said.

"Yes." The whale gave a quiet groan and picked up speed. "Yes, that's good. A little more to the left. A little more. No, left, I said. Miss Byron, left!"

The whale's fin scraped against the other ship's hull. It slid through the wood like a knife through truffle butter. Debris burst into the waters around them.

"Excellent navigating," Ada said cheerfully.

George tore his eye away from the periscope to look at her. "Are you mad? You've punctured it! That ship is going to flood."

Ada's face darkened. "If you use one more breath to defend that nasty industry, I will steer us straight across the Atlantic and drop you off at the nearest tobacco farm."

"As if being wanted for murder wasn't enough..." George grumbled, pressing his eye against the cold metal again.

They sliced through a few more ships on their way out of the dockyard. When they finally emerged into the deeper, clearer waters of the Thames, the periscope was no longer needed. George settled back into the copilot's chair and watched the last bits of debris float by outside the porthole. In a matter of moments, they sped through the Thames and were quickly out into the wide estuary where the river emptied into the North Sea.

"We are officially ghosts now, aren't we?" George said. "How long do you think it will take to find Il Naso and get the map back?"

Ada straightened in her seat. "According to the C.R.U.M.P.E.T.S. invitation, the gathering is in thirty-seven days. Hah!"

"Hah! What?" George asked.

"Don Nadie's not in control of everything. He needs time for the scientists to arrive. They're traveling from all over the world!"

George felt grateful for Ada, who was the picture of confidence in the face of despair. "Let's hope that's enough time to find the map before our nemesis does."

Once Ada had set a course for Spain, there was not much to do except wait. George turned to exploring the rest of the vessel. He found several rooms, including a cramped engine room, a cargo hold, and a pantry stocked with weeks' worth of food. He also found a small berth for

At the time, he meant it with every bone in his body. He hated his father for calling George a spineless coward. He hated him for mocking his grandfather's stories, for abandoning George for days, and for wasting every penny his grandfather had ever made.

The 1st Lord of Devonshire never feared anyone, so he never had cause to hate. If George's grandfather was right—which he always was—then Don Nadie must have been very much afraid of George's grandfather to hate him so fiercely after all this time. The thought gave George a twinge of triumph.

George put the Star of Victory into the leather bag along with the letter and the crime reports from Vice-Chancellor Shadwell. Eventually, he'd be able to prove that they were fake.

Exhaustion rolled over him. He finished his dinner and joined Ada in the front of the ship. He sank into the copilot's chair, finally able to rest. Waves of light from the portholes rippled across the room, moving and changing like a living thing. Occasionally, a school of fish would dart past the porthole in a flash of silver bellies. It was eerie, yet beautiful. If Oscar were here, he would be filling up page after page with all the amazing sights and colors beneath the ocean. George itched with anticipation to see Oscar and Ruthie again.

A loud knock from a closet at the rear of the cabin woke George from his nap that had lasted all night. Remembering how Oscar and Ruthie had stowed away on the mechanical bird during their first Continental adventure, he had the wild hope that they'd appeared again out of thin air. He called out, "Oscar? Ruthie?"

He opened the door—and sprang back. It was not Oscar at all. It was Patty. She'd come loose from her restraints inside the closet, and her porcelain head was bumping against the closet door as she tried to walk forward.

"Oh," George said, his voice thick with disappointment.

The automaton took a step, jerkily. George instinctively reached out to help her. When he'd seen her in Ada's workshop, she'd seemed more like a doll, but now that she'd been repaired and was moving, George remembered why he'd thought she was real when he first saw her in the Jaquet-Droz workshop in Geneva. The curls in her blond wig bounced as she shuffled past George. She was now wearing an elaborate silk gown that reached all the way to her shoes, which were painted a dazzling red. She was roughly the same size as Ada, a few inches taller than George.

Ada ushered the automaton to the pilot's seat and made her sit down. "She's going to make an excellent copilot one day!" Ada beamed.

"I thought you said she couldn't walk. How did she learn how to walk?" George whispered, eyeing Patty nervously. Ada had opened up Patty's back panel to adjust her bright brass gears.

Ada snorted. "Don't be silly, George. She can't hear you ... yet. I gave her some new gears while you were asleep to move her legs. She can only do what she's been given gears to do, remember. She can fire the water cannon, walk, and play music on the organ. And with a few minor adjustments, she can pull levers in a prescribed sequence."

George peered at Patty's serene porcelain smile, then dropped his eyes—and inhaled sharply. "The necklace."

The butterfly gleamed around the automaton's neck— a butterfly that resembled the decorative illustrated wings on the two bottom corners of his grandfather's map. When the map folded along its creases, the butterfly halves came together to form a whole.

George reached up and unclasped the butterfly, studying it silently while Ada tinkered with Patty's mechanisms. The wingspan was slightly wider than his palm. Though he didn't have the map in front of him for comparison, George recognized the intricate patterned web on the wings, and the unique way each tip ended in a curlicue. Certainty filled him. This butterfly was similar to the one drawn on his map. Maybe identical. "May I hold on to this?"

"Be my guest," Ada said. "It doesn't seem necessary to her functioning. I know that you think it's a clue, George, but I don't know how the 1st Lord of Devonshire could have known you'd find it."

He added the silver butterfly to his leather bag. "I know how impossible it seems, but you're the one who taught me to believe in impossible things. Oh—"

George noticed the closet door was still open. He trotted back to close it. A coffin-shaped trunk for Patty and several other pieces of luggage were inside. Large shipping labels were stuck all over the luggage. "Ada, what's the Somerville School—"

Ada dropped her wrench.

George just managed to read the rest of the destination on the labels, SOMERVILLE SCHOOL FOR LADIES OF SUBSTANCE, before Ada shut the closet door.

"*Nothing* of your concern or mine," Ada said through gritted teeth. "But, if you must know, Mrs. Somer*vile* teaches *social graces and other charms for ladies of refinement*. I know because Mrs. Somerville is friends with my mother and my mother will not stop talking about it."

Heat crept into George's neck. "A boarding school? Does that mean you're leaving?"

"Not if I can help it. I'm sure stopping an international criminal organization will be enough to convince my mother not to enroll me," she said primly.

"Right. Of course." George managed a nod. "For what it's worth, I think you're very refined, Ada."

"I agree. For example, this is how a lady holds a wrench." Smirking, Ada retrieved her wrench and held it aloft, lifting her pinky. They burst into giggles.

When their laughter subsided, Ada looked less irritated. "They *do* have science classes and a metalworking course that wouldn't be *terrible*. But my manners are perfectly acceptable. I don't have to clasp my hands a certain way or spiral my hair from right to left. I don't understand why my mother can't let me do things my way. Ever since we got back from Venice, it's as if she's been trying to change me little by little," she said, her voice falling. "What she won't understand is that people don't change. I certainly won't."

"You're perfect the way you are," George agreed. He remembered the lessons his grandfather used to give him. A part of him had always longed to go to school to learn more about accounting. "What if you didn't think about it as change, but more of an improvement—like giving yourself some extra gears? What if you just stayed the same Ada with an increased talent for metalworking?"

"Going to some boring old school isn't going to give me any new gears I couldn't give myself," Ada insisted grumpily.

"I suppose that's true." George nodded. Selfishly, he would prefer Ada not go away. Besides, there was no law that said children *had* to go to school.

A shadow suddenly fell over them. George snapped his head up. They were passing underneath something large. Heart racing, he pressed his face to the porthole while Ada ran to the whale's head.

"A whale," he said breathlessly. "A real, live whale. Or a sea monster. My grandfather's map was full of beasts. Maybe we found one."

Ada pulled back on the throttle to slow their craft, then lowered the periscope from the ceiling so she could investigate. "It's more likely to be a ship. Although it could be an algae bloom or a large patch of flotsam. I'm not sure. The periscope is crusted over with salt and muck already, so all I can see is a great big shadow."

Once they were a safe distance from the shadow, the little whale surfaced with a splash. Ada and George climbed the ladder to the top hatch. Ada scrambled onto the deck and called down, "I was right. It's a ship."

George emerged after her. He shaded his eyes against the low sun. In the northwest, a three-masted schooner bobbed up and down in the vast, choppy ocean that stretched forever in the distance. The flat-topped cliffs of Portugal in the east looked like the edge of a broken sugar cookie. "I guess that's better than a sea monster."

Ada continued to squint at the ship while she scrubbed the periscope lens with the fabric of her skirt. "It's turning about. It's coming this way. George—it's flying a black flag. I think it's Captain Bibble's ship!"

George's heart began hammering in his chest. Something about the situation didn't feel right. "Are you sure? We thought we'd have to search the entire coastline of Spain, and they just happen to be here? With my luck, nothing is ever this easy."

Ada laughed, then clapped her hands together. "It is,

George—look! It's Captain Bibble's flag. Oscar must have a sixth sense for adventure. He's found us! Can you imagine the look on Oscar's face when he sees us? Can you imagine how many new rocks he'll have in his collection to show us?"

George watched as the schooner sailed toward them. It was indeed flying Captain Bibble's black mermaid flag. His ship, the *Kylling*, had been destroyed during their battle with the Society, but according to Oscar's letters, he'd found (or, more likely, stolen) a new one. "I just hope Captain Bibble doesn't fire on our ship. He can be a bit touchy."

This was a serendipitous turn of fortune if there ever was one. George's days of being cursed with bad luck were clearly a thing of the distant past. Joy swept through him at the thought of Oscar's gap-toothed smile and Ruthie's hairy arms hugging him. He jumped up and down and waved at the ship. "It's about time something happened in my favor, don't you think? Look, they're waving at us!"

Ada didn't wave back. Instead, her eyes grew wide as the wind whipped her curls around her pale face. "George, something's not right."

The ship's sails billowed furiously in the wind as it gained speed. It was getting closer and closer, but it wasn't slowing down, not even when it was only a whale's length away from them.

The people who were waving at them leaned over the edge of the deck, but they weren't smiling in greeting. Oscar's face was nowhere to be seen. In fact, none of the pirates looked familiar. Bibble's crew had been fearsome— battle-scarred and tattooed from head to toe—but these pirates looked lethal. Their teeth were capped with silver sharpened into metal spikes. Silver knives were woven into their long, braided hair. And each and every one of them was pointing a gleaming weapon down at George and Ada.

A silver arrow whizzed by Ada's head and embedded itself in the whale's hull with a swift *thunk*.

"Dive!" Ada yelled, throwing herself onto the hull.

George lunged for Ada's arm and dragged her inside the whale. She tumbled down the ladder as George slammed the hatch shut behind them, breathing hard.

Ada scrambled to her feet and clutched George. "We'd better..."

She trailed off, her eyes drifting to the ceiling. A faint buzzing came from a spot above their heads. The sound grew louder and louder until something pointed and silver poked through the hull above them. It grew like a flower emerging from the soil.

The arrowhead.

The arrow drilled completely through the outer hull in an instant, dropping clean through the hole it had made in the whale, spinning around itself with an angry buzz. Instinctively, George picked up a metal wrench and smashed the arrow to pieces. Tiny springs and gears exploded onto the floor.

Ada turned to George, her eyes wild with excitement and fear.

The Society had found them already.

Chapter Ten

Thunk. Thunk. Two more arrows hit the hull above them. George brandished the wrench like a cricket bat, waiting to smash the arrows as soon as they drilled through.

"We have to get out of here," George said.

Ada, however, was already dashing toward the storeroom in the whale's tail instead of the cockpit in the whale's head. "We're not going anywhere if we're leaking like a sieve. We've got to plug up those holes so that we can dive!" she shouted.

Thunk.

"But if we stay here, the pirates will keep putting

holes in the ship and eventually start putting holes in us!" George said as he whacked another arrow into a million shining pieces.

"Stop smashing those arrows. Maybe I could use them for something," Ada's voice called out faintly through the walls. She reappeared lugging a heavy bucket and a paintbrush.

Thunk.

"I know what you're going to say," she said. *Thunk. Thunk.* "But this is not paint and we're not redecorating. Remember the barnacle glue you borrowed from me? This is even stickier. It's a highly viscous adhesive that is modeled after snail slime. It's also waterproof, but it has to completely cover the hole from the outside like a patch. One little swipe across each hole and we'll be as good as new. Are you ready?"

"Ready?" George screeched. Another arrow broke through the wooden hull and clattered to the floor by his feet. Spears of sunlight pierced the air around them. "How could I possibly be ready?"

"I count eight holes." *Thunk.* She shoved the bucket into his hands. "Nine."

Ada climbed up the ladder to open the hatch. George grabbed the hem of her skirt. "What are you doing? If we go out there, we'll die!"

"And if we go under full of holes, we'll die!" she said, pulling her skirt from George's grasp.

Thunk.

"Ten. We'll go up together. I primed the water cannon's pump and opened the valve. I'll handle the cannon because we both know you have terrible aim. Don't worry, George, I won't let those pirates make you into Swiss cheese." Ada looked down at him, both of her eyebrows lifted in warning. "Oh, and one more thing. Don't get the snail slime on your skin. Trust me. It's very sticky."

Ada opened the hatch and disappeared into the sunlight. Now it was George's turn. "It would have been nice to know there was a water cannon on the ship earlier," he said grumpily to himself. *Thunk.* "Eleven."

When George emerged onto the whale's back, the roar of the water cannon filled his ears. The pirate ship now loomed above them, as immovable and imposing as a mountain. Ada aimed the nozzle of the water cannon so that its powerful jet of water spurted directly at the archer and his arrows. The pirates screamed.

George picked up the brush and began quickly dabbing the snail slime over the round holes dotting the hull. He counted each patch to himself. *Three. Four.* Beads of sweat rained down from his forehead. *Eight. Nine. Ten.*

He whipped his head around, frantically looking for the last hole. There it was, at the bow of the ship close to where the top of the periscope poked out.

George took a step toward the hole but found that he could not move. He looked down and saw a wet face half-covered by sopping hair. It was a pirate, climbing over the edge of the whale from the ocean, a long, sharp knife clutched between his teeth. But the pirate wasn't the reason George couldn't move.

He'd stepped on one of the holes he'd already patched with snail slime. No amount of jerking, twisting, or pulling loosened the sole of his shoe from the glue.

"Miss Byron, help!" George screamed as he knelt down to unlace his boot. His shaking fingers fumbled with the laces. The pirate was already up over the edge of the deck, his face twisted in a vicious snarl. He removed his knife from his teeth and raised it high.

A torrent of water hit the pirate square in the chest, sweeping him into the sea.

"Thank you," George called out weakly. He limped unevenly toward the last hole and dabbed it with a glob of slime. "Done!"

Ada looked back at him, tipping her chin to beckon him closer. "Cover our retreat while I prepare us to dive. As soon as the front of the whale is at a forty-five-degree angle, get back inside the hatch."

They exchanged places. He grabbed the handles on either side of the water cannon and aimed at the pirate ship. Ada took the bucket of slime and climbed into the hatch.

A flock of silver-tipped arrows soared across the blue sky. George swiveled the cannon upward to intercept them. He whooped for joy when the stream of water knocked them off course. There wasn't much time to celebrate, though. A window opened near the pirate ship's prow. A new weapon emerged through the window.

A cannon. Not a water cannon. The kind of cannon that shot huge, round, heavy cannonballs.

"Hurry, Ada, hurry," George pleaded in a desperate refrain.

A billow of white smoke rolled out of the cannon's mouth with a loud boom. George aimed his stream of water at the cannonball. The black ball slowed just enough to fall short of hitting the whale. It sent up a spray of water as George triumphantly yelled, "Huzzah!"

George felt himself rising as the front of the ship angled down. The whale was beginning to dive. Just then, the pirates' cannon fired again. George gripped the handles of the water cannon as if his own strength could flow into the stream, but it was no use. The iron ball collided with the jet of water but was still spinning, spinning, spinning right for him.

George let go of the handles seconds before the massive ball struck the water cannon with an earsplitting crunch of wood and water and metal. The device exploded in a shower of splinters, but it protected the ship from suffering any more damage. The cannonball rolled into the ocean on the other side of him with a splash and sizzle.

Head ringing, George skidded down the deck, and only just managed to grab on to the hatch to stop himself from plunging into the water below. With a final tug, he pulled himself through the opening, then slammed the door down on top of himself and scurried down the ladder.

"We survived the Society!"

George wiggled his stockinged toes with a laugh, grinning so much that his cheeks began to hurt. The water cannon was destroyed, but they were alive.

"And the only casualty was your boot!" Ada called back.

"And your water cannon," George said, letting his body collapse against the rungs of the ladder. He watched as Ada settled in the captain's chair. The whale rumbled pleasantly under his legs, bringing the feeling back into them.

George had opened his mouth to let out a breath of relief when he spotted something that made his hair stand on end. A trail of water snaked from the porthole to the other side of a pillar—three paces away from where Ada sat.

George did not have time to cry out a warning because the pirate shrieked first.

Chapter Eleven

The man launched himself toward Ada, silver teeth bared in an earsplitting howl.

Sliding forward on his stockinged foot, George charged the pirate. On the way, he ripped one of the wooden spoon levers from the control panel. He collided with the pirate's chest.

The pirate grunted but didn't fall. George jabbed the spoon into the softest part of the pirate's belly, but the pirate was quicker and stronger. He grabbed the spoon and shoved it back into George. As George fell into Patty, Ada sprang up from the captain's chair to escape. Again, the pirate was too quick. He seized her by the waist, pinning her arms to her sides. Ada thrashed and kicked, but the pirate's grip was firm, and he was able to lift her in the air. As the pirate carried her away, Ada hooked her feet around the ladder to stop him. "George!"

Still dizzy, George seized Patty, then flung her forward with all his strength. "Catch!"

The pirate was so shocked to see a porcelain-faced girl flying toward him that he dropped Ada. Patty's heavy mechanical body knocked the wind from the pirate's lungs when she crashed into him. He spun the mechanical girl around like an awkward dance partner before pushing her back into a corner. Ada vaulted off the ladder in a graceful cartwheel, landing next to George.

Ada and George looked at each other. Then, at the same time, they looked at the bucket of snail slime at their feet.

George kicked the bucket of snail slime over with his booted foot. A sharp pain radiated up to his shin, but it worked—the slime oozed between him, Ada, and the pirate. The scraggly man froze in his tracks as soon as he set foot in the slime. While he attempted to free his leather boot from the layer of snail slime, Ada grabbed a chair from the back of the ship, frantically coating it in more slime.

"Sit," Ada said, shoving the chair hard into the back of the pirate's legs. The pirate's black eyes darted around the room, looking for an escape. He squinted menacingly at George. The dry, sunburned skin around his eyes cracked. Finally, he sat.

George looped a rope around the pirate's chest and arms and tied him to the chair for good measure. Everything had happened so fast, he'd had no time to be scared. Blood was pumping in his ears louder than the ocean outside.

"Who are you?" Ada demanded.

Emboldened by the pirate's captivity, George shouted, "Tell us your name!"

The pirate ran his tongue across his sharp teeth. He thrashed against the ropes, but they held firm. "Cabeza de Perro," he said proudly. "My name is Cabeza de Perro."

"Dog Head? Your name in English is Dog Head?" Ada asked.

"*Sí*. My mother named me Ángel, but the name did not fit me. I am no angel. This name fits better. But my name should not concern you. I am a Nobody," said Cabeza de Perro.

George felt himself go pale as he imagined Oscar and his father facing an entire crew of Nobodies, but Cabeza de Perro didn't seem to notice. "What is this liquid? Poison? Please, do not kill me."

George scoffed. "You were going to kill *me*!"

Cabeza de Perro wriggled his wet shoulders as much as his position would allow. "I do not want to kill. My captain says only to capture you and the girl. Everyone else..." He trailed off, then tossed his head to the side and made the universal throat-cutting sound.

"Your captain? What about the true captain of that ship, Captain Bibble the Beastly, the Bane of Britain?" George asked.

The pirate grimaced and spat on the floor. "That is not my captain. That is my enemy. We took his ship from him and left him to die."

"To die?" George repeated. His heart stuttered, and his chest felt as tight as if a giant fist had squeezed all the air out of his lungs. He met Ada's eyes. They were dazed with surprise and shock.

George whirled on the pirate, anger roaring in his chest. "Were a boy and an orange ape on board? What happened to them? Did you hurt them? If you hurt them, I'll—"

"No boy, no boy, only the men with no arms, no legs," said Cabeza de Perro. "We take the ship easily. The crew is lazy. They leave their boat in the Bahía de Algeciras and think they are safe and that no one will touch them. Well, they are wrong. My captain gave us special weapons that no one else has."

George let out a shuddering breath. Oscar and Ruthie were safe. He cracked his knuckles and straightened up. "Tell me who you're working for. Who's giving your orders?"

Cabeza de Perro threw his shoulders back proudly. The snail slime squelched underneath him. *"El gran jefe* Nobody, Don Nadie, the pirate of all pirates! He is a pirate of the land and the sea and the sky. The king of all criminals. He has suffered more than any of us. He would grind your bones between his teeth and then feed the powder to the sharks."

Cold gripped George's chest. He tried to swallow his fear, keep his voice calm. "We're familiar with him. Is—is he on your ship now?"

The pirate let out a braying laugh. "No. He is not the captain of my ship. He is my captain's captain. My captain's captain's captain. My captain's captain's—"

"Yes, he's very high up, I get the point," George said.

"Well," Ada said, a note of relief in her voice, "why didn't you say all that in the first place? You could have saved us the trouble of tying you up."

With a skeptical frown, the pirate asked, "So you let me go?"

"Of course. I'm terribly sorry. If these ropes weren't stuck to the chair, I would untie you right now. As soon as the glue unsticks, we'll let you go," Ada said sweetly.

George looked at Ada. "We will?"

"Yes. We wouldn't want to harm one of our compatriots, would we?" She shot George a pointed look, then turned back to the pirate and continued, "I *deduce* that you *also* received an instruction to attack any unfamiliar mechanical creatures? Those were our instructions, too."

Cabeza de Perro's eyes narrowed suspiciously at Ada, but when he turned his gaze to George, they narrowed even further. "Ha! You? You are a Nobody?"

Although Ada was lying, George was still offended by the pirate's disbelief. "Why not me? My grandfather was a maritime war"—Ada elbowed him—"criminal. Yes, he was a pirate, too. The fiercest, most pirate-y of pirates." He cleared his throat, trying to keep up with the deception. "A mechanical bat delivered the message to us earlier this morning. Isn't that right?"

The pirate's black eyes darted between Ada and George. "The messenger was not a bat, it was a bird."

Ada scoffed. Her hands flew to her hips as if she were deeply offended. "Of course it was. Are you saying that the fearless Don Nadie couldn't make a mechanical bird that could also transform into a bat?"

"No, no—I am only testing you," the pirate said quickly. "I knew it could do that."

"Of course you did. We received the same message, which is why *we* boarded this whale only thirty minutes before you did. But that bald boy and very short girl escaped."

"Bald boy? Short girl?" Cabeza de Perro's glance bounced back and forth between them. "That is not how I remember the message...."

A sheen of sweat broke out on George's forehead. He quickly wiped his sleeve across his face. Ada turned her back on the pirate, leaned over, and whispered into George's ear. "See if he knows Don Nadie's true identity, and be *quick*."

Just then, the clock on the wall began to chime. "Teatime!" Ada announced.

Ada bustled to the kitchen to prepare a cup of tea. George pulled a chair next to Cabeza de Perro, leaning in as close as he dared. The damp pirate smelled as if he'd been smeared with fish guts. Though the smell made his insides churn with disgust, George plastered on his most engaging smile. "Isn't being a Nobody simply the greatest? My friend and I are rather new, but I think we're doing well, don't you? What has your crew captured lately besides that old pirate ship?"

Cabeza de Perro lifted his chin defiantly. "Nobodies do not capture anything. Nobodies take back what was rightfully ours all along."

"Yes, that's what I meant," George agreed, deepening his voice to keep it from squeaking from fear. This had the unexpected consequence of making him sound eerily like his father, and doubly pompous. "I heard old Don Nadie is sending us to London soon to steal inventions from some place called S.C.O.N.E.S. Or was it M.U.F.F.I.N.S.?"

George snapped his fingers as if he couldn't remember the name. Cabeza de Perro stared at him blankly.

"C.R.U.M.P.E.T.S., that's what it's called," George said. "I guess Don Nadie hasn't given your crew that information yet. Or maybe he never will. He must not trust you rusty-guts fishermen the way he trusts me. I bet you don't even know Don Nadie's real name, do you?"

Cabeza de Perro leaned forward, flashing his silver teeth. The rope strained against his chest. "Nobody is the only name I need to know. If that is the name he calls himself, then that is who he is. You know nothing about trust. Nobody's plans are bigger than the sea itself. He will give this *mundo injusto*, this unjust world, to the pirates and thieves. He says we will be able to walk free again. Wherever we want, we go. Whatever we want, we take. We are Nobodies, but soon we will be Somebodies again."

Ada returned, offering a cup of tea to Cabeza de Perro. Since the pirate could not hold it in his hands, she put the cup to his lips and let him sip it.

Cabeza de Perro licked a drop of tea from his cracked lips. "Don Nadie is unlike any other man. What he does not have, he finds. What he does not possess, he takes. What he does not like, he destroys. There is only one thing that is his, and his alone."

George tried to suppress a shiver. "What is it?"

"His revenge." Cabeza de Perro's lip curled. "He will never give up until he has his revenge. Until he has taken back what was taken from him, what rightfully belongs..." The pirate yawned, exposing several teeth in the back of his mouth that flashed like diamonds.

"What has been taken from him?" George interrupted. "The map? Is that what's been taken from him?"

The pirate blinked slowly. His eyes settled on George, unfocused and bleary. "The map..." A growling laugh escaped his throat. "Much more has been taken from him...."

The pirate's bearded chin drooped onto his chest as he fell fast asleep. George pounded a fist on his chest. "No! Wake up!"

Next to him, Ada peered into the drained teacup. "I hope that was the right amount of laudanum. He should sleep for a while."

George shook the sleeping pirate's shoulder. "Did you hear what he said? We need to wake him back up."

"He won't wake for hours," Ada said, lifting up the pirate's eyelid to peer at his pupil underneath. "I heard enough. I don't think he can help us, George. He clearly doesn't know Don Nadie's true identity."

"Do you think Don Nadie can really do all that, Ada? How can he give the world back to thieves? How can Nobodies be Somebodies?"

Ada murmured something to herself; then her face glowed with understanding. "Well, I'm sure he meant it figuratively. Don Nadie's plan isn't bigger than the sea, nor is he literally planning on giving the world back to thieves.

I've been studying my father's poetry. Poetry is full of figurative language and metaphors."

"I don't think the pirate was speaking in poetry," George said.

"No, but he wasn't making much sense, either. Neither does poetry sometimes, at least until you look deeper. What does it mean to be a nobody?" Ada held out her hands as if she were slicing the air between her syllables. "A no...body."

George wrinkled his forehead. "It means you don't have a...body? You don't belong anywhere? Maybe that's why Don Nadie wants my house. He wants somewhere to belong."

Ada tapped her fingernail against the teacup as she considered what George had said. "Maybe it's not just your grandfather's house he wants. Your grandfather was a nobleman. He belonged to the ruling class. Or a body can also mean a larger body, a group of people, like a political body or government. Maybe Don Nadie feels as though he doesn't belong to any group."

She drew in a sharp breath. "The Organization! When I didn't know what the Society of Nobodies was, I called it the Organization. I thought they were trying to take

127

down the government. I was wrong about their name, but maybe I was right about that! There are all sorts of people who don't belong—pirates, criminals, the poor, the enslaved, the imprisoned, the forgotten people everywhere who don't get a say in how the government works."

"But—"

"Even women can't vote. What if the Nobodies want to change that? What if taking their lives back means making a better world where everyone belongs? A world where a woman can be anything she wants to be."

George watched Ada's eyes begin to sparkle. Her mind had leapt ten thousand steps ahead, as usual. "You're talking about a revolution."

Ada rolled her shoulder as if a revolution did not cause her any great concern. "If Don Nadie is planning to overthrow the government, then what would he need? An army. And what does an army need? Weapons."

"That's an excellent theory, Ada. There's just one problem with it."

Ada frowned. "What?"

"Don Nadie is not a good person. If he's going to overthrow the government, he's not trying to make a better world."

She nodded. "I suppose. Don Nadie is dangerous, but he won't win. He has an entire society of people to carry out his bidding. But we have—"

Ada paused and looked around, waiting for George to finish her sentence. George knew exactly what she wanted him to say, which wasn't that they had a ship and food and favorable currents. What George was supposed to say was that they had *each other*. The problem was that without the rest of the *others*—Oscar and Ruthie—George couldn't say it.

Ada bit her lip. "I wish Cabeza de Perro had been able to tell us where Oscar and Ruthie are. And I hope Captain Bibble is safe."

With a lurch of his stomach, George recalled what Cabeza de Perro had told them about attacking Bibble's crew at Bahía de Algeciras. The pirate hadn't seen Oscar or Ruthie . . .

A spark ignited in George's brain. He grabbed Ada's shoulders. "Oscar. Ruthie. I think I know where we can find them."

Chapter Twelve

"Slow down. We've rounded the peninsula. The caves should be just ahead!" George exclaimed.

About an hour after they'd encountered Captain Bibble's stolen ship, the whale passed through the Strait of Gibraltar, the narrow channel of water that connected the Mediterranean Sea to the Atlantic Ocean. On a map, it looked like two fingertips—the pointer finger coming down from Spain, the thumb coming up from Morocco—that were almost pinched together, but not quite touching. In real life, there were still miles of water between the two sides of land. George couldn't even tell they were passing through the strait until he saw a hazy pyramid-shaped rock appear on the northern horizon.

He swiveled the periscope around to scan the shore-line of the Rock of Gibraltar, a towering peak whose sheer white cliffs rose up mythically from the sea. The cliffs reminded George of the walls of Chillon Castle, which they had invaded in Geneva, but built by nature, not man. Hollowed arches of stone lined the base of the cliff as if a gigantic mouse had nibbled away at the rock.

"Excellent navigating," Ada remarked from the pilot's chair. "You're almost as good as having a map, George."

Ada's unexpected praise caused a prideful flush to creep into George's cheeks. He dipped his head to hide the smile that tugged the corners of his lips. "I was just lucky that Mr. Cabeza mentioned that Bibble's crew was in the Bahía de Algeciras and that I remembered that its English name is the Bay of Gibraltar. My grandfather had a map of this area, including the bay and the rock. If Oscar wasn't on the ship when they were attacked, he *must* have been exploring the rock. It's probably the most famous hunk of limestone in the world."

"Your deduction makes perfect sense to me. I have no doubt that if Oscar wasn't on board his father's ship, then he must be here," Ada said.

Finally, through the periscope, George saw a small

131

rowboat anchored near the mouth of one of the caves. Until he saw the boat, George hadn't dared to trust that his luck would let him find his friends. But now a strange thrill tickled his ribs and puffed out his chest. If this was how Ada felt every time she correctly deduced the answer to a problem, it was no wonder she chased adventure. She didn't belong at the Somerville School for Ladies of Substance.

Ada steered the whale as close to the rocky shore as she could without puncturing the ship. As soon as they breached the surface of the water, George raced to the hatch and climbed out into the warm, salty air with Ada trailing close behind. He already felt lighter and happier, knowing that in a few moments, he would see Oscar's smiling face.

"Oscar! Ooooscar!"

The shore was strewn with gray and green-pocked boulders where the narrow beach met the water. Above, the edge of the cliff sheltered the beach like a massive overhanging porch. It was an alien landscape built for giants, and George had never felt so small. He picked his way over jutting rocks to the entrance of the caves, wading through the shallow waters until they reached the spot where the small rowboat was anchored—but the boat was empty, save for the worn-down nub of a pencil.

"Look, Ada! This must be theirs!" Cupping his hands around his mouth, he called, "Oscar! Ruthie!"

The cave answered with an echo: *Oscar, Ruthie, Oscar, Ruthie, Oscar, Ruthie.*

An orange flash caught his eye.

"I see Ruthie! Ruthie!" he shouted, flapping his arms wildly to attract her attention. The little orangutan shot out from the cave, climbing down the sheer wall of white limestone. Her fur was hard to miss as she swung like a pendulum from rock to rock, screeching loudly. At first, George thought this was some dream, that he couldn't possibly have been right. But then the orange blur scampered across the shore, flung herself onto George's back with a happy grunt, and wrapped her hairy arms around his neck.

"Hello, Ruthie," George said into her fur. Her arms were longer and her grip tighter than the last time he'd seen her, though she was still about the size of a human toddler. He'd never thought he'd be so happy to see an ape. "Where's Oscar?"

Ada wheeled her arms around to speak to Ruthie in semaphore, the language Oscar had taught her. Ruthie stood up with one foot on each of George's shoulders and responded.

"He's in the cave, looking for rocks," Ada interpreted.

"Just as I suspected," George said. "We'd better go in there and rescue him. We need to get Captain Bibble's help as fast as we can."

Ada and Ruthie had another short exchange of hand waves. "Ruthie will stay here. She says there are bats in the cave. Lots of bats. She doesn't like bats."

"On second thought, maybe it would be faster if we shouted to Oscar to see if he can come to us," George said. He hadn't traversed the sea just to be devoured by an army of bats.

They moved cautiously into the mouth of the cave. The fissured entrance grew smaller as it tunneled deeper into the rock, but it was still larger than a cathedral doorway. Ahead, George could see only blackness. "Oscar! Are you in there? Oscar! It's George and Ada!"

George, Ada, and Ruthie waited. There was no response.

"Are you sure he's in there?" George asked.

Just then, a dust-covered figure emerged from the cave, lugging a lantern in one hand and a heavy, lumpy bag in the other. His fingers were covered with chalky white powder and his legs were smeared with something that looked like mud.

George's heart leapt. Even under the layers of filth, he recognized his friend. "Oscar!"

Oscar blinked in the sunlight. He looked confused and a little sad. But a second later, his face broke into a broad grin. "Ada? George!"

He ran to them, falling into an embrace as soon as he was close enough.

In a tumble of words, Ada and George told Oscar the story of the last three days. Just as Ada was describing George's spoon fight with Cabeza de Perro, the crisp, clear sound of a ship's bells clanged over the water. All four of them turned to see where the noise had come from. A small boat with a single sail appeared from behind a rocky outcropping that jutted into the sea.

"OSCAR!" a familiar, booming voice called. The new boat sailed into the shadow cast by the enormous cliffs onto the choppy water. As it neared, a figure dressed all in gold waved furiously. It was Captain Bibble the Beastly (Junior), the Bane of Britain, Oscar's father, who had accidentally abandoned him as a baby and then miraculously returned just in time to save all of their lives.

Oscar smiled tightly in response.

After he dropped anchor near the mechanical whale, Captain Bibble jumped out of his boat and splashed through the shallow waters toward his son.

"I came as QUICKLY as I COULD," he said, alternately shouting and speaking as if he lived inside an invisible swirling hurricane that sometimes muffled his voice, even though everyone else could hear him perfectly well at a normal volume. "And—if it isn't the LORD of Devonshire and ADA Byron."

"Nice to see you again, Captain," George said, hunching his shoulders uneasily. Bibble was Oscar's father and was a trustworthy ally, but he was still a pirate. George couldn't shake his first memory of the fearsome captain. Only months ago, Bibble had threatened to kill George multiple times after finding out that George was partly to blame for allowing the Society to kidnap his son.

"I wish I could SAY the SAME," Captain Bibble roared. "I'm having a TERRIBLE week. My new ship was STOLEN, and my crew was ATTACKED. I had to steal this FISHING BOAT to go rescue my SON from these BLASTED caves."

"Yes, I heard there were quite a few bats. Bats carry horrible diseases," George said politely.

Oscar pulled away from his father. "Rescue me from what? You stole that ship? Are you going to give it back?"

"It's hardly a SHIP. I'm EMBARRASSED to be SEEN in such a state. What sort of PIRATE doesn't have a pirate SHIP?"

"A land pirate?" George suggested.

"It was a RHETORICAL question," Bibble shouted. His left leg, which was an oar, slipped on moss-covered driftwood. He regained his balance with a string of salty curses. "I told you, SON, to stop WANDERING off. Now let's get off this CURSED rock. I need to get my SHIP back."

"It's not a cursed rock." Oscar folded his arms. On his shoulders, Ruthie folded her arms as well. "I will not stop wandering off, and I'm not getting on that ship. You stole it. I told you how I feel about you stealing things from people."

"I'll give it BACK once I have MY ship back," Bibble said, his single eye throwing a frustrated glance at his son. He stumbled. "BLAST this leg. It's broken AGAIN."

137

Ada stepped into the middle of the group, warily glancing from Oscar to Bibble and back again. "Why don't we all take a moment to compose ourselves before we make any decisions about who is going where with whom? Captain Bibble, I'd be happy to fix your leg for you if you let me take a look at it. In return, I would be very obliged if you would take charge of one of my passengers."

"I've no ROOM for an extra crewman. I have enough MOUTHS to feed," Bibble grumbled. He glared pointedly at Ruthie, who had wandered away to munch on a fistful of yellow flowers she had plucked from the cliffside. Oscar glared back.

Ada leaned in conspiratorially. "What if I told you he's a captive member of the crew that stole your ship?"

Captain Bibble's eye gleamed fiercely at the mention of a captive. He sat down on a boulder and removed his leg with his one arm, then handed the golden oar to Ada. "Very well."

With Oscar's assistance and an elaborate pulley system, George and Ada hauled the sleeping Cabeza de Perro out of the whale and onto the shore, laying him out on a flat stretch of sand. All the while, the pirate's head lolled back and forth, his chest rising and falling in a gentle snore.

Ada knelt in the sand next to Captain Bibble so that she could ratchet the joint of his wooden leg while Oscar watched. A few feet away, George tightened the ropes around Cabeza de Perro's wrists, working up the nerve to ask Captain Bibble for help. It would be easier if Captain Bibble were in a better mood. The friction between Oscar and his father was rougher than sandpaper. Finally, George said, "Captain Bibble, we're glad to see that you and your crew are safe—but we were hoping to ask you for a favor. Have you heard of someone named Don Nadie?"

Captain Bibble stood up in shock but, without his left leg, ended up hopping wildly before plopping down on the rock again. "Have I HEARD of HIM? Every pirate CAPTAIN has heard of him. He's a LEGEND, a GIANT, famous among pirates for stealing CREW MEMBERS."

As if in response, Cabeza de Perro began murmuring between his sharpened teeth.

"Stealing crew members? What do you mean?" Ada asked.

"He's spent the last FORTY years in PRISON, where he built up a MASSIVE following with his SILVER tongue. His LACKEYS are everywhere," Captain Bibble said, jutting his chin toward Cabeza de Perro.

Bibble's eye moved uncertainly to George. "Surely your GRANDFATHER, Lord Devonshire, told you about him?"

George's heart leapt into his throat. "He never said a word. But I wish he had, because Don Nadie hasn't forgotten me. I think my grandfather was trying to protect me."

"He came after George in London," Ada explained.

The color washed from Captain Bibble's face. "Do you MEAN to say that the BEAST is out of its CAGE?"

Ada nodded grimly. "It seems so."

Bibble winced. The wind suddenly changed direction, gusting against the face of the rock and whipping the sea into choppy waves that crashed against the boulders at the cliff's base. "Children, the world today is a GARBAGE heap. The best times are behind us. The seas used to be aflame with glorious battles. Pirates PILLAGED. Navies pursued. Cannons BOOMED. Those were the days when men were free to ROAM as they pleased and there was treasure to be found for those who DARED to seek it. Heroes and villains were EQUALLY matched. They fought each other with HONOR. Except ONE. One particular PERSON gave the REST of the villains a bad name. That person was Don Nadie. I know, because my FATHER met him once, in prison long ago."

Ruthie climbed down from the rocks and joined them. Bibble leaned forward, bringing his face so close to George that he could count the flecks of green in his wild blue eye. "My father was no SAINT. He was a pirate, after all. But even a PIRATE knows there are SOME men who shouldn't be crossed. He said Don Nadie was CONSUMED by the desire for REVENGE. REVENGE is a road best walked ALONE."

Ada clamped Captain Bibble's golden leg onto his stump. He stood up and flexed his leg, then tested it by splashing around in the shallow water.

"THANK YOU," the captain said.

George followed Captain Bibble down to the water. "What did my grandfather take from Don Nadie to make him so angry? It's not fair. My grandfather was a hero. He was only doing his duty."

Bibble's face fell. "Well..."

George's pulse raced as he prepared to hear the story his grandfather had kept from him. "Go on."

"Don Nadie told my father that Lord Devonshire

destroyed his family," Bibble said softly. "I ASSUMED he meant he killed them. By throwing them in JAIL to ROT. To DIE."

The air left George's lungs. Ada dropped her small wrench in shock. Oscar inhaled softly. Ruthie, glancing at all of them in turn, loped over to George and climbed into his arms, nuzzling into his chest. For a long moment, the only sound was the wind howling through the caves.

"Impossible," George said, shattering the silence. He squeezed Ruthie fiercely.

"Naval officers did TERRIBLE things in the name of JUSTICE," Bibble said sagely.

"It's not true," George couldn't help but shout. Tears pricked his eyes. "Of course it's not. My grandfather was a hero. Don Nadie told your father lies. He wouldn't—he wasn't capable—"

"Sometimes a HERO is only a HERO to some," Bibble said, eyes darting at Oscar. "My FATHER was a HERO to ME, but your GRANDFATHER would have called him a SCOURGE and a SWAB—"

"Stop," George said. Anger had crept into his voice. "Just stop."

After a few moments, Oscar broke the silence. "What

if he wants the Star of Victory? We can give it back, and everyone will be happy."

George pulled the Star out of his pocket and waved it angrily in the air, clutching it so tightly that the metallic rods dug into the skin of his palm. "We already thought of that. But they don't want this. They want the map. It has to be hiding something dangerous. My grandfather must have hidden it to keep it safe."

"I only know ONE thing for sure. If Don Nadie is FREE, then no one except those who are LOYAL to him is SAFE. Forget about the MAP and find somewhere to hide before he FINDS you. Start a NEW life somewhere."

"No. I LIKE my life," George bellowed, drawing himself up to his full height before realizing that he was doing so. "My grandfather saved the world from this villain once. It's my job to do it again."

Oscar, who had been listening intently to the story, jumped to his feet. "I thought you'd say that," he said. "Father, they've come for our help."

"Have they?" Captain Bibble asked, his voice suddenly quiet.

"Yes, Captain Bibble," Ada replied.

Bibble averted his eyes as he brushed dried seaweed off

his shirt and pants. "Well, I'm sorry to say that I don't have a ship to run off to battle with. As you saw yourself, mine's been stolen from me, and the new one's not yet equipped for fighting."

"I have a solution for that," Ada said. She gestured to where the mechanical whale bobbed above the water. The burnished metal hull glinted in the sun, as if winking at them. "My ship can comfortably hold eleven fully grown adults. Since three children and one juvenile orangutan equal the weight of two adults, that means we can take nine of your crew, given you're all the median height and weight. . . ."

"Batten down the hatches!" Oscar whooped. He splashed into the water toward the whale.

"Stop, son. We're not going," Bibble said.

"What?" All of George's hopes came crashing down. What chance did they have against the Society of Nobodies without Bibble's help? Ada's lips parted in shock. She looked as stunned as George felt.

Oscar waded back to his father, wearing the expression of someone who'd just had the air knocked out of him. A spotted lizard darted across the rock inches away from his hand and he didn't even notice. "You're not going to help my friends?"

"I made a promise to stay away from Don Nadie. I intend to keep that PROMISE," said Captain Bibble forcefully, the volume returning to his voice.

Oscar clenched his fists. "But you fought them before! When they kidnapped me, you came to save me!"

"I didn't KNOW they were NOBODIES," Captain Bibble bellowed. "Now that I DO, I want to get us as FAR away from them as possible. Let's GO, Oscar."

"I made promises, too," Oscar said. "I made promises never to abandon my friends the way my father abandoned me."

"That was an ACCIDENT. I'm here now," Bibble roared.

"Then you can stay here, but I've made up my mind. I'm helping my friends." Oscar hoisted the rock-filled bag over his shoulder. "Ada and George, I'm coming with you."

Chapter Thirteen

George felt whole again.

Nothing that had happened in the last three days compared to the riotous joy George felt when Oscar climbed down the whale's ladder with Ruthie atop his shoulders. It would have been even better if Captain Bibble had agreed to help, and he felt very sorry that Oscar and his father had parted on bad terms...but the four of them were together again. Even without Bibble's crew, George felt invincible alongside his friends.

By the time Oscar got settled in the cabin that Ada had designed for him—with a hammock with a built-in nest for Ruthie, a desk filled with art supplies, and even a small box for his rock collection—she had already set a course for Il

Naso's last known whereabouts according to Ada's sources in Spain: Granada, which, George knew from his extensive studies of his grandfather's map of Andalusia, the southernmost region of Spain, was only a few hours away by sea, then another few hours' journey inland.

While they sailed east by northeast across the warm Alboran Sea, George and Ada told Oscar everything that had happened since they'd last seen him. They introduced Oscar to Patty and reenacted their epic capture of Cabeza de Perro. Ada chatted about C.R.U.M.P.E.T.S. and how she hoped she could convince her mother not to send her to the Somerville School for Ladies of Substance. When they ran out of things to say, George asked Oscar to draw him a picture of the children in the portrait at No. 10. Don Nadie knew too much about George, so it was only fair that George collected every scrap of information on Don Nadie that he could. Using only the details from George's memory, Oscar began to draw an eerily accurate picture of the girl. As her round face and pointed chin appeared line by line, George pressed Oscar for details about his last two months on the pirate ship with his father.

"I thought I'd be spending more time with my father. But he was always ordering me around: hoist this, swab that. Or he was busy shouting and eating and sailing and pirating...he didn't even have the time to teach me about coral." Oscar paused, eyes swimming with unspilled tears. "You were right, George. I'm not a pirate. I don't belong with my father's crew."

A pang of guilt moved in George's stomach. When they had first met, he'd told Oscar that his dream of reuniting with his pirate father was silly and naïve. But he had been wrong. More than finding half of the Star of Victory in Ruthie's belly, discovering Captain Bibble in the middle of the sea was nothing short of a miracle.

George swept his arm around Oscar's shoulder and squeezed. "Don't say that! Your father loves you. He searched the world to find you. He never stopped looking."

Grunting softly, Ruthie ambled toward them and slung her arm around Oscar's other shoulder, a mirror image of George's embrace.

"Only after he abandoned me," Oscar added glumly.

"He's made some mistakes, but that's no reason to give up on him. No one is perfect. Take me, for example," George said. "I was a disaster before I became friends with you and Ada. I couldn't even leave my house for fear of something awful happening. But look at me now, sailing the open seas like my grandfather! My luck is improving by the day. I won't let you and your father lose each other again. As soon as we get the map back from Il Naso, we'll find Captain Bibble and fix whatever's gone wrong between you."

Oscar's pencil pressed harder into the paper. "I don't know if that's possible. You don't understand, George."

"I guess I don't understand," George replied earnestly. "My entire family is dead. I didn't know how lucky I was to have them when they were alive, but I'd give anything to have a family again."

Even though it wasn't George's intention to sound pathetic, Oscar's eyes opened wide with pity as he quickly began to comfort George by patting his arm. "You do have a family. Me, Ada, Frobisher, and Ruthie! You'll always have us, remember?"

"And you have us, Oscar. If you don't want to go be a pirate, then we'll be here for you."

"Yes..." Oscar nodded once in agreement, but for the first time since George had met him amid the gigantic fronds and chirping parrots of the royal menagerie, there was not even a hint of a gap-toothed smile on his face. He put his head down and concentrated on finishing the portrait of the children in No. 10 until Ada surfaced the whale.

"We're here!"

George sprang to the porthole to see a palm-studded coastline. The white peaks of the Sierra Nevada mountains hovered in the distance.

They'd arrived in Andalusia. Somewhere in the city of Granada, far inland, Il Naso had the treasure map.

George cleared his throat. "This looks like a good place to come ashore. The city is in those mountains about fifty miles north. We have a long hike ahead of us."

Ada swiveled around in her chair, a huge grin plastered on her face. "Lucky for us, this isn't just a ship, it's also a carriage. I bet Don Nadie doesn't have one of these. The trip to Granada won't take more than two hours." She cranked a handle at the base of the steering wheel. Below the floor, gears began to whir, creating the noise of a thousand pepper grinders in unison.

The ship rolled out of the water onto the beach on four wagon wheels that had previously been hidden beneath its broad metal underbelly. Riding over the dry, rocky soil studded with small patches of brown grass was bumpy, and Ada seemed to be playing tug-of-war with the steering mechanism, but soon they were rumbling over the mountainous path toward the city. It was like traveling inside a snail shell. Amazingly, Oscar and Ruthie fell asleep in their hammocks, rocked back and forth by the lurching of the whale.

The minutes crawled by as the mechanical whale climbed the terrain. George's stomach rocketed into his throat as they careened down into the valleys. The road became more crowded and twisty the closer they came to the city. Ada turned the whale off onto a dusty lane surrounded by barley fields.

"Why are we stopping?" George asked. His leg jiggled with nerves.

"We're at the edge of the city. We should go the rest of the way on foot. Let's find somewhere to hide the whale," Ada said.

They pulled up to a barn. Oscar woke from his nap, his mood greatly improved. He climbed outside to negotiate with a farmer, using the bits of Spanish he had learned during his brief time as a pirate.

"¡Vámonos!" Oscar said when the whale was safely stowed out of sight.

Granada stood on a flat plain inside a bowl of

mountains. The city itself was spread out like a picnic blanket at the base of a green hill, and every one of its buildings seemed to have the same white walls and tiled roof. Atop the hill, rising above the treetops, was a magnificent building very unlike the ones below it: a fortress with flat, smooth walls made of reddish stone and perfectly square towers with perfectly square windows.

George had never seen anything like it. The angular geometry reminded him of the elaborate castles he and his grandfather used to build with toy blocks.

Ada inhaled sharply, pointing up at the fortress. "The Alhambra."

"That's the Alhambra? The last Moorish palace in Spain?" George asked. The sun broke through the clouds, and a thin beam of sunshine struck the roof of the glorious building. "I didn't think it was real. I heard it was supposed to have walls of gold and that treasure was buried beneath it by the Moors before they fled."

Oscar shaded his eyes with one hand. "What a lovely shade of gray!"

"The fortress isn't gray...." But George soon saw that Oscar wasn't referring to the magnificent reddish Alhambra. Drifting far across the valley, a gray balloon hovered like a strange cloud. As they watched, another dirty-gray balloon passed over their heads, slowly gliding toward the fortress at the top of the hill. Then they spotted another emerging from behind a far-off peak. George felt a swirl of fear in his chest. He would recognize those balloons anywhere.

"It's the Society! They're the same spy balloons we saw during our first flight over London months ago!" His heart sank. "That must mean that they've already found Il Naso."

Ada narrowed her eyes. "Or they haven't found him yet, but they know he's here in Granada somewhere. I count...seven balloons in plain sight. That's not taking into account any that might be hidden from view. I bet that if we found the right materials, I could make a balloon with a mechanical frame that squeezes like a jellyfish. It would fly circles around those boring old bubbles!"

George recognized the glint in Ada's eyes. It was only a matter of seconds before she'd run off to construct a jellyfish balloon. "Ada, concentrate! We can't take down the entire Society by ourselves in a jellyfish balloon."

Ada tore her eyes away from the balloons. "Of course. Il Naso. But if we had more time, I could construct a vacuum apparatus that would suck the balloons out of the sky, or I could fix the water cannon, but where would we find the water?"

George groaned. "Where will we find Il Naso?"

Suddenly Oscar cried, "Sharks!"

"Sharks?" George repeated.

Ruthie hopped onto Oscar's shoulders, chattering softly. "On my father's ship, we used to track sharks in order to find the best fishing spots. Wherever the sharks were, we were almost guaranteed to find prey. If we follow those balloons..."

George felt a rush of gratitude for Oscar and Ruthie. "We'll find Il Naso."

"Oh, fine, be *practical*," Ada scoffed. She took a pair of binoculars out of her pocket and brought them to her eyes. "They all seem to be converging on the Alhambra. There's one that's almost there. It looks like it's dropping something onto the ground below."

George's insides somersaulted. "So we follow the balloons and, hopefully, find Il Naso before the Society can. But...the Society knows who we are. How are we going to keep them from attacking us?"

"Disguises!" Ada said gleefully. "It looks as if they're

doing construction on the palace—we'll grab something along the way so that we can blend in as workers. It only has to work long enough for us to get inside the Alhambra without being noticed. We'll find Il Naso, you'll convince him to give you the map, and we'll be on our way."

Oscar clapped his hands delightedly. "We can leave through the secret tunnels! Fortresses always have secret tunnels."

They hurried through the maze of streets toward the Alhambra. There was chaos everywhere. People were gathering in the middle of the roads to gawk at the balloons or rushing to get inside their homes. It was hot and the air was full of strange smells. As they reached the road that led up the hill to the Alhambra, the crowds only increased. Groups of people were streaming down the wide path toward the city, fleeing the fortress. George was surprised to see so many people, but he saw that Ada was right—most of the people fleeing were workmen in dust-covered aprons, along with some children in rags and well-dressed women and men in braided jackets, which George thought looked very smart. Ruthie plucked a few hats from atop the distracted workers' heads while Oscar picked up four smocks that they had dropped in their rush. Most of them were coughing and holding cloths to their faces.

"What's happening?" George asked. Oscar repeated in Spanish, "¿Qué pasó?" but they received no reply from the stream of people.

As George, Ada, Oscar, and Ruthie came closer to the fortress through a dense thicket of trees, they heard a loud bang followed by a muffled explosion. The ground shook slightly beneath their feet. They were almost at the top of the hill, and above the walls of the fortress they could see that one of the Society's balloons was being anchored with thick ropes. A bald man leaned over the side of the balloon's large basket, which looked as if it could hold at least ten people. He was holding something that resembled a cannonball over his head threateningly.

"Surrender now or I'll drop it!" the man shouted in English, followed by a halting string of Italian: *"Arrenditi adesso o lascerò questa cosa cadere sulla tua testa!"*

With a start, George recognized the bald man from their last battle with the Society. His name was Shaw, and he was one of the Nobodies who had chased them across the Adriatic Sea a few months ago.

"They're going to bomb the fortress. We have to hurry," Ada said. She began running, clutching the construction hat to her head. George followed, heart pounding.

When they reached the top of the hill, they ran through the keyhole-shaped entrance in the fortress walls. Inside, they found themselves directly underneath the balloon's carriage-sized basket in a courtyard that was overgrown with elegant toffee-colored trees and lush green plants that spilled out of stone planters. All four of them slowed to a halt, necks craned to marvel at the high stone walls, which were lined with archways carved with intricate leaves, flowers, and curlicues. It was wildly beautiful. Since they were invisible to the Society fifty feet above them, George allowed himself to be transported, just for a moment, his troubles blown away on the gentle breeze.

Then the smell hit him.

Ruthie wrinkled her brown nose and gagged. She buried her face in Oscar's neck. "Cover your noses," Oscar said.

"What *is* that?" Ada choked out between coughs.

"Rotten eggs," George said. "And fish carcasses. And something else I don't even want to guess. Now we know why those people were running away as fast as they could."

Oscar gasped. "Look out!" he shouted as he covered his head and rushed toward a tree to shield himself.

Ada and George dove for cover behind a stone planter just as Shaw hurled the small black sphere from high overhead. It hit the ground a few feet away and exploded into a puff of smoke that carried a new, disgusting odor—rotting vegetables.

"*Stink* bombs!" Ada practically shrieked, pinching her nose between her fingers. "Brilliant! Perfectly harmless to us, I'm sure. The Society wouldn't risk damaging the map with real bombs or weapons."

"They're not harmless to Il Naso, though," George replied. The Italian policeman was called Il Naso, the Nose, because he had the most finely tuned sense of smell of anyone on earth. He could even smell *feelings*. "He'll be in utter agony. We have to find him before the rest of the balloons get here and he surrenders the map to save his nose."

Ada turned in a circle. "Okay—we need to get away

158

from this balloon and find higher ground. I'm sure Il Naso will have gone upwind and gotten as high as possible to avoid the stench."

George peered up once more at the high walls surrounding them. A few towers peeked over the trees, but some had large cracks running through them or had crumbled, their tops lying in ruins. On the far side of a wall, one large square tower rose above the rest. It seemed to be fully intact. He pointed to it and shouted, "There!"

They all pinched their noses and ran as fast as they could toward the tower. Beyond the wall was another long courtyard surrounded on all sides by the smooth white faces of buildings. Stacks of tiles and buckets of mortar lay abandoned around a drained pool at the center of the courtyard. The workmen must have been in the midst of their repairs when the stink bombs started falling—they had left their tools scattered on the ground in their desperation to get away. At the far end of the pool, a carved wooden door appeared to lead inside one of the tall towers.

George, Ada, and Oscar ran across the courtyard at full speed and crashed into the door, but it was locked. As Ada worked on the lock, Shaw caught sight of them and hurled a stink bomb in their direction. There was a loud bang as it crashed and exploded, sending the stench of sweaty feet into the air.

Oscar gagged. "I'm going to be sick."

"Hurry!" George said into his elbow, which he'd used to cover his nose.

"I am!" Ada said.

Ruthie launched herself off Oscar's shoulders, then climbed up the arches and disappeared through a window. The door opened suddenly to reveal a grinning Ruthie on the other side.

"Ruthie, you brilliant ape," George cheered as they all scrambled inside in a tangle of arms and legs and vines. Ada shut the door and quickly locked it behind them.

Inside, the tower was cool and dark. The air was slightly clearer, though faint hints of skunk had permeated the walls. George breathed, taking in his surroundings.

From floor to ceiling, the walls were covered in patterns and interlocking shapes. They were every bit as intricate as the designs they'd seen earlier—except these had been carved right through the stone in some places. Sunlight filtered in, cutting the outside world into geometric swirls and shapes. Oscar ran his hands along the faded paint, barely visible anymore between the lacelike carvings.

"Cinnabar, azurite, and gold. If only I could see them as they once were," he murmured to himself.

Ada gestured to an oval carving filled with symbols and dots. "Those are Arabic inscriptions. Isn't it beautiful? I wish I could read it."

The floors suddenly creaked above them, followed by a loud sniff. A fine mist of dust drifted onto the carvings.

They were not alone.

Chapter Fourteen

The loud sniff echoed a few times, then faded into silence.

"Il Naso! It must be!"

Ada turned to George. "I have a plan to take down the balloons, but first we have to find Il Naso and get the map. He knows us. Let's start calling to him until he answers."

George glanced up at the carved wooden ceiling. "How are we going to get up there? I don't see any stairs."

"The stairs are over there," Oscar said, pointing at a door behind an arched alcove. "But I'm sure there are secret passages here, too."

"The regular stairs will do. No time to look for secret ones. Come on!" Ada ran ahead.

They made their way to the upper floor, which was an enormous square room in a state of disrepair, although it was obvious that the interior had once been beautiful. Water stains dripped over the stone carvings. George felt a sudden pang of sadness. It reminded him of his own home before he'd restored it to its original splendor, although his house had been nowhere near as sumptuous as the Alhambra. A palace as beautiful as this one deserved to be restored.

"Il Naso," George called out cautiously. "It's your old friend George. The 3rd Lord of Devonshire? We've come to help you."

Oscar gestured to a square window an arm's length above them. "See those windows up there? From the outside they were right beneath the roof. We can't go any higher. He's not here."

"But he has to be here! We heard him," George insisted.

"Maybe so, but I have an idea for getting rid of Shaw first. A simple idea," Ada added before George could protest. "Which way is the courtyard we came from?" Ada ripped the hat from her head and began taking objects out of her pockets and arranging them on the floor.

"Out there. George, help me take this off." Oscar knelt down beside a window covered in more geometric patterns.

Together, George and Oscar removed the heavy wooden screen. Circular bubbles of light within rectangular borders flashed across his eyes and cast strange shadows on their bodies that mesmerized him. He felt an unexpected idea loosening in his brain at the same time the screen popped out of its frame. They gently placed it at their feet.

Below them lay the drained pool. From this height, George could see over the walls of the Alhambra's courtyard like a mouse that has been lifted out of its maze. The fortress was a city unto itself, with gardens and trees and buildings all woven together at the top of the hill. Searching every corner of this place for Il Naso would take weeks. To George's left, Shaw's balloon floated high above everything. If they tried to leave the building the way they had come, Shaw would see them for sure.

While his brain was still spinning like a wild compass needle, George spotted something blinking at him from a small window in the wall on the other side of the pool. Il

164

Naso. He must have taken a different path inside the labyrinthine fortress. Their eyes locked for a brief moment. A gray balloon slowly rose up behind Il Naso's wall like an evil moon. The policeman's black mustache twitched once, twice—and then he disappeared from view.

George pointed to the window to show Oscar and Ada. "Look! He's inside there, but if I call out, Shaw will know where he is, too. There's another balloon coming fast. I think Il Naso saw me, though."

"Well done, George! Now it's time to get rid of those balloons." Ada finished emptying her many pockets, including a few hidden ones. On the floor in front of her she'd placed a glass vial, a pencil, a hairbrush, three hard-boiled eggs, and ten cherry pits. "Empty your pockets, boys. Oscar, if you have any rocks, put them here. I think we can destroy that balloon with what we've got on hand."

Oscar added six rocks of various sizes to the pile. From his leather bag, George withdrew a length of rope, the Star of Victory, Patty's butterfly pendant, a few receipts, *The Proceedings of the Old Bailey*, and three shillings. Ruthie didn't have any pockets, of course, but she plucked a few small pebbles from her fur and added them to the pile.

Ada rocked back on her heels and observed the pathetic

collection of objects with a sigh. "If only I'd thought to bring a crossbow and arrows... but this will do. A rock stuck inside one of my eggs with a few drops of acid from my vial should make the perfect projectile. All we need is a projectile weapon and something sticky."

"I can make George's rope into a sling," Oscar said.

"And I saw some wet mortar in a bucket in the courtyard. Is that sticky enough?" George asked.

"That's perfect! Ruthie, go get that bucket," Ada said, gesturing to a small wooden bucket. The little orangutan raced down the wall and grabbed the bucket with her strong arms. By the time she returned, Ada and George had pierced the eggs with Oscar's pointiest rocks to improvise arrowheads. Oscar, meanwhile, braided the rope into a sling. George coated the eggs with mortar using Ada's hairbrush.

Ada made everyone stand back as she uncorked the vial of acid she had used to break out of the prison carriage. "A few drops will eat through anything," she explained. "Even hot-air balloons."

As soon as the acid was dripped into the rocky center of an egg, Oscar took aim with his improvised slingshot. The egg soared through the air toward Shaw's balloon, which was still anchored in a far courtyard. It missed, sailing past the gray balloon into a tree. Oscar squinted and aimed again. This time, the egg stuck to the fabric balloon with a satisfying *whomp*. Faint yellowish smoke rose into the air as the acid ate away at the fabric, creating a gash that let the gas inside *whoosh* out.

Ada and Oscar cheered as the balloon deflated, whooping when Shaw and the other members of the Society frantically pulled at the ropes, trying to keep the basket level as they drifted to the ground. In a matter of seconds, the balloon had sunk behind the walls, out of sight. Oscar aimed another egg at a second balloon and hit it on the first try.

"George, look!" Oscar said. "I think Il Naso's seen us! He knows we have a few minutes to escape without being spotted while the balloons crash." In the courtyard below, Il Naso had emerged, crouched at the far end of the pool next to a small fountain. He'd wrapped a cloth around his face, but tears streamed down his cheeks from enduring the terrible stink bombs. He seemed to be waiting for them.

But when Ada and Oscar sprinted ahead toward the stairs, George tripped over the wooden screen they'd taken out of the window frame earlier.

They doubled back to help George to his feet, but his feet wouldn't move. The world had narrowed to a single pinpoint and nothing else mattered. He sat, transfixed by the screen. Or, rather, transfixed by the pattern carved into the screen. Because the pattern wasn't only in the wood itself, but in the *absence* of wood—in the holes.

The gears in George's brain had at last clicked into place, and he finally knew what had been nagging at him ever since he'd seen the butterfly pendant around Patty's neck in Geneva. He picked up the butterfly pendant and cradled it in his palms.

Of course.

"George, what are you doing? We have to hurry, or the Society will get to Il Naso first!" Ada said, tugging on his arm, hard.

George's head snapped up. Oscar was already at the window, a glum expression twisting his face. "It's too late."

The gears in George's mind had taken too long to click. He followed Oscar's gaze. Shaw and his cohort had found their way to the courtyard on foot and spotted Il Naso where he was waiting for them. Red-coated figures stampeded toward the Italian policeman, their hands outstretched, ready to grab him. Slowly, Il Naso raised his hands to the sky.

The policeman had surrendered.

"No, no, no . . ." George groaned.

Below, as if he had heard him, Il Naso patted his breast pocket and gave George a silent nod. Then, as George watched from above, Il Naso took the map from his sleeve, ripped it in half . . . and set it on fire. Flames licked up the parchment as it dropped from the policeman's fingers and fluttered to the ground.

The air left George's chest all at once, as if he'd been struck by a blow.

A howl went up from the Society, and they dove for the burning fragments of the map, completely ignoring Il Naso.

Il Naso pushed the stone fountain next to him with all his might. To George's shock, it slid aside, revealing a black hole underneath. Then Il Naso jumped into the hole and was gone.

"I knew there were secret tunnels!" Oscar whispered to himself.

But no secret tunnel would lead them back in time. The last flicker of fire consumed George's map, then died out completely.

Chapter Fifteen

Their escape from the Alhambra was a blur.

While the Society members howled and cursed over the loss of the map, Oscar slid open a panel next to an alcove to reveal the entrance to a tunnel. Ada dragged George through, all the while remarking how lucky it was that Moors had built the first irrigation systems and how wonderful it was that there were channels for water everywhere, even underground. When they finally reached the mechanical whale and secured the door behind them, Oscar, Ada, and Ruthie collapsed onto the floor, panting.

But George was slowly winding up, like a spring ready to burst into action.

After catching her breath, Ada fixed her gaze on him.

Her face was flushed with anger. "What on earth came over you, George? That should have worked! That map was our advantage over the Society."

"You don't understand," George said. His head was a storm of rotten smells, and he couldn't yet calm his heartbeat, let alone put into words what he'd figured out. "The shapes. I saw the shapes."

Ada let out a frustrated sigh. "Not another breakdown. For my sake, George, please don't fall apart. If it helps, I'm starting to think you were right. There's something wrong with your luck. It has become increasingly difficult to ignore your talent for disaster. When we get home, I'll study it and help you. But now is not the time to let that get you in a dither."

"It's all right about the map," George said, shaking his head, though his gut was still wrenched from the sight of his grandfather's map set aflame. "We don't need it."

Ada tilted her head at him. "What?"

Clutching the butterfly pendant tightly against his chest, George was giddy with excitement. He began to pace. "It wasn't for nothing. All those patterns everywhere on the walls and the floors and then the tiles. It was just what I needed. All along I knew there was something I was missing, something that was just out of reach. But I see it. It was meant for *me*. My grandfather knew that one day I might go to the workshop in Geneva and that if I did, I would see the butterfly. It's another layer of the puzzle. Another path to the map's secret."

"But…" Oscar bit his lip. "Didn't you say Don Nadie needed the map as the final piece of the plan to attack C.R.U.M.P.E.T.S.? It's destroyed now, so he can't have it. We're done. We've saved the world."

George stopped to catch his breath. "It's not that simple, Oscar. All we know for sure is that Don Nadie is a scoundrel and a liar and he can't be trusted—and he's determined. He spent forty years in prison forming the Society. He's not going to give up, and neither can we."

"That's all well and good, but the map is gone, George. So what do we do?" Ada asked.

Ada, Oscar, and Ruthie stared at him, waiting for an answer. Luckily, he had one, because his grandfather had left it for him to discover, like bread crumbs in the forest.

George opened up his palm and let the butterfly rest on it so that the others could see its delicate wings and the familiar shapes that at last were so clear: two sea horses and a man taking a bath. On the left side was the larger, curving sea horse. It was about to be trapped by the hand of a man lying sideways in a bath with his body outstretched in an X shape. The man's round belly poked out of the water in the middle; his face, hands, and feet surrounded his belly like the five points of a star. A few other tiny bits of the man, such as his armpit, poked out, too. The farthest shape was a baby sea horse, curved like a peanut, swimming away. George pointed to each of them in turn. "There are the sea horses and the man in the bath. Isn't it amazing? They were here all along."

"Lord Devonshire, what on earth are you talking about?" Ada asked.

"Losing the map again was too much for him," Oscar whispered loudly. "I'll go make him some tea."

George frowned. "I can hear you. I don't want tea. I'm trying to tell you that it's all right. I didn't see it until now. These shapes between the metal on the butterfly, the glass bits here. They represent *islands*. There's a set of islands hidden in the butterfly's wings."

Ada peered down at the pendant; then her eyes flew wide. "The Galápagos."

Triumph flooded through George, quick and sure as the beat of his heart. "Yes! They're the Galápagos. See, that big sea horse is Albemarle Island, and the little one, that's Chatham. But this one, right here below the little sea horse, I don't recognize it. It's not one of the twenty-one islands in the archipelago."

Ada's lips parted slowly until her mouth was hanging open. She took the butterfly from George's palm to examine it more closely. "An extra island?"

A grip of certainty seized George and turned his doubt into unshakable sureness. "A lost island."

Ada shook her head in wonder, curls bouncing. "How clever. It was staring us right in the face. The butterfly on the map and the butterfly here. I thought the Star of Victory was showing us an island, so why didn't I see it?"

George grinned. "I would imagine it's because only someone whose grandfather spent hours and hours tutoring them in geography would recognize it. It doesn't matter that Il Naso burned the map. The map is in my mind. The butterfly was the last piece of the puzzle. I can see it so clearly now!"

Oscar's face was scrunched with confusion. "See what?"

George spread out an imaginary map on the floor in front of Oscar. He drew the invisible lines of Australia and South America with his finger, then jabbed at a spot between them. "The Galápagos are islands in the Pacific Ocean off the coast of South America. Whalers stop there on their way to hunt in the open waters. The islands are covered in volcanoes and massive tortoises the size of ponies."

"Is this another one of your stories?" Oscar asked suspiciously. "It doesn't sound real."

"Oh, it's very real," Ada said. She produced a blank sheet of paper from one of her notebooks. Using a rag dipped in her inkpot, she smeared ink on the metal form of the butterfly, then pressed it quickly against the paper. The ink left a perfect impression of the islands.

George borrowed a pen from Ada and labeled each island with its proper name. When he was done, there was one tiny dot of an island just below the little sea horse that wasn't on any map of the Galápagos that George had ever seen.

A thrill raced over George's skin. "Whatever Don Nadie needs, whatever my grandfather hid, must be on that island. Or we'll find the next clue he left for me. Oscar, you can help me draw the map again. We'll make it just the way it was before."

"Another treasure hunt?" Oscar asked glumly. "It's all my father talked about. Treasure this and treasure that.

If someone else can steal it from you, then it's not really yours, is it?"

George's short time as a convicted felon had taught him that his life could be snatched away at any moment. If he didn't hold on tightly to what belonged to him, it would be ripped away. "I don't believe that, but more importantly, that's not the law. Stealing is wrong. My grandfather wanted me to protect this treasure from Don Nadie. He mustn't find it before we do."

"I agree," Ada said.

George stood up. "Well, what are we waiting for? Next stop, the Galápagos!"

Oscar pushed the paper with the butterfly stamp aside. "But—what if we go back to London first? Or somewhere else?"

"London?" George echoed. "I can't go back to London! If we go back to London without finding something that can stop Don Nadie, he'll win. Then we can never go back because we'll be killed in whatever revolution that maniac is going to incite."

"And I'm not safe there either until we stop the Society from hunting scientists," Ada said.

"All right, but maybe Ruthie doesn't want to go to the Galápagos, either," Oscar said combatively.

George pouted. "You really don't want to come with us to the Galápagos, Oscar? It wouldn't be the same without you. We can drop you off at whatever port you want on the way," he offered, even though it was the exact opposite of what he wanted.

"Why, so you can go find your fancy treasure and Ada can go to her fancy school and I can wander the earth alone for the rest of my life? Or go back to the pirate ship and learn how to tie knots and cut throats?" Oscar crumpled to the floor, spread out like a starfish, and Ruthie lay on top of him like an orange blanket, trying to comfort him.

A tear slid down Oscar's cheek.

Ada and George exchanged befuddled glances, then both crouched down next to Oscar. Softly, Ada said, "Oscar, what's wrong?"

"I—I don't know. George said I belonged here, but... I don't feel as if I belong anywhere, really. I thought once I was with my father I would know what it felt like to be home. But I wasn't like the rest of his crew. I didn't fit in there. They didn't need me. I was the loneliest I've ever been. All I had ever wanted was to be with my family. But if being with my family didn't make me happy, then what will?"

"Oh, Oscar," Ada said.

"Maybe I should go to Borneo to reunite Ruthie with her family. Or Tahiti to find my mother."

George looked at his friends' distraught faces. Oscar's chest was heaving with barely contained sobs. This was no way to start the greatest adventure of their lives.

George offered Oscar a handkerchief and tried to find the right words to provide comfort. "You don't have to know where you want to go, Oscar. You'll figure it out. Some people know right from the minute they're born what makes them happy, and some people have to search for years and years, I think. That's nothing to be upset about. My grandfather always said that happiness is the hardest treasure to find."

"That's right," Ada added. "George and I are on a quest to stop the Society of Nobodies from attacking C.R.U.M.P.E.T.S., but you're on your own quest to find where you belong. We'll help you along the way. We'll follow the clues and never give up on you, Oscar Bibble, not until we discover where you want to be. Maybe you'll want to be in Borneo, or Tahiti, or maybe even merry old England after all."

George clapped Oscar on the shoulder. "When you get close to your happiness, your heart will know what to do, just the way my heart is telling me that my grandfather's treasure is on the lost island. Are you ready to start your journey and join us in sailing to the Galápagos?"

Oscar's tears had stopped, but he looked skeptical.

George held out his hand gallantly. "Will you come with us?"

Eventually, Oscar took George's hand and let himself be pulled upright again. Ruthie wrapped her arms around his waist. "All right, George. If I learned one thing from my father, it's that you never know where the tides might take you. I'd rather go out and look for where I belong with the two of you and Ruthie than anyone else."

Sadness flitted across Oscar's eyes again, but disappeared in a flash. A smile lifted the corners of his mouth. "Though I'm not sure if I want to be caught with London's most wanted truffle assassin."

George chuckled at Oscar's joke. But at the same time, he couldn't help but glance out the portholes, half expecting to see the British navy on the horizon.

"Once you see the Galápagos, Oscar, you'll feel much better, I promise. There's nothing like a long trip in a mechanical whale to raise your spirits," Ada said.

Oscar smiled. "I do want to see the giant tortoises and the volcano rocks. Who knows, maybe I'll find my happiness there."

Ada hopped to her feet and beckoned the boys to join her as she marched to the pilot's chair. "Anchors aweigh! Next stop: the lost island."

COMMANDER'S LOG
FOR THE WHALE

Day 1

Fair winds and favorable currents.

I have plotted our course to the Galápagos following the fastest route and most favorable currents, which flow from the southern tip of Africa, then along the Indian Ocean to the Pacific.

Our captain, Miss Ada Byron, has insisted that I promote myself from lieutenant to commander based on my heroic actions during the Battle of the Alhambra. I humbly accepted. I also serve as cook. We are joined by our boatswain, Oscar Bibble, the most experienced sailor among the crew. Ruthie is the boatswain's mate, and she has proved very helpful at swabbing the decks. Another crew member, Patty, is undergoing repairs after being damaged by a nasty pirate. The captain is hopeful she will be an able lieutenant and pilot once her gears are properly aligned.

Day 2
Light winds and favorable currents.

The boatswain and I have completed an inventory of all supplies and have concluded that we are well stocked for our journey, but we will need to find fresh fruits whenever possible due to the boatswain's mate's dietary preferences.

Patty has been repaired and now holds the rank of midshipman after a brief discussion about her ability to advance.

We sailed through a very large group of Portuguese man-of-war jellyfish today. There were over a thousand of them floating in the ocean with their long blue tentacles brushing our portholes. The captain has looked over my shoulder and just informed me that they are not in fact jellyfish, but siphonophores, which she has made sure that I spelled correctly and which she informs me are groups of unrelated polyps that form a single organism. Oscar has drawn some very good pictures of these not-jellyfish and has now been promoted to ship's artist.

Day 3
Calm winds and unfavorable currents.

The ship's artist–boatswain and I are making a map to replace the one destroyed by Il Naso during the perilous Battle of Alhambra. Progress is slow, as the artist likes to ignore reality in favor of "what looks good."

Day 4
Blustering winds and unfavorable currents.

We anchored in Cape Town today. The captain asked the boatswain and me to go ashore and purchase supplies. Next time we make landfall, we will be in the Galápagos!

Day 6

Strong winds and favorable currents.

The boatswain and I spent most of the afternoon pumping water from the lower decks after a leak formed around a loosened bolt. Progress on the map continues, but it is slow.

Day 7

Strong winds and unfavorable currents.

More pumping.

Day 8

Strong winds, rain, and favorable currents.

The captain has changed Patty's gears, and she has taken over pumping duties today.

Day 9

Fair winds and favorable currents.

We surfaced for some fresh air today because the sea was calm. The boatswain remarked that the sky was a perfect cobalt blue.

Our food stores are running low. I have checked the inventory and suspect the boatswain's mate is consuming more than her fair share. The captain and boatswain disagreed with me, and I have exiled myself to my cabin for the rest of the day.

Day 10

Light winds and favorable currents.

I have demoted the boatswain's mate to the rank of seaman because I still suspect her of stealing food. When I consulted the captain on the matter, she said, "Oh, really?" and went back to her cabin to read a book on her latest mathematical spiffle-spaffle.

We also saw a group of dolphins. The boatswain is angry at me because I told him that he was neglecting his duties to draw the dolphins in his sketchbook rather than help me with my map and he said, "I can draw if I please." He's probably still upset at me about the boatswain's mate, but it's not my fault that she's stealing food!

Day 11

Freezing winds and favorable currents.

We have run out of all salted meats, dried fruits, and eggs. The boatswain pointed out that we are surrounded by food. He made a fishing pole and caught several large mackerel after our ship surfaced.

Day 12

The captain has suggested that I end this log, as the boatswain is keeping a far superior record of the voyage in his sketchbook. Here ends the logbook of the commander of the WHALE.

Chapter Sixteen

I don't know, it's just not right!"

"Which do you want? Curlier or straighter?"

"Can it be both?"

Sighing, Oscar rolled his eyes. For the millionth time since they'd started re-creating George's grandfather's map, he picked up his eraser and rubbed out an hour's worth of work. "It was a cracking good sea monster."

"It was, but the tail wasn't *right*," George said. "Any of the details on the map could be part of the puzzle. It has to be exactly the same as it was."

"Mine is probably better," Oscar mumbled under his breath.

"I heard that," George said.

Ruthie was curled up in her hammock in the corner of Oscar's cabin. George couldn't see her eyes, but he could feel them watching him. She'd been avoiding George since he'd accused her of stealing food. Grunting, she sat up and whirled her arms around to catch Oscar's attention.

"Ruthie wants to know if we're there yet," Oscar said.

"Patty is taking us to the precise coordinates of the lost island based on my hours and hours of latitudinal and longitudinal calculations. She'll stop us when we arrive just south of Chatham Island. If we were there, you'd know it," George replied steadily.

Inside, though, he was quivering with nerves at their nearness to the Galápagos. What would be there when they landed? What if Don Nadie was waiting, poised to spring at them on his devilishly long legs?

Oscar began tracing the outline of the sea monster on the map again. Although George could picture the map in his mind, the patchwork quilt of countries and the rivers threading through them didn't look quite the same when spilling from the end of Oscar's pencil. No matter how detailed George was with his instructions, it wasn't right. Having excellent penmanship, he himself had written the words *Tabula ad Stella Victōriae*, or "Map to the Star of Victory," in an exact replica of his grandfather's handwriting. He'd spent hours getting the lettering just right. He'd rather re-create what had been lost than be left with nothing at all. But no matter how hard he tried, it didn't change the fact that the real map was ash and smoke. He could pretend all he wanted that this map was the same heirloom his grandfather had made for him, but when he held the parchment in his hands to admire their work, it never felt the same.

"Make its tail a little thinner so the loops have more open space between them," George directed.

Oscar's pencil glided over the page, and like magic, the sea monster appeared. Still, though the image on the paper and the image in George's brain were the same, George's stomach sank. The map was beautiful, but it was only an imitation.

Seeing the hopeful look in Oscar's eyes made George jump to his feet anyway. "That's it! That's just right!"

Oscar dropped his pencil in surprise. "It is? I did it?"

"You did it!"

Oscar tossed the eraser in the air and opened his mouth

to let out a whoop of triumph. George beamed. Ruthie screeched in her hammock. The whale suddenly surfaced and ground to a halt with an earsplitting mechanical groan, bucking under their feet. George and Oscar were thrown against the wall. Ruthie tumbled out of her hammock on top of them.

George sat up, spitting out a mouthful of Ruthie's orange fur. "We're here! We're at the lost island!"

"Thank goodness," Oscar said. "I was starting to worry I might get permanent sea legs."

George grabbed the map from Oscar's desk. They raced up to the hatch and found that Ada was already climbing out onto the upper deck. "Boys, get up here right now!"

Her voice was tinged, not with excitement, but with panic.

"What, what is it?" George asked, huffing and puffing up the ladder as fast as he could. When he got to the upper deck, he saw exactly what had made Ada sound so upset.

Before them stretched blue water and blue sky. No treasure. No lost island. Just waves that were rising and falling, rising and falling, endlessly forever.

Chatham Island was to the north, as they'd expected. That matched the map created from the butterfly's wings—but where was the lost island they'd seen? They should be right on top of it. The island wasn't there, though, nor was there any sign that any human had ever passed this way before. There were no buildings, no ships, no lighthouses, no towns, no castles, no rulers. Chatham Island looked like an abandoned beach, a strip of sand and rocks and scraggy grass that someone had dropped into the middle of the ocean.

Worse, so much worse, the ocean around it was completely empty. Miles and miles of water reached from horizon to horizon to horizon. A deep, ringing hollowness seeped into George from his head to his toes. They were so far from civilization that he doubted they could find their way back. A whale could gobble George up right now, and he would never be found.

There was no lost island.

George reeled, suddenly light-headed. His grandfather had once owned a globe, and George's hand had been too small to span the width of the Pacific Ocean. How silly of him to measure this ocean with his own hand. It was at once empty and full, everything and nothing.

They were on the edge of the world.

They were nowhere.

"It's lovely and warm. Look at the sea lions. I feel quite...happy," Oscar said, smiling broadly as the stiff breeze tousled his hair. Curious whiskered faces poked over the side of the whale. Ruthie swatted them away. "You were right about one thing, George. You'd said I'd find my happiness if I came to the Galápagos."

"It's not what I expected." Ada's voice was shaky and uncertain. Her skirts whipped around her ankles.

"It's—it's..." George stuttered, spinning from the shock of not finding the lost island. Perhaps it was Don Nadie's plan all along to drive him into the wilderness because the 1st Lord of Devonshire wanted George to save the world. "We're going to die here! No one will ever find our bodies! Our bones will turn to dust and blow away in the wind. Don Nadie will take over my house and kill Frobisher. It's all my fault!"

George's outburst evaporated into the air. He pulled the butterfly out of his bag and resisted the urge to chuck it into the ocean. Under her breath, Ada said, "It seems more your grandfather's fault, not yours."

George glared at her. The wind howled a mournful dirge. Choppy waves slapped against the hull of the whale.

Oscar breathed in deeply and blew out his breath in a loud huff. "Can we get off this boat, please? I'd like to go for a walk on that island over there," he said, pointing to Chatham Island. "Before I die and turn to bone dust."

"Absolutely," Ada said. "I'd like to spend my last night on earth under the stars."

George knew that they were making fun of him, but he was too miserable to care.

They anchored in a small bay at the southern tip of Chatham Island. There were a few stretches of flat, sandy beach between piles of black, craggy boulders. Sea lions were sprawled out on every flat surface like giant slugs that had washed up onshore. They didn't care one bit when three children and one orangutan pitched tents on the ridge just above the beach. Neither did the bright red crabs that scuttled over the black rocks. Ruthie chased a baby sea lion around the beach before settling down on a boulder to watch the sun set over the water.

While Ada set up the last tent, George and Oscar walked along the beach to collect driftwood for a fire. George dumped an armful of wood onto the sand. "Do you know what's worse than having bad luck?"

"Being friends with someone who has bad luck?" Oscar replied.

George tried to pull the end of a piece of driftwood from beneath a fat sea lion, but the sea lion twisted around and screamed *Oark!* "It's thinking your curse of bad luck has gone away and you have good luck, only to find out your luck was bad all along."

"You're not cursed. Curses aren't real, and neither are miracles. Those are just excuses for how you end up somewhere," Oscar said. He brushed a red crab off a piece of driftwood before tucking the wood under his arm.

"There's no lost island out there. There's not even a lost islet or a lost peninsula. I thought I could defeat the Nobodies. And look where it's gotten us," George said.

He returned to the pile of wood to add another load—but the sticks and small logs were gone. "Where did the firewood go?"

Oscar shrugged at the empty sand. "Maybe it's on the lost island."

Anger rose in George like a fire, burning him from the inside out. He threw down the wood. "This is serious, Oscar!"

"You think I don't know that? I'm here with you in the middle of nowhere! Don't blame me because you're unhappy now."

Before George could respond, Ada came charging down from the tents, holding her satchel. "There you both are! Which one of you did this?"

She turned her satchel upside down and a cascade of small black rocks tumbled out onto the sand.

George exchanged a confused glance with Oscar. "We've been collecting firewood."

"Really? Then where is it?" Ada asked. "I don't see any. I'm not in the mood for pranks. My favorite pair of boots were in this bag. I don't want to walk on these rocks in slippers, if you don't mind."

Tears sprang into George's eyes at the thought of Ada having her boots stolen. "My bad luck has brought us to this cursed place. I should have known the last two months were too good to be true. I'm no hero. My grandfather would be so disappointed in me."

George's legs wobbled, and he was about to sink dramatically onto a black rock when Ruthie screeched and sprang up from where she had been resting. She grabbed George's arm and yanked him forward onto the sand. Then she flung herself onto the rock where George had been about to sit.

"What in the world has gotten into you, Ruthie?" George asked.

Oscar burst into laughter. "You were about to sit on a turtle!"

Sure enough, the black rock was the curved shell of a large turtle. With Ruthie on its back, the turtle lurched forward and crawled toward the water.

"Look, it's missing a leg. Just like my father," Oscar said.

"Are we sure that's not a tortoise?" George asked. "She looks sturdy enough to sit on."

Oscar gasped. "We can't sit on Shells! That's her name—Shells. We aren't sitting on a friend."

Ada watched as the animal struggled across the beach, turning in lazy circles. "She's a turtle, not a tortoise. Look at her feet. They're flippers. She's meant to swim in the water."

"Let's help her into the water, then," Oscar said.

Ada shook her head. "She can't steer with only one front flipper. She's probably been swimming in circles since she lost it. Look, she can't even walk in a straight line."

"Well, don't stare at her," George snapped. "She didn't ask to have her flipper chewed off. She washed up here all alone, and now she's stuck, wandering in circles, looking for her way home. No matter how hard she tries, she can't get back."

"Ada can help her," Oscar said sharply. "She can make Shells a new flipper like my father's leg."

Ada grinned. "I think I can! A bit of wood, some canvas, and a little snail slime ought to do the trick. It would only be a prototype, but it's a simple form. Excellent idea, Oscar."

Ada hiked back up to the tents and fashioned a flipper while Oscar and Ruthie kept Shells safely on the beach. Determined to do something useful, George finished collecting firewood near the tents. He stacked the light wood as Frobisher had taught him, and used Oscar's flint stone to light a pile of kindling underneath. Gently, he nurtured the small flames.

Tears of frustration dripped down his nose. One fell onto the fire, extinguishing it with a *hiss*.

"Brains of porridge," George scolded himself. His father's favorite insult slipped out of him easily. Burning with self-loathing, he grabbed the rest of the twigs he'd collected for kindling, and once again lit the pile with Oscar's flint stone. It sparked, burned—

And went out.

"Brains of porridge," he muttered again, pounding the sandy ground in frustration. If he couldn't light a simple fire, how did he think he could follow his grandfather's clues and defeat Don Nadie?

George cast his eyes around for twigs or leaves and found nothing but a scuttling crab. Determined, he reached into his bag, looking for anything that could catch a flame. His hand closed around a sheaf of papers—the crime reports Vice-Chancellor Shadwell had thrust on him in London. The terrible phrases leapt from the page.

... George Devonshire ...

... robb'd and gagg'd Captain Romaine on his ship ...

... a wreck of devastating proportions ...

"Lies," he whispered. He crumpled the paper into a ball of kindling, stuffed it into the nest of driftwood, and set the flint stone to it. He made a spark that landed on the paper. It flamed, then sizzled out. Spark. Flame. Sizzle. Spark. Flame. Sizzle. Spark. Flame. Sizzle. Over and over again, until the last scraps of strength and bravery George had been clinging to sizzled away, too, leaving him feeling raw in the stinging wind. But then—

A small orange flame licked the edge of the paper. Dark smoke rose from the kindling like the most beautiful gray ribbon George had ever seen. He'd done it! He'd made fire!

Oscar called out to him from the waterline. "George, come say goodbye to Shells!"

The western sky was ablaze with a violently beautiful orange sunset. Fitted with a new flipper, Shells waved the white canvas paddle in the air a few times before scooting into the waves. Ruthie whimpered sadly as the turtle disappeared into the water.

"Who says my inventions are useless?" Ada muttered.

George slung his arm around Ada and leaned his head on Oscar's shoulder. "No one says that, Ada. You're wonderful. You're both wonderful. I'm sorry I was cross with you just now."

"Me too," Oscar and Ada said at once.

Smiling, Oscar pointed across the water. "Look! Shells is saying goodbye!"

George squinted into the glowing sunset. Far offshore, Shells was waving her white flipper at them. He watched the waves smooth around her sleek back. Odd—the turtle seemed to be standing on top of the water, not swimming in it.

Beside him, Oscar said, "Can turtles walk on water?"

"Not that I know of..." Ada pulled a pair of binoculars out of her skirt. "It's as if she's perched on an object *in* the water."

The gears of George's mind began to whir and click. Without a word, he sprinted toward the fire, then dove toward the flames.

"George!" Ada and Oscar screamed for him in unison.

George collided with the fire. Smoke filled his lungs. Flames licked at his arms, hands, fingers as they fumbled, searing with heat, for the paper that he'd used as kindling. He felt a sharp tug on his jacket as his friends hauled him back onto the cold, hard ground.

"Have you gone mad?" Ada demanded.

Faint smoke rose from his clothes. Slowly, he opened his fist to reveal the paper torn from *The Proceedings of the Old Bailey*. Though it was singed brown around the edges, George could still make out the passage he'd been looking for. He began to read out loud.

"22 March 1782. Yesterday George Devonshire, the son of the respected shipbuilder Thomas Devonshire, was accused of being one of the persons who robb'd and gagg'd Captain Romaine on his ship, *La Isla*, bound for the port of Guayaquil—"

"Guayaquil," Ada repeated. "That's in Ecuador on the mainland, not far from here."

Beaming, George continued. "—causing a wreck of devastating proportions, for which he now hangs in chains at the Gatehouse, being concerned with a large gang of thieves in several felonies, burglaries, and acts of piracy."

Ada gasped. "A shipwreck near Guayaquil?"

George nodded. "What if the lost island isn't an island? What if it's—"

"A shipwreck! *La Isla*." Ada's eyes brightened. "We could have sailed right over the top of it and never known."

"Shells is brilliant!" Oscar exclaimed.

"Let's get out there," George said. "It's just beyond the bay."

"First thing in the morning. It's going to be dark soon," Ada answered.

Chapter Seventeen

It is impossible to sleep soundly the first night on the edge of the earth. The sky is too dark. The air is too warm. The sounds are too strange.

For a moment, when George awoke from his restless sleep the next morning, he forgot where he was. He looked up at the white canvas tent above him and thought it was peculiar that his bed curtains had changed color. Then the *oark oark* of sea lions fighting on the beach below and the crashing of the waves reminded him that he was camping on Chatham Island, halfway across the world.

Whatever Don Nadie wanted, whatever his grandfather had hidden, was just out of reach, tucked beneath the waves.

As George buttoned up his shirt, he was filled to the brim with faith that he would tear off the mask of Don Nadie, revealing the villain in his grandfather's story. Yesterday, he'd been as drained as the dry pool in the courtyard of the Alhambra. He'd let his doubt siphon away his faith. But this morning, even his jacket felt lighter when he picked it up from where he'd thrown it last night.

Outside, in the muggy morning air, he could see that none of his friends had slept soundly, either. Ada's cheeks were sunken. The curls she'd kept perfectly spiraled at all times, even in the whipping winds of her airship, were as limp as overcooked noodles. Ruthie and Oscar were sprawled at the edge of their camp, dejectedly staring out at the open sea where they'd last seen Shells.

"Huzzah and good morning," George said, beaming. "It's a fine day for a treasure hunt, isn't it?"

Ada looked up from her notebook. "It's not ideal conditions. The ocean is calm, but it's teeming with sharks. We'll need to be careful when we go in the water."

George was not disturbed in the least. If anything, his knees buckled with the desire to dive into the waves headfirst. "Excellent. I have no doubt you'll keep us all safe from whatever sea creatures we encounter, Miss Byron. Right, Oscar?"

Oscar eyed him warily. "I suppose."

George's smile faltered. Oscar's confidence in Ada was usually unshakable. Could something be wrong?

But George was determined to play the role of the hero. He filled his lungs and addressed the group. "Just yesterday, I was like a boat sailing against the wind. I thought I was doomed to never fulfill my destiny because of a curse. But I won't make that mistake again. Oscar, you said that curses and miracles aren't real; they're excuses. I can't think of truer words spoken by a truer friend. No more excuses. No more doubt. I've come this far. My destiny is in my grasp. My sails are unfurled, and I'm pointed toward the future." He threw his jacket on with a flourish and grabbed the lapel as he faced out toward the water.

The corners of Ada's lips lifted into a smile. "Impressive use of metaphor, Lord Devonshire. Perhaps you should consider becoming a poet."

George grinned. "Maybe I will. Someone ought to write down our adventures one day. Hey! Where did my buttons go?"

All of his jacket's bright gold buttons were gone. Wispy little threads hung where the buttons had been the last time he'd seen them, which was yesterday.

"Don't look at me!" Oscar said, throwing his hands up.

Ada shrugged. "I have better sources for metals."

George emptied out his pockets. Nothing. "Well, someone took them."

"Or ate them," Oscar said, turning to look at Ruthie. The orangutan blinked sadly at the waves.

George prickled with unease. Someone had taken Ada's things yesterday. And their firewood. The Society could not have followed them—could they? But the Society wasn't interested in buttons or driftwood. Nor had they been attacked. Pushing the uneasy feeling away, George took his jacket off and folded it. "No matter. It's too warm for a jacket anyway."

"Yes, and it's not the best outfit for swimming," Ada said. "I packed two diving helmets in case of an emergency. I didn't think Oscar and Ruthie would be joining us. The helmets aren't meant to be used for more than a few minutes underwater, but that should be plenty of time to find the treasure, since we have all day."

"We're swimming ourselves? I thought the whale—"

"The whale is only a mode of transport. We won't be able to see well out of the portholes. We'll need to do this by hand."

After a quick breakfast of dried biscuits, they returned to the whale, leaving Ruthie behind to guard the campsite from any overly curious sea lions. The whale roared back to life, and they cruised out of the bay. In no time, they were wandering over the reefs where Shells had seemed to find dry land yesterday.

The deep waters were a dark cobalt, while the shallow reefs surrounding the island were a light aquamarine. The water was so clear that they had no trouble finding *La Isla* where it lay just beneath the waves. It was a great, hulking mass covered in coral.

If not for the unmistakable curves of a hull, they might have thought it was just another ridge of the reef.

Looking down at the shipwreck in the water, George felt an undertow of sadness beneath his elation at having correctly followed the trail his grandfather had left. *La Isla* was on its side, its masts sheared off just beneath the waterline. Even beneath the coral, George could see that it had been a beautiful ship once, a two-masted schooner, perhaps a packet boat carrying letters across the sea.

"Do you think anyone died down there?" Oscar asked, leaning over the railing.

George watched the ghostly shadows of fish dart in and out of the open hatches and portholes. "They wrecked in shallow water. It's possible they were all able to get out safely." Ada carried over one of the glass diving helmets and laid it on the deck in front of Oscar with a *plonk*. The helmet looked like an upside-down fishbowl with a padded leather gasket that closed tightly around the neck with a cord.

Oscar picked up the helmet and put it over his head. "I'm inside a bubble!"

"Take that off, Oscar. It's not a toy, and this is not a game. Listen closely—you'll have about five minutes of air after you put it on and unless you come up, you'll suffocate. Keep your head upright at all times or water will get inside your helmet. I'll tie ropes around your waists and pull you back up if you stay down too long," Ada said.

George picked up the second helmet. "You're not going?"

"If you must know, I'm a rather poor swimmer. My mother never let me learn how to swim properly because I told her I would swim across the English Channel if I did.

Plus, she's afraid I'll catch a fever if I get wet outside. That's how my father died, apparently. He went horseback riding in the rain. Besides, there are only two helmets. I'll be manning the smaller water cannon in case any sharks get too close." Ada fixed a serious gaze on George. "This isn't like my other plans, George. There are too many factors to take into account to fully guarantee your safety. Are you sure about this? We could keep looking for another way—"

He grabbed her gently by the shoulders. "Ada, I'm sure. Just as I'm sure that my grandfather meant to guide me here. He's been leading us here this whole time. I know it."

Though the rippling water below sent a shiver through him, George plastered on a brave face and followed Ada's instructions. Along with Oscar, he strapped on a weighted belt, which was attached to a long rope. They each filled their lungs with a deep breath of air, then put on the helmets and pulled the leather cords snugly around their necks.

Oscar reached out and gripped George's hand. Together, they plunged feet-first into the cold ocean.

Beneath the surface was an entirely new world. Sunlight filtered through the clear water in radiant beams.

Fish darted around them in rapid flashes, like hundreds of moving, blinking lights. George could hear nothing except his own heartbeat pounding in his ears. Using a mast as a guide, he descended to the wrecked boat, willing himself to breathe calmly. The helmet kept his face dry, and besides a little circle of fog from his breath on the glass, he could see everything. With a gentle tap, his feet touched down on the hull of the drowned ship. Oscar touched down next to him.

Over the next few hours, they slowly searched the ship inside and out, five minutes at a time. Because the ship had sunk sideways, they entered through a tear in the starboard side, careful to keep their helmets upright and away from any sharp bits of metal. They followed fish through open hatches and portholes into the dim, topsy-turvy cabins.

Each time Oscar and George explored the ship, all they discovered was more water and fish. No barrels or crates or treasure chests to be found.

By afternoon, their breaks between dives were growing longer and longer. The sea lions had grown curious and began following them down into the ship, then jostling them, trying to play. Ada had to scare away a couple of slithering sharks with her water cannon. George was slapped by a manta ray's wings, but for once, he hardly noticed any of the bother or the danger. While Oscar concerned himself with yanking George back from collapsed portions of the ship and dragging him to the surface well before their oxygen ran out, George wasn't focused on anything other than solving the trail of clues that his grandfather had left for him to piece together.

Oscar, however, was ready to quit. When they surfaced into the heat of the late afternoon, he set his helmet down and sprawled out on the deck of the mechanical whale.

"I'm exhausted," he said.

Ada untied the rope from around his waist. "It's nearly nightfall. I think we should pack up and head for shore."

George lingered in the water. "Pack up? You mean give up?"

"There's nothing down there," Oscar said.

"There's an entire ship down there," George replied, sweeping his hands across the water. "You stopped me from searching a few of those cargo holds, Oscar."

"They were pitch-black!"

"I can find my way in the dark—"

"Your grandfather wouldn't have meant for you to kill yourself looking," Ada interjected.

"My grandfather—" George began, but suddenly the whale tipped violently to one side. Ada and Oscar were flung across the deck while George bobbed in the water. Ada grabbed hold of the water cannon, but Oscar slid into the railings. Oscar's helmet slid, too. It rolled across the deck and hit the railing with a *bang*. George grabbed it after it splashed into the water, but it was no use: a shining crack appeared in the glass bowl.

"Looks like the sea lions have made the decision for us," Ada said. "Time to go."

"My helmet is still perfectly fine," George argued after swimming to the ladder but refusing to climb aboard. "I'm not giving up."

Oscar's face contorted with worry. "What if that wasn't a sea lion bumping the whale? First Ada's bag, then George's buttons. Someone or *something* on this island is trying to send us a message. You might get hurt."

George felt a brief swell of uncertainty, but he'd vowed not to let his doubts overwhelm him again. "I promise that I'll be safe, Oscar. There's no such thing as ghosts or bad luck or curses, remember? According to Miss Byron, there is a logical explanation for everything. The supernatural is the mind's way of explaining connections it doesn't understand. Everything will be fine."

Ada cocked her head to the side. "I did say that, but I'm not so sure anymore. You do have awfully bad luck, George. It's beyond logical explanation."

"I can't believe I'm hearing what I'm hearing," George said. "I do *not* have bad luck. I have the proper, average amount of luck just like everyone else. My only mistake has been doubting myself and doubting my grandfather. The map contained a secret, and I gave it away. The butterfly contained a clue, and I ignored it for too long. You once told me to trust my gut, didn't you, Miss Byron?"

"Yes, but this is getting ridiculous. Give me a few days to modify the periscope or build a device that will do the searching for you."

"We don't have time for that, Ada," George insisted.

Oscar untied the belt from around his waist. "I'm tired. And hungry. And I want to stop. This isn't fun anymore."

"It's not supposed to be fun!" George replied.

"It's not supposed to be dangerous, either. Let Ada find a better way that doesn't involve us drowning," Oscar argued.

The concern in Oscar's voice gave George pause, but he

pushed his doubts away again. His grandfather's map was his quest, not Oscar's, not Ada's. All the tools he needed were already inside him. Heroes had no room for hesitation and fear. "Well, my gut tells me that the answer is down there, and I have to find it before Don Nadie does."

George took a deep breath and jammed the helmet back onto his head. He heard Ada's and Oscar's muffled protests, but he knew they wouldn't follow where he was going. Alone, he stepped off the ladder and splashed into the water.

He slipped through an open hatch, dropping down, down, down into the heart of the ship. George strained his eyes to see. The water had begun to eat away at the wooden hull, leaving gaps for light to pierce into the dark interior. Oscar hadn't wanted to go this far into the ship, where the light hardly penetrated, but Oscar wasn't with him now.

There had to be something here. George kicked aside a loose plank, startling a fish with a bright yellow tail. The fish bumped its nose into George's glass helmet, then darted in the opposite direction, where it disappeared—straight into a wall. As he approached, he saw a thin seam in the wood...in the shape of a small door. A hidden cabinet. This was what he'd been searching for! All his persistence and hope were paying off. The circle of fog on his helmet grew as George let out a warm sigh of relief. At last!

George felt the rope around his waist tugging him up, up, up. Ada was trying to pull him to the surface, but George grabbed the wall and propelled himself across the cabin. He kicked at the wood with his heel and it gave way, revealing a small compartment. Inside was a smaller sea chest. The outer wooden layer of the box was rotting away, but the inside had been lined with silver metal. His heartbeat thrummed against his ribs, which were starting to feel strained from the lack of fresh air.

George reached down and grabbed the box, but in his excitement, he forgot that Ada had told him to keep his head upright at all times.

Salty water rushed up underneath his helmet. It splashed into his mouth. George gagged from the taste, coughing out a string of spit. Panicked, he twisted his head, but there was no escaping the water pouring into his helmet, which was now up to his nose.

With one last gasp of air, he yanked the helmet off. The ocean rushed into his ears, so loud, and yet there was no sound.

Wooden chest clutched under his arm, George pushed off the bottom of the cabin, kicking wildly to drive himself toward the surface. Sand and slivers of rotting wood exploded around him. In the swirling murkiness, he lost all sense of what was up or down. He tested the rope around his waist, but it had gone slack.

Seconds passed like hours as George's lungs burned. He jerked and flailed but never seemed to move. The box was heavy. It was dragging him down, back into the depths of the ship. But he couldn't let it go. If he let it go, he'd have failed his grandfather one final time.

He kicked his legs hard again. Above him, there was a square of light. The distance to the surface might be a few feet or a thousand miles. A bubble of air escaped George's lips. Sharp pain stabbed between his tightening ribs. With each lost breath, the edges of his vision faded to gray. He couldn't hold the darkness off much longer.

He took one last breath of salt water just as something yanked the box out of his arms.

Chapter Eighteen

Oscar's grip on the box and George's elbow didn't loosen until they broke through the surface. By then, George's lungs felt as if they were being devoured by flames. He coughed up a mouthful of water, then sucked in breath after glorious breath until the stabbing pain in his chest eased.

Oscar threw the box up to Ada on the whale. Ada threw over a rope to haul George onto the deck. George's eyes stung from the salt water dripping from his hair. It felt as if a horse was sitting on his chest.

Splayed next to each other, George and Oscar shook with nerves as Ada silently rubbed their heads with blankets, then wrapped the soft cloth around their shoulders.

She chewed on her thumb, her face pale, as she watched them recover. When George finally sat upright and drank some fresh water from a canteen, she let her head sink into her hands.

"Oh, thank goodness," she moaned quietly.

Once he had caught his breath, George reached for the box—but Oscar snatched it up first, his eyes blazing with an anger George hadn't known he possessed.

"Is this all that MATTERS to you?" Oscar bellowed in George's face. He sounded exactly like his father. "So what if it's full of gold, or silver, or jewels? Was this worth losing your life, or me losing MINE?"

"It's not about treasure, Oscar, I don't even know what's inside. It's about destroying that blasted Don Nadie—"

"You SAID that nothing would HAPPEN to you! You PROMISED!" Oscar shouted.

"Not now, Oscar," Ada chided gently.

Oscar turned his fury on her. "Yes, now! You can't wait to see what's in there, either. I'm surprised you dried us off first. What do YOU think is in that box? Another adventure you can chase?"

Ada seemed to shrink under Oscar's glare. She shot George a worried glance. "I don't know, but whatever it is, it's important. Let's all calm down. I'll take us back to the camp."

"I AM calm," Oscar said. "I didn't come with you on this journey just to watch you DIE. I've spent TWO months with my FATHER, and I'm SICK of people risking their lives for TREASURE. I'm tired of seeing people FIGHTING and CHASING. I—I thought it would be different if I was with you two," he finished, his voice raw and full of hurt. "I thought we could be friends, and that would be enough."

"It is different, Oscar, you belong with us—" George said just as Ada left the deck.

"No, it's NOT! Getting REVENGE on Don Nadie is not worth giving up your LIFE!"

"He started it!" George cried, before pushing down his frustration. He extended his hand, one eye on the box. "I'm sorry, Oscar. I didn't mean to put us in danger. We'll all open it together. Didn't you once say that pirates share everything?"

"I'm not a pirate," Oscar answered angrily, pressing the box to his chest.

Below them, the engines rumbled to life. They both jumped at the unexpectedly loud sound. George desperately wanted to snatch the box from Oscar's hands as they sailed away from the shipwreck, but he was afraid that if he moved an inch, Oscar would fling the box back into the sea.

"I've apologized. I don't know what else to say," George pleaded. "What do you want from me?"

But Oscar only hunched his shoulders miserably and said nothing. Wordlessly, they reached the shore, where Oscar jumped down onto the sand and carelessly cast the box to the ground. Screeching, Ruthie ran to him immediately and wrapped her orange arms around his leg, clinging to him as if he were a raft in the middle of the ocean.

George strode over to the box, with Ada close behind. It was a small comfort that George knew they were thinking the same thing: they had circled the globe to find out whatever was inside that box. George knew the treasure would be worth the journey. It had to be.

Oscar crossed his arms. "Well, are you going to open it?"

George exchanged a glance with Ada. She nodded, then retrieved a lit lantern and set it next to the box. The sun had almost set over the smooth, calm sea that had tried to kill George less than an hour before. The dazzling blues had cooled to smoky purples and grays as the honey-kissed clouds faded into the evening sky. The horizon was so flat and straight that it could have been a line in one of Oscar's drawings.

"It's rather small," George said warily.

"A number of dangerous and important things are small," Ada observed. "Open it."

Carefully, George picked up the box and put it in his lap. It was time to learn what his grandfather had wanted him to find. What Don Nadie wanted so badly, and what they might use to stop him.

A hundred butterflies flitted in his stomach.

Water from the box dripped onto his cotton trousers. The thick outer wood layer of the box crumbled under his touch, revealing more of the tin lining. After he'd brushed away the loose wood and bits of mud, George could see that underneath the wooden casing, the metal structure of the box was slightly rusted but still intact and locked tight. It was about the size of a loaf of bread, with a hinged lock that secured the top. The rusted hinge was easy for George to break off with a sharp rock.

George held his breath and lifted the lid, which popped off with a puff of musty air. Miraculously, the interior of the box was bone dry. There were two items inside: a soft leather portfolio with a sheaf of papers in it and a rusted compass.

Ada picked up the compass between her index finger and thumb to inspect it. After a few seconds, she declared, "Ordinary."

George reached inside the box and gingerly pulled out the papers. Careful not to tear the parchment, which had grown almost translucent with age, he flipped through the pages. There were inventories of the cargo and a list of crew members and passengers, all documents for the ship called *La Isla*.

George turned the box upside down, but nothing fell out. He used the Star of Victory to see if there was a hidden message to be decoded, but looking through the gem proved useless.

A bundle of documents. That was all there was.

A hard lump formed in George's throat, but he swallowed it down. He'd nearly died for this box and it appeared to be...nothing. He looked to Ada, expecting some miracle to come tumbling out of her mouth—but she just stared back at him with sad brown eyes.

"I think this is a dead end, George," she said.

A few paces away, Oscar scoffed. "What a surprise."

Frustration made George spring to his feet. Ada held his elbow to stop him, but George yanked it out of her grasp. "Oscar, what is wrong? Making rude remarks is not helping right now."

If Oscar's stare could cut, the whole world would be sliced into ribbons. "I've done nothing but help you—both of you—since I first met you! And for what?"

"For what?" Ada repeated softly, surprised. "What do you mean?"

"You said I belonged with you. But so far all I've done is draw *your* map and search for *your* treasure and fight *your* battles. I don't want to fight villains. I don't want to be a hero if this is what being a hero looks like." Oscar met George's eyes. Confusion and anger and pain were all mixed together on his face. "You almost died. I'd rather collect rocks on a deserted island for the rest of my life than have you or Ada or Ruthie die on some pointless intercontinental adventure."

"What are you saying, Oscar?"

Oscar hoisted his rock-collecting sack and a blanket over his shoulder. "I'm saying that this is not where I want to be. I don't have to be a hero or a villain, because from what I can tell, you're all acting the same. Maybe there's something in between that I can be. Or maybe I'm supposed to be a Nobody. What if that's where I'm meant to belong?"

George's jaw dropped. The thought of Oscar becoming a Nobody hit him like a punch to his stomach. "You can't be a Nobody!"

"Why not? We can't all be somebodies."

Without another word, Oscar turned his back to them and tramped off across the island, Ruthie still clinging to his leg as if she were stuck with barnacle glue.

Chapter Nineteen

Oscar would come back. He had to.

And when he did, George would show him just how wrong he'd been.

After Oscar stormed off, Ada disappeared into her tent. The lantern's glow cast a silhouette of her writing in her notebook against the canvas. George remained on the beach, the contents of the ship's box spread on the sand in front of him. He wouldn't stop until he'd studied every inch of every object in that box, backward and forward, upside down and right side up. The sun had set, and the dark was pressing in all around, so he set the lantern on a rock and read each line as carefully as if it were poetry, or an enticing double-column ledger.

According to the documents, *La Isla* had been a packet ship bound for the Ecuadoran port of Guayaquil carrying mail, passengers, and supplies. There were thirty-two crew members and fifty-five passengers aboard the ship. Among a constellation of water stains, the passenger manifest's list of names was legible.

With the dedication of an aspiring accountant, George ran his finger along the column of names, dissecting each one in turn. Nothing seemed remarkable until the fourth time George scanned the page, when he came to the twenty-seventh entry: *Estelle D.*

The tip of his finger stopped like an arrow that had found its target. The name. *Estelle.* It was so familiar. But why? George shook his head as if he could dislodge the answer. Damp strands of blond hair fell into his eyes.

Suddenly, a shuffling sound to his left jolted him upright.

"Ada? Oscar? Ruthie?" he called out.

He glanced over, hoping to see Oscar and Ruthie. But all he saw was the sleeve of his jacket being dragged across the ground and disappearing into the scrubby bushes that lined the beach.

"Hey! Stop!" George sprang to his feet and swung the

lantern in an arc to illuminate the underbrush. He saw a flash of brown ankle and the white bottom of a foot as its owner ran into the wild unknown of the island's interior.

George plunged into the rough scrubland after the mysterious foot. Flocks of tiny finches exploded ahead of him, blooming into twittering clouds as the thief darted forward, faster than George could follow. George quickly realized that he was being led down a narrow path beaten into the ground. His lantern clattered loudly and the flame flickered, but he dared not slow down in case he fell too far behind.

"Give me back my jacket! And my buttons! And my friend's shoes!"

After a while, the footsteps in front of him faded into the other sounds of the night. Hoots. Chirps. Growls?

George slowed to a stop to see that he was standing at the base of the long-dead volcano that towered like a mountain at the island's center. The ground ahead was getting steeper and steeper, and the path seemed to vanish as the plants became taller.

George turned to go back the way he'd come, but the path had disappeared.

He closed his eyes, trying to remain calm. When he

opened them, he spotted the bright pinpoint of the camp-fire Ada had made. Above him, stars glittered in the night, lavishly decorating the darkness like jewels, or the shiny minerals that Oscar collected, thrown into the sky. Together, the lights would guide him home.

Under the sky, the black ocean writhed and moved in the distance, scattering the silver starlight and moonlight—and another small constellation of yellow lights in the bay he didn't recognize.

George lurched back. The yellow lights in the bay. They weren't reflected from above. They belonged to a ship. No, a *fleet* of ships.

A fleet of ships heading straight for Ada's campfire.

George snuffed out his lantern and stumbled toward the campfire as fast as he could. When he got near the camp, he saw that the ships had launched smaller boats that were swarming toward the shore. Did Ada know they were coming or was she too busy writing in her notebook?

George kept his eyes locked on the ships. They were six large and well-armed two-deckers, each with several dozen cannons at least. When he finally managed to creep to the edge of the camp, the shore was already teeming with invaders. They had organized themselves into tidy formations, each headed by a man wearing a familiar style of dark blue naval jacket with gleaming rows of gold buttons.

He rubbed his eyes in disbelief, but the scene did not change. It couldn't be, he told himself. It was impossible.

But, as Ada had told him countless times, nothing was impossible.

In a moment of wild hope, George let himself believe the navy had come on behalf of the King to apologize for the truffle incident. But immediately his hopes were dashed. A contingent of officers escorted Ada out of her tent like a prisoner. She looked so small pressed between the soldiers. Her hair was loose around her shoulders, which made her appear even younger than she was. Finally, he saw that her wrists were bound with rope. The sight of it filled George with fury such as he'd never known.

A portly man with bushy eyebrows stepped off the last boat and strode onto the beach. George's stomach seized as he recognized him. The last time he had seen him was through the bars of the prison carriage, just after he'd sentenced George to prison for trying to poison the King of England.

Vice-Chancellor Shadwell had found them even on the other side of the world.

After five seconds of carefully considering all his options, of which he could only see two—*stay* or *run*—George made a decision. The bravest one he could muster. He wouldn't let Ada be taken into custody alone.

The 3rd Lord of Devonshire strolled into the middle of the British navy with his palms facing up.

"I surrender."

Chapter Twenty

Don't talk," Ada whispered under her breath to George when they brushed shoulders on the narrow rowboat. The fresh-faced soldiers on either side of them talked over their heads as if they weren't there at all.

"*That's* the London Truffle Assassin? He's just a child."

"I know. Scrawny, ain't he? Kind of dull looking, too. Wouldn't have thought he had it in him."

"It's a pity the girl got mixed up in his schemes. She must not have known who he was."

"Shadwell says the girl's the smart one. Faked her death, broke him out of prison, and helped him escape here. Anyway, the whole world knows who he is now. He's been on the front page of every newspaper in the empire. It's the biggest news of the year."

"Ghastly shame, is what it is. What is this world coming to? Children trying to murder kings and gallivanting around the world? Nothing like that ever happened when I was a boy."

Unable to listen any longer, George shouted, "I'm innocent!"

The nearest soldier rapped George in the skull with an oar, then shouted, "Quiet!"

Grumbling, they were taken aboard one of the sleek ships. Thankfully, there was no sign that Oscar or Ruthie had been captured. The mechanical whale also seemed to have vanished. At any moment, George expected it to come bursting through the surface, mechanically transformed into a shark or something similarly ferocious, to rescue them. But the waters below them remained dark and still.

Ada and George were then brought belowdecks and put in separate iron cages. Although they could see each other, they were an arm's length away. Guards were stationed around them so that even if the two somehow escaped the bars they would be immediately captured again.

George only dared to speak when the bells for the next watch sent the guards hurrying to the upper deck. He pressed his face between the bars and whispered a frantic string of words. "Adahowwillweescape!"

"I'll just invoke Princess Victoria's name. That should get us back to London alive, at the very least." She smiled. "On the bright side, if we are hanged, I won't have to go to the Somerville School for Ladies of Substance."

George did not have time to scold Ada for making such an awful joke before footsteps sounded above them and a handful of fresh-faced guards flowed in.

"We demand to see the vice-chancellor," Ada said to the nearest guard.

"Prisoners don't make demands," he replied curtly.

George leaned against the bars. "Can we make polite requests?"

Ada lifted her chin and stretched herself to her full height. "Please inform the vice-chancellor that his presence is demanded in the name of Princess Victoria."

"Princess Victoria is not the Queen yet, nor do I answer to her," said the vice-chancellor as he descended the narrow staircase into the prison hold. "You'd do well to remember that, Miss Byron."

The guards suddenly snapped to attention. Smiling, Vice-Chancellor Shadwell approached the cells. Though his eyes still crinkled kindly beneath his bushy brows, George saw that there was a cruel slant to his smile.

"She *will* be the queen one day, and then you *will* answer to her. You'd do well to remember that, Vice-Chancellor," Ada replied calmly.

The vice-chancellor smiled. "One day is a very long time from today. Yet, it is also true that a lot can change in one day. I hope you are not implying that you have ill wishes toward our current elderly sovereign and his equally elderly brother. Because then it would seem that you have something in common with your friend here, the London Truffle Assassin."

"But I didn't—" George began.

"This is outrageous!" Ada interrupted. "The King was not assassinated. He's alive and well. No crime was committed, and I think you are clever enough to see that *he*"— she pointed angrily at George—"is no type of assassin. I demand you release us at once."

Vice-Chancellor Shadwell turned his back to Ada and strolled over to George's cell. He reached through the bars and put a firm, strong hand on George's shoulder. "My boy, I'm very disappointed in you. Your friend thought she was doing the right thing by helping you escape, but you know deep down in your heart it was a cowardly thing to do. A real man accepts the consequences of his actions."

The words reached into George's very core and twisted.

Ada rattled the bars of her cell. "Don't listen to him, George. You didn't do anything wrong. He's manipulating you."

"If anyone's manipulated you, it's that girl," the vice-chancellor said in a quiet voice, leaning even closer to the bars. "I can see that she's thoroughly muddled you with her fanciful notions. Has she filled your head with tales of adventure plucked from her father's poetry? It's quite understandable that you'd be seduced by her pretty words. She is a Byron, after all."

George gritted his teeth. "A real man would not speak ill of Ada Byron."

The vice-chancellor waved his finger at a guard, who clamped his hand over Ada's mouth. "I only want the truth. Is she hiding the map for you? If you admit that it was her idea to poison the King, then I can spare you from the gallows."

George met Vice-Chancellor Shadwell's gaze. "How did you know about the map?"

The kindly twinkle completely vanished from the vice-chancellor's eyes, and now his face was entirely cruel. His fingers tightened around George's shoulder, gripping his muscle like a vise. "I can make things easier for you, if you tell me where it really is."

George wrenched himself from the vice-chancellor's grasp and backed up, all the way to the rear wall of the cell. The hair on his arms and neck stood on end. "So you do know about the map. You're working for Don Nadie?" he asked, horrified.

The guard who'd been holding Ada's mouth closed yelped and drew his hand back. She must have bitten him. She shouted, "How did you find us?"

The vice-chancellor sighed. "One of his men put a device on your ship back in Spain that left a trail of phosphorus in the water. You've heard of cold light, haven't you? It was quite pretty, and it led us straight to you."

"The map is long gone. It burned to ash in the Alhambra," said George smugly. "No matter what you do to me, your boss Don Nadie will never get what he wants."

The vice-chancellor licked his lips, then smiled. "That wasn't a trick, then? The map really burned?"

George nodded defiantly.

"That's a shame, Lord Devonshire. I was almost growing fond of you. No map, no mercy. Those were Don Nadie's orders. Now I have to kill you." The vice-chancellor nodded at one of the guards. "Tell the captain to prepare the noose. We will be executing the London Truffle Assassin on the yardarm as soon as possible."

The vice-chancellor left George and Ada alone in their cells. They could hear the ship stirring to life around them, the clank of chains and the crisp snap of the sails in the wind.

"Let's get out of here," George said. He shook the door of his cell. "What do you have this time? Some more acid? Will the whale turn into a mechanical beaver to chew us out?"

Ada sat down in the middle of her cell and buried her head in her hands. Her shoulders began to shake miserably. "They took everything when they searched me on the island. Even my hard-boiled eggs. The last time I saw the whale it was where I left it on the beach, but I can only assume that Shadwell has already set his men on it."

"Maybe Patty..."

This only made Ada's shoulders shake harder.

George stomped his feet on the floorboards, testing them for any weaknesses. "We'll! Think! Of! Some! Thing! We! Have! To!" he cried, punctuating each word with a stomp.

"I never suspected—never actually thought—that the Society had someone working for them in the government at such a high level already," Ada said.

Her chest heaved with sobs. When she looked up, her eyes were red and tears dripped off her nose. George tried to reach through the bars for her, but his fingers only touched the air between them. "Don't cry, Ada. It will be all right. I'll save us," he said, although he had no idea how.

But not long afterward, the guards came and dragged George and Ada onto the top deck. The morning sun was dazzling on the blue ocean. Overnight, they had sailed away from the Galápagos, and there was nothing but blue water and sky for miles in every direction. The naval officers were assembled on the ship's deck in a menacing line of navy blue. Only one figure stood out—a man dressed in a long black robe. A matching black hood covered his face.

George's executioner.

With a turn of his stomach, George saw that the lower sails had been raised and a simple noose hung over the yardarm. His legs went weak, and bright lights danced at the edges of his vision. But George was a gentleman, and a gentleman did not cringe in the face of death. He stood upright as the guards led him onto a small platform, directly in front of the noose. The executioner sidled up next to him.

Vice-Chancellor Shadwell stood at the foot of the mast, his hands clasped behind his back. A smile played at his lips. "Miss Byron, I'm sorry to subject you to this unfortunate event. But I believe your friend's fate will ensure that you won't soon forget what happens to enemies of progress and justice."

Ada suddenly burst forward and collapsed at George's feet, sobbing and clutching the hem of his pants. Even though he was the one to be hanged, he was alarmed by Ada's emotional outburst. It was so unlike her. He'd never seen her so upset—she wailed and thrashed, causing many of the officers to shift uncomfortably. Indifferent to Ada's pitiful cries at George's feet, the hooded executioner brought the noose forward inch by inch. When he was about to lower the noose onto George's head, he leaned in close to whisper,

"It's time to jump, little rabbit."

The executioner grabbed George by the arm, and Ada sprang up to grab George's other hand. In a chain of three, they dashed to the side of the ship before any of the sailors could react and took a flying leap over the railing, vaulting into the air.

George, Ada, and Il Naso plunged into the swirling waters.

Chapter Twenty-One

George surfaced and saw Il Naso, unhooded, helping Ada swim to the mechanical whale, which was floating just below the surface. Then he untied the tether that attached the whale to the navy ship's stern.

Bullets whizzed over their heads, peppered by confused shouts. The whale was too close to the ship for the sailors to get a good shot. While they reloaded their weapons, George glanced up to see the vice-chancellor glaring down at them. The air around him was strung with puffs of smoke.

"Go lick Don Nadie's boots, you canker sore," George shouted, emboldened by the distance between them. "Tell him the 3rd Lord of Devonshire sends his regards!"

George climbed onto the whale's deck, opened the hatch, and dropped inside. Il Naso and Ada followed him down the slick ladder. In her hand, Ada held the tracking apparatus that had been placed on the hull.

George tackled the Italian policeman in a hug. Just a few months ago, Il Naso had tracked them through the streets of Venice like a dog hunting a fox. And after Il Naso had burned his grandfather's map, George never would have imagined that when next he saw him, he'd want to squeeze him and never let go. But Il Naso had saved his life. George's gratitude wiped away every other feeling.

Il Naso stumbled back, surprised, his boots slipping on the wet floor. George hugged him harder. "You saved my life! Thank you. Thank you. Thank you."

Il Naso smiled broadly. He patted George on the head. "It is all right, little rabbit."

As they all gathered around the pilot's chair, George wiped salt water from his face. "Where did you come from? How did you get here?"

Ada wrung water from her hair with one hand while the other moved in a blur over the controls. "Yes, not to sound ungrateful, but how *did* you get here on *my* ship?"

Il Naso chuckled. Tiny drops of water sprayed from his

black mustache. "There will be plenty of time for stories soon. First we need to get away from these terrible men."

"Agreed," Ada chirped. Patty was sitting motionless in the copilot's seat. Ada flicked a switch in Patty's back and she jerked to life.

"I will never get used to that thing," Il Naso muttered.

"George, man the periscope," Ada said. "We're going to make sure the vice-chancellor never bothers us again."

"How? He has a fleet of the British navy's finest ships and enough cannons to blow us to bits! Let's get out of here while we still can," George pleaded.

"We will. But first, we ought to do a little damage. Remember what we did to those tobacco ships in London and what the Society did to Captain Bibble's ship at Levrnaka? That was nothing. I've got a new weapon I want to test."

George heard the *clunk* of a lever. His eyes widened as he swiveled the periscope. A gleaming silver horn shot out from the whale's prow with a loud hiss. Ada turned a dial, and the horn began spinning furiously, just like the arrows that the Society had fired at them from Captain Bibble's stolen vessel.

Diving deeper, Ada steered the whale through the

fleet, darting around and underneath the large ships like a minnow between porpoises. Ada jabbed the horn into the bottom of each ship with satisfying muffled crunches, condemning the fleet to founder in the middle of the ocean or pump the lower decks until their arms fell off. The naval fleet was too close together to fire their cannons without risking striking each other.

George whooped. "Shadwell will be limping back to London like a dog with his tail between his legs!"

When they'd finished turning the bottoms of Shadwell's ships into Swiss cheese, George plotted the course back to Chatham Island, hoping the destruction of the navy boats would give them time to track down Oscar and Ruthie. The thought of leaving them behind with no explanation was impossible to even consider. With the fleet destroyed and the vice-chancellor's crew in lifeboats, they would have time to look for Oscar and Ruthie, and with Il Naso on their side, they had a nose to track them down. Ruthie couldn't be hard to sniff out, George reasoned.

Once they settled on a plan, Il Naso wrapped himself in a blanket with a cup of tea and began to tell the story of how he'd rescued them. "When last I saw you in

Venice, little rabbits, I had finally closed the case against the English poet which had plagued me for many years. I had not taken a *vacanza* in all that time. I love my city of Venezia, you must understand, but I needed to get away.

"The treasure map, it fell into my lap in such a way, I think it is the *perfetto* thing. I will go to Spain in the sunshine and solve a riddle, perhaps find a treasure. This would be fun for me." Il Naso lurched forward and, in a rough whisper, said, "But then I found out other people wanted this treasure, too. Bad people."

George grinned sheepishly. "When I gave you the map, I didn't know how much trouble it would cause."

The policeman arched an eyebrow at him. "I smelled them coming, but I did not know what they wanted. Then I understand. They are looking for this map. Every step I take, they are right behind. I hide in the Alhambra, where I have many ways to escape, but still they trap me."

"So you destroyed the map," George said, filling in the rest of the story.

Ada raised her eyes from the control panel. "What's the Society's smell?"

"Ada, that's disgus—"

"The Society of Nobodies smell like smoke and corruption and greed and sadness and misery," Il Naso interrupted, pounding his fist into the palm of his hand for emphasis. "They are rotten like spoiled fish. On the outside, they look like us, but on the inside, they have festered and grown rancid. This is because they are unhappy and lonely like their leader."

George scoffed. "Unhappy and lonely? How do you know that?"

Il Naso tapped his nose. He continued, "When I saw you at the Alhambra, I did not know yet if I could trust you. So I followed you to your whale and stowed away. As I did with the Society, I study the map and I study you. Both things I have solved. I know that you are silly, petulant children, but you are good. I want to help you stop the Society. This will be the greatest case of my career."

The story riveted George, but there was one thing he didn't understand. "Mr. Naso, how could you study the map? We saw you burn it."

With a grin, Il Naso stood. He strode into the belly of the whale, then returned a short time later holding a square of parchment.

Ada's hands flew to her mouth. "Is that..."

"My grandfather's map," George confirmed, taking the delicate paper from Il Naso. He unfolded it tenderly, as if afraid of shattering it. The world bloomed in front of him in ink and chalk and paper. The map was no worse for wear after its time in Il Naso's care. Warmth rushed into George's cheeks as he realized all at once that the time he'd spent trying to re-create the map with Oscar had been spent in vain. They could never have made a map identical to the one he now held in his hands. But the hours had not been wasted. Now he only appreciated the real one more. Plus, he'd spent that time with Oscar, he thought with a twist of his heart.

"I knew that if the Society realized I did not destroy the map, they would hunt me forever—or come after you. This treasure must be very important. And still, I did not know if you could be trusted with the map." The Italian policeman hung his head. A tear trickled down his cheek. "The Society destroyed my nose with their awful stink bombs. It will never be the same. Maybe if I could have smelled your intentions, I would not have stayed hidden in the cargo hold for so long. I am sorry that I did not trust you sooner."

"What changed your mind?" Ada asked.

"I am not usually so trusting of Truffle Assassins or Byron children," Il Naso said. "But your ape stole food to feed me while I was on board your ship. I was thinking of your father, *signorina*. Lord Byron was a great lover of animals. In his apartment in Venezia he had cats and dogs, and also monkeys and peacocks, yes, and many others. I could see he loved these animals. I did not like your father, but on this one thing we agreed: animals are more easily trusted than people. And if this kind animal loved you, then you must be not so bad."

The hard line of Ada's lips softened into a half smile. "I heard my father loved dogs best of all."

George's cheeks burned with shame. All that time on the ship when he had been angry with Ruthie, she had been stealing food for Il Naso, not herself. Il Naso must have been the one stealing things around the camp as well, so that he could survive. George patted Il Naso's sopping shoulder with his free hand. "It's all right, perfectly all right. We have the map, everything is going to be fine. Now all we need is the Star of Victory to decode it."

When the whale returned to the beach on Chatham Island, the three of them raced to the camp, where the Star of Victory lay among George's things. Finally (finally!) he would have the map and both parts of the Star of Victory assembled. He'd never had all the pieces of the puzzle together in one place at the same time. There would be no more secrets, no more wondering, no more indiscernible clues hidden in sunken ships. Whatever his grandfather had meant for him to find—whatever he wanted to protect from Don Nadie—George would be able to discover at last. He would finally be the hero his grandfather had meant for him to be and defeat Don Nadie for good.

George slapped his forehead. "I almost forgot to ask— were you stealing our driftwood? And my gold buttons? I'm thankful to you for saving us, but I *would* like my buttons back."

Il Naso shook his head. "I did not steal any gold buttons. Only food."

"Then who did?"

"I don't know," Il Naso replied. "The smells of this place are not familiar."

The tents had been ransacked by Shadwell's men. Their supplies and possessions were scattered across the dirt, but there was no sign of Oscar or Ruthie.

Hands trembling with excitement, George retrieved the Star of Victory from where it lay on the ground outside his tent. Its silver rods sparkled, and the blue sapphire shimmered as if it knew it was finally going to serve its purpose. His heart began to thump like a drumbeat behind his ribs. With Ada and Il Naso crouched beside him, George unfolded the map on his crossed legs. He turned the Star upside down so that its silver sprays served as a tripod on which the blue sapphire stood. He peered into the gem.

"What do you see?" Ada asked.

Looking through the Star of Victory wasn't very different from peering through the periscope. George took a deep breath and allowed his eyes to adjust to the distorted image he saw through the glittering gem. The lines of the map seemed to lift up and float above the paper in three dimensions. This didn't surprise George—he'd seen it before, when they'd examined the small scrap of map back at his house. Now, though, it was clear that the floating map was not what he was meant to see. What he sought was hidden underneath.

George slid the Star across the page, moving his lips

silently as he discovered the message hidden beneath the continents teeming with rivers and the oceans swirling with beasts.

It did not reveal a lost island, or shipwreck, or hidden weapon.

It was a birth record.

For the 1st Lord of Devonshire.

Chapter Twenty-Two

CHRISTENINGS AND BURIALS 1763

*George, the son of Thomas Devonshire of
Greenwich and Victoria his wife, was born the
16th and baptized the 28th of August by the
Reverend Mr. Gilbert Crocker.*

"I don't understand," Ada said when she had finished looking through the Star of Victory.

"Neither do I," George said truthfully.

"Don't look at me," Il Naso said. "I told you everything I know."

George stared blankly at the map. Dread filled him.

He didn't see how they could stop Don Nadie and save C.R.U.M.P.E.T.S. with his grandfather's birth record. In his imagination, he saw himself walking into C.R.U.M.P.E.T.S and waving the paper in the air while scientists laughed in his face. "In the letter he wrote to my grandfather, Don Nadie said that my grandfather stole something from him. But how could he steal his own birth record?"

Il Naso scratched his mustache. "This is what I do not understand: Don Nadie needs the map for the final step of his plan. How can this be useful to him?"

Ada sprang to her feet and began to pace. She always claimed walking stimulated the brain. "The simplest hypothesis is always the best," she said. "But nothing about this situation is simple. According to all the evidence we've gathered, your grandfather stole something very valuable from Don Nadie, then hid its whereabouts in the map. We have found that the map is in fact your grandfather's birth record. Don Nadie needs the map to complete the last part of his evil plan. Hence, Don Nadie needs your... grandfather?" She stopped so abruptly that her feet kicked up a cloud of dirt. "Are you sure your grandfather is really dead, George?"

"He's very dead," George said, shivering at the memory

of his grandfather's stiff body being placed in his coffin. "I'm sure of it."

Il Naso began to pace around the camp with his nose lifted in the air as if the answer could be smelled on the breeze. "Maybe this Don Nadie is having some fun with you. Criminals like to do this sometimes with their victims. You have a saying for this in English, I think. Cat-and-mouse game?"

"Or a wild-goose chase," Ada offered.

While George pored over the map and Il Naso stalked away to try to sniff out Oscar and Ruthie, Ada rattled off a few other options:

"A prank?

"A distraction?

"I said all along it might be a diversion."

George's careful examination of the birth record uncovered an odd clue. "Aha! Wait—stop!"

Ada halted in her tracks. "What is it?"

"Something's wrong," George said, waving the birth record in the air. "First, this states that my grandfather was born in Greenwich, when I know for a fact that he was born on the seaside. Greenwich is not on the seaside. Second, he was born on a cold winter's morning. The

254

twenty-eighth of August is not winter. Lastly, he was about to turn sixty years old the year he died in 1826. Turning sixty-three is not the same as turning sixty, which means that the birth year is wrong."

Ada leaned over the birth record, eyes furiously scanning the words.

George pulled out the crime reports and compared the documents side by side. "It must be a fake—right, Ada? Another piece of my grandfather's puzzle. Just like these crime reports! I *knew* my grandfather didn't do all those terrible things."

"A forgery?" Ada looked from one document to the other. "I don't think so, George. Trust me, I've forged plenty of documents. This seal would be very hard to replicate. Plus, *someone* was responsible for sinking *La Isla*, remember?"

"He would never have done that. Only a villain deliberately sinks a ship," George said sternly, trying to erase the glee he'd felt while drilling very large holes in the vice-chancellor's ships earlier that day. He racked his brain to put all the evidence he'd found together in a way that made sense.

Ada tilted her head and began to tug on one of her

curls, which she always did when puzzling over an invention. "George . . . what if we're both right?"

An uncomfortable sensation swam in his chest. He wanted to defend his grandfather's honor until his last breath, but all the things he'd just learned were casting a shadow on the bright light of his memories. "What do you mean?"

"What if the reports are real but your grandfather didn't do those things?"

"You mean someone stole his identity? An impostor?" He thought of Frobisher's fake identity. It was possible for one person to live as someone else.

"Yes, but"—she gestured with the birth record—"what if your grandfather was the one who stole someone else's identity? What if he was the impostor?"

"What? That's ridiculous." His gut shifted inside him, making him feel sick. Ada couldn't be right.

But . . .

George picked up the leather bag where he'd stored all his clues: the portrait Oscar had re-created, the butterfly pendant, and the poisonously written letter. Slowly, as if pulling a venomous snake out of a tank, George took the letter out of his bag. One phrase lashed out at him, alive with new meaning.

I curse your true name, 1st Lord of Devonshire.

Cold and heat raced over him in alternating waves. He glanced up from the letter to find Ada staring wide-eyed at him. "'Your true name,'" she quoted. "Your *grandfather's* true name."

George began to shake. Everything he knew about his life, every image in his memory, began to peel away and fall into a black abyss. The ground swirled beneath him. The sea lions barking on the beach below grew distant, as if they were barking in a dream.

"My..." George began to ask out loud. "My grandfather wasn't the 1st Lord of Devonshire?"

A sharp bark of laughter made them both spin around.

Fear stoppered George's throat. Ada clutched his hand.

An impossibly tall man stood within arm's length of them. They'd been so absorbed in their discovery that they hadn't heard him crossing the sand.

He stepped forward. Instinctively, George pulled Ada behind him.

Just as he had in No. 10, the man carried a long stick that he used to help himself balance. His tall shadow fell across the papers in George's hand, blocking out the sun.

"Your grandfather *wasn't* the 1st Lord of Devonshire," the tall man said. "I am."

Chapter Twenty-Three

"Tie him up."

Snapping to his senses, George scrambled to get away, but red-coated ruffians grabbed him and pinned his arms to his sides, holding him in place. Beside him, Ada yelped as she was pushed to the ground at Don Nadie's feet. George looked back and glimpsed a familiar sneering face surrounded by bright red curls.

Roy. The thief who'd first stolen his grandfather's map.

Don Nadie was soon joined by Roy's sister, Rose, a sopping wet Vice-Chancellor Shadwell, and other members of the Society, who were restraining Il Naso. The policeman was glowering underneath his black eyebrows with barely contained rage. After their initial fright, Ada mostly looked annoyed and impatient, while George was afraid he would soil his trousers from fear.

Still, he managed to meet Don Nadie's gaze. *"You."*

Don Nadie tipped his chin proudly. His shock of white hair fluttered in the warm breeze, and his gray eyes wandered over the scene in a detached inspection. "Astutely observed. I'm also the rightful 1st Lord of Devonshire. Your grandfather stole my family, my future, and the commission in the Royal Navy that was supposed to be mine. Everything that's yours is mine."

"That can't be true," George insisted forcefully. He struggled against Roy's iron grip. "This is all part of your game!"

"I told you, George. Your grandfather was the one who played games. But after forty years, the game is now concluded." Don Nadie waved his walking stick at another Nobody, Shaw, whose bald head was already beading with sweat in the hot sun. "The map, if you please, Mr. Shaw. And the rest of the papers."

Shaw gathered up the papers from where they lay at George's feet. He handed them up to Don Nadie.

"What are you going to do with those?" Ada asked, eyes darting from George to the papers to Don Nadie.

Don Nadie peered down at Ada. "This is a family

matter, Miss Byron. Your interference is most unwelcome and will no longer be tolerated." He tapped Ada's shoulder with his walking stick and a blue spark flickered from its tip.

"Ow!" Ada cried as she clutched her shoulders.

"Don't you dare hurt her!" George screamed.

Don Nadie tapped George's shoulder with his walking stick. A stinging pain coursed over George's skin. "Settle down, children. If either of you misbehaves again, the other will be punished. Is that clear?"

Ada's eyes were aflame with rebellion, but she held her tongue. George nodded grudgingly.

"Now," Don Nadie continued, "if you had been a little more patient, I would have been happy to tell you what I plan to do with these papers. I've thought of nothing else for the past forty-two years, two months, and eleven days. Unfortunately, we don't have much time before I have to return to London for a certain scientific gathering, so I'll have to give you the short version. Your grandfather liked to tell stories, did he not? He was an orator?"

George could only nod.

Don Nadie tapped his walking stick on the ground. "His father taught him as a child—correct?"

"How do you know that?" George asked, voice trembling.

The man sighed, as if bored. "Because the same person taught me."

He cleared his throat and began.

THE VERY TRAGIC TALE OF GEORGE,
THE TRUE 1ST LORD OF DEVONSHIRE

My story begins in the city of Greenwich, the most elegant city in all of England. My parents, Thomas and Victoria, were both from distinguished families of minor nobility and—

No, no. Too early. I shall start again.

My story begins when I was three years old. My mother died and the widow Foote arrived to be my little sister's nursemaid. The widow was poor, very very poor, and had a son not much older than my sister. His name was Arthur. The three of us— myself, my sister, and Arthur—we loved to—

No, still too early.

My story begins when my beloved nursemaid, the widow Foote, died, when I was thirteen years old. She was like a mother to me because my own had died.

The widow's son, Arthur, was the same age as my sister,

Estelle. We grew up together as children, as close as siblings could be. When the widow Foote died, my father adopted Arthur. In spite of the tragedies that had marred our lives, we were happy. Arthur was as much of a brother to me as if we'd shared the same blood.

I couldn't have known how wrong I was about that.

As we grew older, some people began to say that my father favored Arthur and loved him best of all. Arthur was handsome and clever and charming—and I was not.

The tall man stopped, bringing a hand to his chest, as if he'd been struck by an invisible blow. He cleared his throat, then continued.

What Arthur did best was make words dance like butterflies. He flattered my father no end: "Sir, how can I ever repay you? It is my greatest honor to be your son." Codswallop! He was a liar. He said the words, but he didn't mean them.

Soon my sister fell under Arthur's spell, too. We used to all play a game together. We pretended to build a house or a castle, and then one of us would hide a treasure inside, and the others would have to find it. Arthur and Estelle would use all sorts of riddles and clues. My father even gave my sister that silly gem so she could encode and decode messages.

"The Star of Victory?" Ada asked.

Yes, something special from my father for his little star, his beloved wife Victoria's Estelle. Stella Victōriae, another toy for their games—but they made it so complicated! They invented the most outrageous story that it was a priceless stone and that whoever owned it would win any battle.

Arthur and Estelle's fantasies grew wilder as time went on. They said they would find the lost gold of Montezuma, the crown jewels of King George, and the third Sacred Treasure of the Japanese emperors. But what was even wilder was that my father believed them! He thought they could do anything.

But me? No matter what I did or how many friends I made, nothing I did was worth anything in my father's eyes. I would always be a nobody to him. Some of my new friends told me I didn't need my father to get what I wanted. There was money to be made all sorts of ways. Not everybody hides their money or buries it behind riddles and games. In fact, they barely protect it at all. Can you believe that?

There's not enough time to tell you about the trouble I got into with my new friends, the first members of the Society. It was all in good fun, and nobody was meant to get hurt. But my father was looking for any excuse to cut me off. When I turned twenty-one, he had promised me a commission in the Royal Navy. I was the oldest; it was my birthright and a sure path to knighthood. But the third time he posted my bail to free me from prison, he said I didn't deserve it.

With his dying breath that same year, he told Arthur he was the son he'd always wanted, and gave him everything.

Well, if Arthur could take things that didn't belong to him, then why couldn't I? Everyone was fleeing England for the colonies, taking all they owned with them. My friends and I took a ship and decided we would head to Australia to see what we could find. And who followed us there? Arthur and Estelle, of course. They couldn't bear the thought that I would go around the world before they did. They completely ruined my first adventure and sank the ship we were planning to rob. Everything would have been fine if they hadn't been there! She would not have gotten hurt!

He stopped abruptly, staring somewhere over George's shoulder. An image of the brother and sister in the portrait in No. 10 flashed through George's head. He'd been so focused on the Star of Victory in the girl's hand that he hadn't thought about the boy in the portrait at all. "Estelle? Your sister? She … died?"

Don Nadie's gaze fixed on him, eyes blazing, and George knew the answer was yes.

We weren't going to fire on the ship. We didn't even think it had cannons. But they fired on us first. When La Isla went down, Estelle and most of the other passengers didn't survive....

Don Nadie paused again, swaying on his long legs.

Arthur made sure I got all the blame even though it was his fault. He took over my ship during the battle, and afterward he threw me into the darkest, nastiest, worst prison he could find. And then what did he do? I'm sure you can guess by now. He took the Royal Navy commission that was meant for me. He took my title, the 1st Lord of Devonshire, as his own.

But that wasn't the worst of it. He kept playing games with me, sending me strange mechanical people and writing me cryptic letters. I behaved terribly in prison, all so I could be moved to a new location, because I didn't want to see him ever again—not until I was ready to take everything away from him.

I made a vow. I would play my own game that was bigger and better than anything Arthur could create. The prize was getting my life back tenfold. I became a Nobody, but I would be better than a lord. I wouldn't just leave prison and return to an empty life without my sister; I would take back what was rightfully mine and more besides. Your grandfather took Estelle away, and he deserved to suffer along with the rest of the world.

He thought that throwing me in prison would make me disappear. Well, I turned my prison into my palace. I found other

people whose families were dead or who didn't believe in them.
Other Nobodies. I became their king. Through letters and sto-
ries, we grew and grew into the biggest society in the world.
That's the kind of family loyalty that your grandfather could
never understand. . . .

"Now, the end of the game is finally here," Don Nadie
finished. "It is so much sweeter because you're here to see
it. I'm out of prison and free as a bird. Perfectly legal. Perfectly proper. I can take whatever I like and go wherever I
like. Soon you will see."

"He'll be king of everyone!" Roy cheered.

A smile curled on the 1st Lord of Devonshire's lips. "To
start."

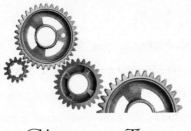

Chapter Twenty-Four

While Don Nadie told his story, a crowd of mechanical beasts gathered around him on the shore like an army of giants amassing on a battlefield. He had steam-powered whales like Ada's and others that George had never seen before, including a glass bubble driven by a shining silver propeller and a ship that seemed to skate across the water on thin legs like an insect.

"You won't get away with this. We'll stop you," George spat out.

Don Nadie's shoulders shook with a silent chuckle. "You can't stop progress. I *am* progress. I'm taller, faster, and better than anyone alive. After I invade C.R.U.M.P.E.T.S., I'll be in possession of the newest and best technology. A new army. Unstoppable."

"That's preposterous," George said.

"The best plans always are," Don Nadie replied. "Your grandfather taught me that. My one regret is that he's not alive to see this."

"Don't you dare talk about my grandfather. He was twice the man you are, even if he wasn't as tall as you are." George's jaw clenched with anger—but questions swirled in his head. How could his grandfather have lied to him? The disappointment put a dull ache in his chest. He felt like an egg that had been cracked.

"He's wearing stilts," Ada said scornfully. "He's not really taller than anyone else alive."

Don Nadie took one large step on his stilts and was in front of George in the blink of an eye. "Your grandfather never told you who he really was, did he?"

A lump the size of a fist curled in George's throat. "I know who my grandfather was."

"But he didn't tell you he had a brother? A sister whose death he was responsible for?"

"I—he—" George stopped. He couldn't go on. His lower lip was trembling too hard.

Don Nadie shook his head slowly. "How does it make you feel to know you were just another pawn in his games?"

Something shattered inside George. All the cracked pieces of himself that he'd been so carefully holding together fell apart. The one thing about himself that he'd always known to be true—that he was the 3rd Lord of Devonshire—was a lie. He was nothing.

He was a nobody.

George's body went limp, and he nearly fell to his knees. He wished he could crawl into a deep, dark cave and never have to face the world again. Ada's voice called to him from very far away—"Stand up, George. Stand up."— but George's spine seemed to have turned into jelly. His father had always said he had the spine of a snail, hadn't he?

Don Nadie took out a small perfume bottle. He sprayed a light misting of liquid over the map, which he had pinched between two fingers. All of George's grandfather's beautiful work vanished, leaving behind a page that had been ripped from a parish register long ago to erase the record of the *real* Lord of Devonshire from history—by his grandfather, George realized with a terrible jolt, who claimed the identity as his own.

George let out a little sob that sounded like the whimper of a puppy.

"I know exactly how you feel, my boy," said Don Nadie, his voice flat. "It's very sad, isn't it? But you'll survive. I've been thinking about killing you, but that doesn't seem right. I'm going to punish you by the book. Nothing illegal. Just like your *upstanding* grandfather would have wanted. I would rather you live and suffer, stripped of your name, like I suffered all those years."

"I'll never help you," George said.

Don Nadie made a face as if he'd swallowed a fly. "No, of course not. Did I ask for your help? I didn't offer that. I'm disgusted by the sight of you. You look just like your grandfather, you know."

Behind them, Shaw cleared his throat. "Excuse me, sir. We need to leave now. There's no time to waste if we're to be in England for the start of the scientific gathering."

"Load up the ships. I'll be along in a moment," Don Nadie said with a wave of his hand. Roy released George with a hard shove and followed the rest of the Society as they moved toward the strange mechanical fleet, taking Il Naso and Ada with them.

"Ada! No—" George ran after them, but Don Nadie lashed out with the tip of his stick.

"You can stay here. Start a new life for yourself on this barren island with nothing, just as I had to do. You'll probably die fairly quickly, but maybe you won't. Either way, if I ever see or hear from you again, I will find a way to make sure you die a slow, horrible, legal death." He spread his hands wide and smiled. "There can be only one Lord of Devonshire, and starting from this very moment, he's standing in front of you."

George gathered his last shreds of dignity to fire back: "You may call yourself the Lord of Devonshire, but you'll never be a true nobleman."

Don Nadie bent over and patted George on the head. "I'll remember you fondly when I'm living in No. 8 Dorset Square. Thank you for taking such good care of my house."

"No. 8 is not your house!" George cried.

Don Nadie took a deep breath and smiled at the sky. "I'll need to expand it soon, of course. A new palace for a new king. You see, the great Truffle Assassin will be very, very upset about my return. He'll poison the King *and* his brother this time, and he'll probably succeed. Poor little Princess

Victoria couldn't possibly run an entire country. She's only eight years old! Luckily for her, the Lord of Devonshire will be there...the only man in all of England with the technology to make her army the greatest in the world. After I've gotten what I need from the scientists at C.R.U.M.P.E.T.S., I'll buy up all the houses from Dorset Square to Park Road and make Regent's Park my backyard."

With that, Don Nadie strode away. In five long steps, he was walking through the water on his stilts, climbing into the glass bubble ship, and leading his fleet across the wide blue ocean toward London.

Chapter Twenty-Five

At some point in life, George knew, every person asks these two questions:

Who am I?
Why am I here?

Before Don Nadie arrived and turned George's world upside down, George would have answered those two questions thusly: I am George, the 3rd Lord of Devonshire. I am here because my grandfather drew me a map leading to this spot.

But as George watched Don Nadie's fleet slip across the horizon, he suddenly realized he could only answer: I am

George Foote. As to why he was here, that was obviously due to his bad-luck curse, which had been biding its time until it could destroy him finally, completely, and absolutely on a desolate island in the middle of an unfamiliar sea. He was certainly not here to save Ada. George had no doubt she'd already hatched a plan to save herself from Don Nadie.

His stomach growled with hunger, but he ignored it. No more truffle stew ever again. No more Frobisher.

No more George, the 3rd Lord of Devonshire. Not that he'd ever really existed in the first place. Technically, he would have been the 2nd Lord of Devonshire, not the 3rd. Because his father had died less than a day before his grandfather, the title had gone directly to George. He'd thought he was honoring his father by pretending he'd lived long enough to inherit his grandfather's title. There was no reason to worry about that technicality anymore. Did George's father know who his grandfather really was? Was that why he'd always been so cruel?

George crawled into his canvas tent, pulled the blanket over himself, and wished that either he would disappear or the world would blink out of existence. He lay there for hours and hours, images of his old life flashing before his eyes as if they were inside a phantasmascope, a type of spinning wheel Ada had shown him once. His memories were outside him, like a part of his body that had been amputated. Eventually, he fell in and out of sleep, expecting to see nightmare flashes of Don Nadie as a spider, tying him up with threads of silk.

Instead, he dreamed that he and Oscar were playing cricket in the menagerie. Instead of a cricket ball, they were using the Star of Victory. George's grandfather and father were there, too, cheering them on. But George could not bear to swing his cricket bat at the Star. Oscar pitched it to him over and over. "Hit it, George! Smash it!"

George sat up and blinked, awake. A wave crashed onto the shore. The sea lions barked *oark oark*. Dreaming of his family had warmed George's heart. He hadn't dreamed about them in a long time.

George had unraveled as far as he was going to unravel, he thought.

With every ounce of energy he could muster, George crawled out of his tent and pried open a tin of peas. As he ate each green, mushy mouthful, he watched a tortoise graze on the edges of the camp. Ada had once said that dreams spoke to you. Taught you things that your waking brain was not ready to learn. Was dream-Oscar trying to tell him something?

George felt the warm touch of the morning sun on his cheek. In Oscar's opinion, George's title was probably the least important thing about George. He would probably say that George was better off without it. He would say that no matter what George's name was, he was still made of the same substance on the inside. The same rock might be called a lodestone or a magnet or iron, but calling it a different name didn't alter its properties. Don Nadie might have chipped away at some of his outer layers, but his core was as tough as a diamond—his essence had not been changed.

Oscar would have pointed out that Don Nadie had forgotten something—Oscar. Ada. Ruthie. Oscar would have said that friendship doesn't cost anything, so therefore it could not be stolen. Don Nadie thought he'd stripped George of everything he was. But his revenge plan would never be complete because no matter what he did, he couldn't take away George's friends.

"George! George!" Oscar's dream-voice wailed.

George stopped chewing his mushy peas. He was not dreaming anymore. Therefore, it was not dream-Oscar calling out to him.

A terrible, keening cry split the air. George recognized it at once.

Ruthie.

Practically flying, George threw down the tin of peas, grabbed his bag with the Star of Victory, and sprinted toward the sound, which had come from the center of the island. The barren, scrubby island was covered in a white mist that hid the distant slopes of the volcano. If he squinted, George could almost believe he was back home in London on a quiet, foggy morning. But then Ruthie cried out again, and he urged his legs to move faster.

Very quickly, George found himself on the same narrow dirt path he'd seen by lantern light when chasing the thief. With a shudder, he remembered that Il Naso was not the one who had stolen the golden buttons from his jacket. Maybe it had been the Society...though why hadn't they attacked? Had they found Oscar? As far as George knew, the Galápagos were uninhabited. But then again, many people had thought his home in Dorset

Square had been uninhabited months ago, when it was falling apart.

Uneasily, George realized he was the real intruder. They'd landed on the island without permission or welcome.

The landscape around George began to change as he kept running into the mist. The dry, dusty scrubland full of cactus and brambles changed into a lush green jungle fed by bubbling streams that trickled down the hillside. The plants grew taller and thicker. Lacy ferns tickled George's ankles.

"Oscar! Ruthie!"

The sunlight dimmed, blocked out by the canopy of leaves overhead. An enormous bee buzzed around George's head before returning to a bush covered in red flowers. The bee was almost the same size as the tiny birds that darted among the ferns.

A small red berry fell from the sky onto George's neck. He brushed it off and ran on.

Another red berry fell from the sky, hitting him square on his cheek, harder this time.

Still, George ran. All he could see were the slim trunks

of the trees with their leaves unfurled high above, flat as a parasol. The trees here were much smaller than the ones back in London. A berry splatted onto George shirt, leaving a round, red mark.

From deep in the forest, a giggle filtered through the trees.

George skidded to a halt. Something was crashing toward him. The slim trunks swayed and dipped as if they were dancing. George didn't know what kind of terrible beasts might be lurking in this forest. Then a beast hurled itself onto his back.

The beast squeezed his neck with its hairy, orange arms.

"Ruthie!" George cried. He swiveled the little orangutan to his chest and squeezed her tight. "You're alive!"

Ruthie grabbed his hand in hers, then squirmed down to the ground. She tugged George forward, her brown eyes wide and insistent.

"Where's Oscar?" George asked.

Ruthie led him through the forest at the edge of the path. The bushes grew closer and closer until they closed around him like a tunnel made of waxy leaves. George had to push the branches out of his face so that he could see Ruthie, who was only inches ahead of him. A few minutes later, she screeched to warn him before he fell into a deep hole.

He jumped over the hole, and all of a sudden, Oscar was in front of him, sitting beneath a small grove of trees with his head resting against his knees. His head jerked up when he heard George approaching. Though his clothes were filthy and his eyes were sagging with exhaustion, his face lit up in a gap-toothed smile. Ruthie climbed down from George's shoulders and nestled into Oscar's side.

"George!" said Oscar.

"Oscar!" said George. "I heard Ruthie screaming from camp. Are you all right? What happened?"

Oscar lifted up his leg. A rope was tightly cinched around his ankle. "I've gotten caught in a snare."

George eyed the snare. It was fastened with a strangle knot that Oscar could easily have untied. "Are you hurt? Let me help you."

"Don't bother." Oscar sighed loudly and drew his knees up to his chest again. "I'll only step in another trap. I've been trying to get out of this forest forever. First I stepped on a catapult that shot me into a huge net in the trees. After I climbed down from that, I fell into a pit. After I got out of that, my left leg got caught in a snare. After that, my right leg. Forward or backward, it doesn't matter. I'm stuck here. I was wrong. You are cursed with bad luck. It must be contagious."

George burned with anger at the Society. They had left traps all around the island to torture him. He scolded himself for thinking, even for a second, that they'd been safe from Don Nadie's crew. "You're not stuck. We can go back the way I came." George knelt down and began to pick at the knot to loosen it. "I'm glad I found you," he continued cautiously, wanting to make sure that his words came out properly. "I need to apologize to you for putting you in danger. You were right. I was being selfish. There are a lot of other things I need to tell you, too, but first I have to tell you that I'm sorry."

"Did the 3rd Lord of Devonshire just tell me he was sorry?" Oscar asked in mock amazement.

"He should have said it sooner, but the 3rd Lord of Devonshire was an idiot. He thought he knew better than everyone else," George said.

"Why are you talking about yourself as if you've died? Where's Ada?" Oscar asked.

George sucked in his cheeks. Where to begin to

explain everything to Oscar? They'd been apart for less than two days, but in that time, George's life had been turned upside down. "Miss Byron is—Ada is—" George hesitated.

Oscar's eyes grew wide and his chest expanded with a breath he didn't exhale. "No. Don't say it. I thought I'd lost you for one second in the shipwreck. I couldn't bear to lose Ada. And I said all those terrible things—"

"Ada's not dead! She's alive!" George corrected him hastily. "Alive and well, last time I saw her. Don Nadie followed us here. He captured Ada and is taking her with him to C.R.U.M.P.E.T.S. And Il Naso, too. He was hiding on the whale this entire time. And there's more, much, much more, to tell you once we're somewhere safe. But Ada will be fine. I'm sure she'll find a way to escape and save the scientists."

Oscar's shoulders relaxed as he began to breathe normally again. "Of course she will. She's the smartest person I know."

With a final tug, the knot loosened, and George helped Oscar to his feet. He dusted a few twigs from Oscar's shirt and handed him a piece of dried fruit from his bag. Ruthie took some for herself, too. "I wish she were here now to

283

help us figure out what to do next. Don Nadie took the whale and left us with nothing and no way to get home."

"I've been sending messages in bottles to my father so he'll come get us eventually. We'll figure out a way to help her stop the Society. Our plan won't be as good, but it can still work. She's older than we are, so she's had more time to come up with clever ideas. I think I'll probably be as smart as she is when I'm twelve," Oscar said brightly.

"I'm already almost thirteen, and I don't think I'll ever be as good at math and inventing things as Ada," George said. "Should we let her save the world without us?"

George had meant it lightly, but the words weighed on him. Oscar had called his mission meaningless not long ago. A gull screamed overhead, reminding him that he was in the middle of an unfamiliar sea in the middle of nowhere, no better off from his adventure than when he'd left London, no closer to beating Don Nadie. Maybe it wasn't his purpose to be the hero after all. Maybe it was *Ada's*.

Oscar shook his head. "We're not meant to do what she does. We're all good at different things. Ada's good at inventing things, and it makes her happy. Ruthie loves eating fruit and hugging people. I'm good at drawing and collecting rocks, and I thought being a pirate would make me happy, but we both know how that worked out. You're good at—well, you *were* good at—sometimes, it seems like you're good at..." Oscar scrunched his face as he wrestled with his words before finally saying, "You're very good at getting yourself into trouble."

George smiled weakly. "All I ever wanted to be good at was making my grandfather proud, and look where it's gotten us."

"Are you joking? You've traveled farther than most people ever will in their lifetime. Look where we are. This island is amazing! The animals aren't afraid of humans at all. I saw a tortoise yesterday, and it reminded me of you. If you could carry your home on your back, I think you'd be happier." Oscar jostled him. "I've had a lot of time to think while I was stuck here. I figured out why I've been so angry with you."

"You have? Why?" George asked.

"Because I knew that even after you found the treasure your grandfather left, it still wouldn't make you happy."

"It might have if things had turned out differently."

George imagined opening the box to find gold coins or the secret to eternal life instead of a musty passenger manifest.

"It wouldn't have mattered what was in that box," Oscar insisted. "You don't need a treasure, just like I didn't need to be a pirate. What I needed was to know that my father loved me even if I wasn't just like him."

George shifted from foot to foot.

"But I still need a place to belong—and you do, too," Oscar continued. "But you haven't found it yet. The map was like a pair of blinders. You couldn't see beyond it. We spent hours and hours trying to draw it together. We could have drawn anything, but you wanted that. Did it make you feel better when I drew the map?"

"No," George admitted.

"When Ada asks me to draw something, it's a new invention or something she wants to make in the future. If you asked me to draw your future, what would you want to see?" Oscar asked, leaning intently toward George's face to hear his answer.

George gulped. If he imagined his future, he would have to think about all the empty places and missing people in his life who wouldn't be in that future. Thinking about it was as painful as touching a fresh, tender bruise. He didn't want to talk about it. "I don't know," he mumbled.

"You don't know!" Oscar repeated proudly, as if he'd known what George's answer would be. An enormous smile stretched across his face.

"Why are you happy about that?"

"Because I can show you. That's what *I* want to do. I don't want to be a pirate or an adventurer. I want to help other people figure out where they belong," Oscar announced.

George couldn't help but smile. "That's wonderful."

"I want to make a place where people can imagine new lives for themselves. A place where people can try new things. Not a school, exactly—more like a greenhouse to help people grow. There are so many other children like you and me, who get stuck doing what we think our families want us to do because they don't know anything else. If a person doesn't find what they love to do, they could end up as Nobodies or spend their entire life being a pirate when all along they were meant to be a truffle farmer. Everybody should have the chance to be a somebody," Oscar continued. "I don't know exactly where or how I'll do it yet, and maybe you'll tell me it sounds like a silly idea, but I don't care. That's what I want to do. Everyone deserves to find their place in the world. You can be my first experiment, if you'd like. We'll invent lives for ourselves that make us both happy."

"I'd like that!" George replied with genuine enthusiasm. George, the 3rd Lord of Devonshire, didn't think he deserved happiness most of the time. But perhaps George Foote was a fellow for whom happiness would come more easily. "What would make me very happy now is *not* getting caught in any more of the Society's traps."

"The Society? This wasn't the Society." Oscar's eyes darted left to right. He leaned in close to George's ear and whispered, "The girl from the portrait. She's here. Hiding."

Chapter Twenty-Six

By now, George knew how to set a trap. All he and Oscar had to do was act completely natural until the time was right to set the bait.

George carried a long stick in front of him to sweep the ground ahead for any more pits as they carefully picked their way through the trees toward the path. They found snares galore everywhere they stepped in the jungle—stumps stacked like staircases, rope bridges over quicksand pits, and various other hazards both hidden and in plain sight. Between obstacles, George filled Oscar in on everything he'd missed.

A twig snapped loudly in the canopy above them. The girl was here.

That was all George needed to execute his plan.

When they were certain they were being followed by someone walking through the branches, George stopped. He took the Star of Victory out of his bag, making sure it sparkled in the sunlight. Oscar sat down and listened as George drew his story out, embellishing it with every exciting detail he could muster. Still talking, George casually slipped the Star back into the bag, which he then hung over a thick tree vine. Out of the corner of his eye, he saw Ruthie slink up the other side of the trunk.

"Don Nadie rose up like a giant. Inside I was trembling, but I stood straight and tall, facing this enormous enemy the way David faced Goliath. Blue sparks flared from his walking stick like lightning. His eyes blazed with fire as he revealed the truth that would change my life forever—"

George was interrupted by a scream as something heavy crashed down through the trees.

Silently, Ruthie had doubled back and wrapped herself around their pursuer. She must have caught the person quite off guard, because they'd both plunged almost all the way to the ground before Ruthie had managed to save them. Ruthie was hanging by her feet upside down from a branch with her hands gripped tightly around the pursuer's wrists.

"Aha! We caught you!" George declared.

Their pursuer was a girl about Oscar's age. She dangled from Ruthie's grip, her feet nearly level with George's shoulders. Her dark hair floated around her face like a cloud made of tiny ringlets. Though her skin was darker, her round face tapering to a sharp chin was identical to the little girl from Don Nadie's portrait. George's mouth fell open—Oscar was right.

The girl began to giggle.

Ruthie let go, and the girl dropped to the ground as lightly as a cat. She clutched her stomach as her giggle turned into a thunderous laugh. "You did! You did! You tricked me!"

George and Oscar glanced at each other. The girl's delight at being caught was not what they had expected. But George had not expected her to step out of the portrait, either.

The girl in the painting was Estelle—could this be Don Nadie's sister? But that was impossible. Estelle would have been almost as old as Don Nadie. Besides, she'd died in the shipwreck, George remembered with a jolt of sadness.

"How...who are you? Why were you following us?" George asked.

After the girl had caught her breath and wiped tears from her eyes, she shrugged. "Why not?"

Oscar's brow wrinkled. "Why did you try to trap me?"

"I didn't try," the girl protested, then erupted into a fresh wave of giggles. "You were too slow. You were both too slow for my game."

A glint of gold on the girl's tattered dress caught George's eye. "Hey! Those are my buttons. Give those back."

The girl stuck out her tongue. "Finders keepers."

"You didn't find those, you stole them from my jacket," George said.

"Losers weepers," the girl replied. "If you catch me, you can take them back."

Oscar wheeled his arms at Ruthie. The little orangutan dropped onto the girl's shoulders and began plucking the buttons from her dress. The girl grabbed for Ruthie, but the orangutan was too quick.

"Clever clever!" the girl cried delightedly. "I want one."

George pressed her. "Do you know anything about survivors from a shipwreck called *La Isla*?"

The girl grabbed a branch above her head and began swinging on it like Ruthie. "Is this a game?"

"No," George said.

The girl did a backflip and dropped from the branch. "Oh. I was hoping it was a game."

George huffed. He was quite sick of games by now. "We're looking for someone who was on the ship. Her name was Estelle."

The girl jumped up and down. Her hair bounced with her. "That's me. That's me. I'm Estelle."

"Are you really?" George asked doubtfully.

The girl looked hurt. "It *is* my name," she insisted. "I'm called Stella for short. I'm named after my granny."

George's heart leapt. "Your grandmother? Her name is Estelle?"

"Estelle Devonshire," said Stella. "Your name is George. I knew yours before you told me. I found you right away. I watched you."

At just this moment, George realized that Estelle was

293

not just a name, it was a clue. The illustrated ribbon on the map with the words *Tabula ad Stella Victōriae* waved furiously in his head. His grandfather had been leading him not just to the Star of Victory, the object, but to another Star of Victory—his grandfather's sister.

The realization struck George so forcefully that he plopped to the ground in a sitting position. Ruthie, in mock surprise, scattered George's buttons into the dirt as she pretended to faint. The girl quickly scooped up the gleaming golden buttons and dropped them in George's lap.

"Thank you, Stella," he said, staring at her in wonder. In response, she stuck her tongue out at him.

If Estelle was the same Estelle who was on the passenger manifest of *La Isla* . . .

And that Estelle had wrecked near this very island . . .

What if she had survived the shipwreck and had been living here all this time?

"This is too easy." George pressed his fingers to his forehead. "Oscar, is this a dream? It can't be this easy. It must be a trap."

Oscar grimaced. "I wouldn't call it easy, exactly. We had plenty of bad luck getting here."

"You got captured by the bad man, and your friends left you, and you almost drowned," Stella agreed cheerfully. "Nothing so exciting ever happens to me. My whole life and not one bad thing. It's a curse, I think. A curse of good luck."

Chapter Twenty-Seven

Stella did not find it extraordinary in the least that she lived on the side of a volcano in the middle of a jungle. Nor was she impressed by the small village that her grandmother Estelle Devonshire had helped to carve out of that wilderness. A village that wasn't on any map or in any guidebook. Wide dirt paths connected small houses made of stacked stone with thatched roofs. Stacked-lava-stone fences bordered neat garden plots and fields. Goats and sheep grazed on the hillside overlooking the flat beach and harbor below.

Ruthie was drooling at the sight of the orchards that surrounded the village. The papaya, orange, and plum trees all made her tremble with joy.

"Oscar, I can't believe it," George repeated over and over again as they followed Stella—his cousin, his *cousin*—home. "My family isn't all dead. This whole time my grandfather left me a map that was leading me to his long-lost sister!"

As soon as the words rang out into the air, George's stomach lurched. Because if his grandfather knew where his sister was . . . why hadn't he retrieved her himself?

A small knot formed in George's stomach. Maybe his grandfather had been hiding her because she knew something important about Don Nadie. Maybe he had been protecting Estelle, like a secret weapon of his own, hidden where his evil brother would never find her. Hah!

George looked to Oscar to share his triumphant answer, but Oscar was too busy investigating an outcropping of pumice stone along the path. He stuffed his pockets with the airy stones, which he told George were the perfect tool for cleaning his hands of paint.

Though he laughed as Oscar struggled to carry a mountain of rocks in his arms, George was itching with nerves. All he could think about was meeting Estelle—the real Star of Victory. If she was his grandfather's adopted sister, and if she was alive, then she might be able to somehow help them stop Don Nadie from springing his trap on the scientists of C.R.U.M.P.E.T.S. Because that was what his grandfather had intended George to do, wasn't it? To stop his vile brother from wreaking havoc on the world?

George was so preoccupied with what might happen next that he wasn't paying any attention to Stella. She tried to warn him about getting too close to a poison apple tree called a manchineel. But George completely ignored her because a poison apple tree sounded like something from a fairy tale. It wasn't. It was very real. So was the blistering rash on George's arm that appeared after he brushed against the leaves of a manchineel tree.

"You're lucky," Stella said, examining George's red, burning skin. "If you fall asleep under the tree, you can die. The poison gets in your lungs and kills you. My mama told me so."

"I'm not very lucky." George scratched.

Stella frowned. "You are! Mama will give you a nice bandage and some medicine. She never gives me any."

"Not even when you're sick?" Oscar asked.

"I'm never sick," Stella replied. "I'd do anything to get a toothache so I could have a nice white bandage wrapped round my head."

George was grateful to know relief was coming when they turned off the path toward a small house made of stacked stones, beyond which stretched a long row of similarly sized homes. Stella skipped ahead, calling for her mother and grandmother. "Mama! Granny! I told you people were at the farthest beach. Here they are!"

Two women stood up from inside a stone garden fence. They were both lean and wiry, and their rolled-up sleeves exposed strong, tanned arms, which were very unlike the soft, pale arms of the ladies George had seen in London. Immediately George recognized which one was Estelle. Though she no longer resembled her portrait and was far shorter for not having stilts, she had the same brilliant white hair as her brother.

Estelle shaded her eyes to look at the boys as they neared. Her gaze danced over Oscar and Ruthie, then fixed on George—and when her eyes flicked from his face to his sailing jacket, which had belonged to his grandfather, a lightning flash of recognition passed across her face. Her shoulders sagged, and she leaned against Stella's mother.

George stepped into the garden, heart pounding. "Do you know who I am?" he asked hesitantly.

Smiling, Estelle reached out to brush a lock of hair from George's forehead. Her fingers were as rough as lava stones, but tender. When she spoke, her voice trembled. "You look exactly like him."

A warm ray of sunshine melted through George's heart. "I do?"

Estelle's eyes grew misty. "Arthur always wanted children."

Hearing Estelle call his grandfather Arthur, not George, was like having another nail of truth driven into his heart. He wobbled on his feet. "He only had one, my father. I'm his grandson."

"I never thought I'd see him again, but here you are," Estelle said. Her eyes glowed, making her look years younger. "Is he with you? How on earth did you find me?"

George's heart lurched. *Is*, not *was*.

Though he'd seen his grandfather die with his own eyes—though he had buried him—George could not summon the words to tell Estelle that his grandfather was dead. His face, though, must have said it for him. Without speaking a word, Estelle pulled him in close with her strong arms. George buried his face in her shoulder and let

300

himself finally release the tears he'd been holding inside for two years. Estelle's soft cotton shirt was warm and smelled like sunshine and rain.

When they let each other go, George wiped his eyes and said, "He gave me a map that led to you. I didn't understand it at first. I suppose I've been looking for you a long time."

Estelle smiled, but the smile was weak, like watered-down tea. Silent tears slid down her cheeks. "Ah. Did he tell you about the games we played when we were children? Such clever games. You must be very smart to have reached the end of his map."

"I had lots of help," George admitted.

"It's smart to ask for help. Arthur never made a puzzle that could be solved alone."

More tears welled in George's eyes. "So it's true? He was your adopted brother."

"He was my *brother*," Estelle said firmly. "But that was a long time ago. Things became...complicated. Come now, don't be upset."

Stella cartwheeled into the middle of their conversation. "He's crying because he needs a bandage. The man-chineel tree got him."

Renata, Stella's mother, took George inside their small house and put a poultice of herbs on George's itchy skin and wrapped it in a strip of cloth. Stella watched jealously until her mother shooed her outside with Oscar and Ruthie.

Estelle brought George a cup of herbal tea. "It's not the same kind of tea as you're used to, I'm afraid. We make do with what we have here."

Wrapping his hands around the cup filled him with warmth. He held his face over the liquid, letting the steam rise up and sink into his skin. Don Nadie was getting closer to London with every passing second, but right now, all George wanted to do was sit in this cottage over a hot cup of tea and bask in his miracle. "Have you really been on Chatham Island since the shipwreck?"

She smiled and laughed softly. "For forty years, I think. It's hard to keep count. We travel to Ecuador once in a while on the whaling ships that pass by. Some of our friends in the village went last year to celebrate Ecuador's independence," she said, raising her teacup in a toast. "Whalers stop by here fairly often, and we are able to trade for what we need. In return, the whalers keep our village a secret and off maps."

"If you could go to Ecuador, why didn't you find a ship to take you home? Were you hiding?"

"Hiding? No, not hiding." Estelle's eyes locked on to his but went fuzzy and unfocused, as if she were staring at something very far away. "I had no home to return to. My parents were dead, my brothers were at each other's throats about who would inherit the house and our father's title. A silly *house*. Can you believe it? And—"

Estelle turned her head away so George wouldn't see her face crumple like the handkerchief she clutched in her hand. Gently, he squeezed her arm. "What is it? What's wrong?"

She inhaled deeply and turned back to George. "I fell in love."

"Oh." Of all the things he'd imagined Estelle might say, he hadn't expected *that*.

She chuckled. "I don't remember much of the day *La Isla* sank. Arthur and I chased our brother here, to stop him from throwing his life away with a bunch of thieves—and then Arthur fired on my brother's ship, even though he promised me he wouldn't. Cannons started to fire back, and there was a terrible fight, and that's where my memory ends," she said, tapping her temple. "The next thing I can recall is waking up on this island, surrounded by a handful of people who started this village. Jean-Charles was one of the founding villagers. He bandaged my wounds with his strong, gentle hands. One look into his eyes was all it took. We fell in love and got married within a week." She smiled. "He'd wanted to be a doctor ever since he was a boy. He studied by candlelight."

"That's wonderful," George said.

"I'm afraid it wasn't that simple. He was born into slavery in the colonies, and he was here searching for a new life. There were some in London who might have accepted us, but they were vastly outnumbered by the people who wouldn't. And I couldn't be apart from him. I would have died if I'd gone home without him." She pounded the table. "Well, if I was going to die, I'd prefer to do it here with my husband—on my own terms."

The sudden fierce determination in Estelle's voice reminded George of Ada. He could almost hear her saying the same words. Even so, anger bubbled in him. "You pretended to be dead all these years?"

Estelle wavered slightly, then steadied herself. "I had to make a choice, and I chose to make a new family. Haven't you ever had something that you couldn't bear to lose? Something that you'd give up everything for?"

"My friends. My grandfather, if he were still alive." He paused. "My grandfather would have helped you and your husband. I'm sure of it."

"Perhaps." She sighed. "In the beginning I was too angry to return. I was furious at my brothers for risking my life and theirs over nothing. Then, when I had children, how could I bring them to a place where they might not be safe because of the color of their skin? How could I ask my husband to join me in a land where there was still slavery? Besides, home was wherever Jean-Charles was, and we made our home here. Together." Estelle winced from remembered pain. "I was happy here, George. Truly happy, even after Jean-Charles died a few years ago. This is where I belong. It's as if the rest of the world faded away."

Estelle turned away from George, dabbed at her face with her apron. "Was your grandfather happy? Did he have a good life?"

"He must have been happy," George said, searching for some reassurance among the wreckage of his memories.

"He took your brother's name. He brought honor back to the Devonshires. We lived in a beautiful house. And he told me stories. Lots and lots of stories about the most valuable treasure in the world. It turned out to be you." George continued, unable to keep the hurt from his voice, "He never told me you existed."

"Ah." Estelle dropped her eyes to the table, suddenly looking like a sheepish child. She twisted her handkerchief between her fingers. "I didn't disappear completely, you know. I wrote Arthur a letter to tell him where I was and whom I'd married. I apologized, but I said I would never return—that as far as anyone in London should know, Estelle Devonshire was dead. I said some harsh things that I wish I hadn't. But you see, I was afraid your grandfather wouldn't be able to leave me behind. That he'd sail around the world every year to come to see me or try to bring me home. I couldn't live my life worrying about him, wondering if he was at the bottom of the ocean because he'd been on his way to see me. If I know your grandfather, he took my proclamation seriously. I suppose I was dead to him." A smile flickered on her face. "But your grandfather was clever. He gave away my secret to you without breaking his promise."

"What do you mean?"

She nodded toward the map. "Technically, you figured it out yourself."

"I had help," George said, his brain buzzing. He *had* discovered the truth—so why did it still feel as if he was missing something?

The image of her brother—his great-uncle, he reminded himself, though it seemed like something from a dream— stalking the world on his stilts burst into his brain. "Your brother Don Nadie—I mean, your brother George still thinks you're dead."

Estelle's eyes widened. "He—he does?"

"Yes. He told me so himself." George recalled what Don Nadie had told him yesterday: that he'd had himself moved from prison to prison to get away from his grand-father's taunts. "My grandfather must have kept your secret. Your brother was just *here*, Aunt Estelle."

A laugh escaped Estelle's lips, but the sound was harsh, twisted with disbelief. "Well, I never thought I'd have to worry about him looking for me. Sometime during that terrible fight, he told me he hated me for choosing Arthur's side and never wanted to see me again as long as he lived," she finished softly, as if the words had been spoken yesterday and not over forty years ago. "I remember so little about that day, but I remember *that*."

George felt a tug of pity for her. He remembered when he'd said almost the same thing to Oscar, Ada, and Ruthie on a rooftop in Venice. It had been the worst thing he'd ever done.

Ringing with energy now, George set his teacup down on the table. The liquid had grown cold. It reminded him that he didn't have much more time to spare. "I need your help. Your brother is out of prison and is planning revenge for everything my grandfather did. He's going to steal inventions and ideas from all the best scientists in the world and use them to build an unstoppable army. Well, I'm fairly sure my friend Ada Byron isn't going to let that happen, but that won't prevent him from wanting to destroy the world."

Estelle stood up abruptly and cleared away the teacups with shaking hands. "I don't see how I could help."

"My grandfather wasn't perfect, but he was honorable. Maybe he didn't tell me about you because he was trying to respect your wishes." Or maybe, George thought, if he told his grandson the story of Estelle, he would have had to reveal the truth about his identity. "But though he never told me about you in words, he led me to you through this map. Not just to be clever. Because he believed you're the only person alive who can help stop Don Nadie. I don't know why, but I trust my grandfather sent me here for a reason. You can come with me. Look—"

George retrieved the Star of Victory from his bag, placing it between him and his great-aunt on the table. Estelle picked up the Star, wonder dancing in her eyes.

"My father made this so my brothers and I could write secret messages to each other. He said it would bring its owner success in any battle because the enemy wouldn't be able to read the communications. I'm sure he never thought his children would one day be on opposite sides of that battle."

"The Star is more than that," George said. "It was a message from my grandfather to help me find you. It's not too late to stop your brother. You can tell everyone the truth—the truth about who Nobody really is. You're my secret weapon."

"Oh, George, I'm of no use to you." Estelle sighed. "If it were that easy, I would go with you. But I couldn't stop my brother from making mistakes all those years ago, and I can't stop him now. Trust me, George. Sometimes a broken thing cannot be put back together."

Frustration rose in George. All at once, he understood how Oscar had felt when his father refused to assist them in fighting the Society. His next words were more of an accusation than a question. "You won't even try?"

Stella waltzed through the door carrying a spiky yellow lizard the size of a small dog. "Try what?"

"Nothing, dear. No animals inside the house," Estelle admonished.

George couldn't prevent his frustration from seeping into his voice. "She won't even try to help me stop her brother from stealing the throne. She's too afraid."

"I'll help you stop him from stealing the throne," Stella said.

"You'll do no such thing." Estelle took the lizard from Stella and carried it outside. "It's much too dangerous."

"What can we do to change her mind?" George asked Stella.

Stella flopped down heavily next to George. "Nothing. Once she makes up her mind, it's made up forever. It's maddening. You can't believe how many times I've begged her to take me to a city. There are so many things I haven't seen. Is it true that people have stairs *inside* their houses?"

"It's true, George will tell you," Estelle said, coming back inside. "And maybe he'll also tell you that people fall down stairs and die quite frequently. The cities you're so eager to see are just like the manchineel tree. The fruit looks tasty, but it's poison. What you don't know can't hurt you, Stella. There are beautiful things in the world, and there are ugly things, too. I know what's best for our family, and that is to keep you safe by staying right here."

George stood up, straightening his jacket. "I'm sorry to hear that. Because my mind is made up as well. Before I came here, I thought I could stay home and bury my head in the sand, too. But there are people I love in England, and they're in trouble. I may not be a Devonshire by blood, but I am an Englishman, and I am Ada Byron's friend. I'm going to fight by her side, where I belong. I'm going back to London."

George waited for Estelle to leap up from the table and take his hand, but she only dried the teacups, averting her eyes from him and the jewel he'd left on her table. So, though it was truly the hardest thing he'd ever done, he turned his back on his grandfather's hidden treasure and strode out the door.

"Oscar! Ruthie!" he shouted. "It's time to save the world."

George's shouts were lost in the general chaos that was taking place outside. The villagers were screaming for their children to run and hide in the forest. Meanwhile, Oscar was arguing with a group of village men who were setting up a cannon lower down on the hillside. Underneath a white cloud of sails, a ship with a black flag was cruising toward the shore at full speed. George thought he saw a figure glinting with gold dive from the ship and paddle frantically to the shore.

Stella followed George outside. "Pirates!" she whispered, biting her fingertips with fear and excitement.

Ruthie flung herself in front of the cannon. Oscar's face was alight with joy as he bolted toward the shore, crying, "Don't shoot! That's my father!"

THIRD CABIN BOY'S LOG FOR THE *ORDEK*

Day 1

Fair winds and favorable currents.

After I said goodbye to my great-aunt Estelle, Oscar, Ruthie, and I joined Captain Bibble on his new ship, the Ordek, which he captured from Turkish pirates after we left him in Gibraltar. Despite his vow not to help me fight the Society, Captain Bibble had also made a vow never to abandon his son again. He's been following our route since we left Spain, guided by Oscar's messages in bottles.

Oscar is pleased as punch that his father is here. I must say, I am, too. Even so, I'm afraid we may not make it back to

London in time. C.R.U.M.P.E.T.S. begins in less than three weeks, Don Nadie has a head start, and his ship is faster than ours.

Though my great-aunt Estelle refused to join us and save the world from her dastardly brother, she did provide us with fresh fruit and supplies for the journey home.

Day 2
Fair winds and favorable currents.

The position of commander on the Ordek has already been filled by a large fellow named Jan Eendenbloed. Luckily there were some openings for cabin boys. Oscar is first cabin boy and I am third cabin boy. The second cabin boy will not tell me his name, and he refuses to look at me. I fear this will be a long trip.

Day 3
Light winds and favorable currents.

I can see why Oscar did not enjoy being a pirate. Jan Een-denbloed has kicked me in the rear several times for not tying knots fast enough.

Day 4
Blustering winds and unfavorable currents.

We have sailed into a storm off the coast of Chile. Oscar has begun to help me find out what gives me, George Foote, purpose. Because my grandfather was a sailor, Oscar thinks my future may be on a boat. It is hard to think about my future when I'm worried about Ada and Il Naso and my house and C.R.U.M.P.E.T.S. However, we have made some progress. We discovered that my talents are not piracy or tying knots or deck swabbing.

Today the second cabin boy told me his name accidentally. He made me swear not to repeat it to anyone.

Day 5
Strong winds and unfavorable currents.

The storm continues. I have discovered that I do not enjoy mopping vomit. I do enjoy entertaining the crew with educational stories about the Society and tales of our adventures. Today I made Jan Eendenbloed laugh when I told him the story of how we almost outwitted Il Naso in Venice with an army of fire ants. I hope Il Naso is all right.

Day 6
Fair winds and favorable currents.

Oscar and I have decided that when Ruthie is old enough to live on her own in a few years, we will sail to Borneo to reunite her with her family. Ruthie seemed excited by this plan when we told her there would be lots of fruit to eat.

The second cabin boy has told Oscar that he would also like to think about his future, since he is not sure he wants to be a pirate forever. Oscar helped him draw a picture of what he would like his life to be. There were a great deal of fish in that picture, several swords, and a boat, so it may be that piracy is his destiny after all.

Day 8

Light winds and unfavorable currents.

I have neglected my deck swabbing today, and Jan Eendenbloed has kicked me several times. I have too many things on my mind to care about the pain.

I'm afraid that we won't reach London until it's too late. We are still at least a week away, but we'll only arrive in time if we have favorable weather the whole way. I don't think I'll be that lucky. Oscar says that Ada will protect the scientists at C.R.U.M.P.E.T.S. and that I shouldn't worry. I haven't told him that's not all I'm worried about.

Day 9

Fair winds and favorable currents.

I have been informed by several members of the crew that cabin boys do not keep logs. Here ends the third cabin boy's log of the Ordek.

Chapter Twenty-Eight

When they arrived in London, it was as if they had never left. The Thames River was humming with activity. Ships riding low in the water, their bellies full of cargo, were pulled into the docks with thick ropes. Ships leaving for distant lands passed by in the opposite direction, unfurling their sails to catch the winds that would carry them away.

The *Ordek* weaved its way around other vessels, cutting in front of an East India Company ship to take its spot at an open dock. They stowed their sails just in time to avoid a rushing wind that swirled up out of nowhere. As they pulled closer to the dock, the wind grew louder and louder until they realized it was not a wind at all. Every sailor, seafarer, longshoreman, waterman, harbormaster, and dockworker had gathered at the waterfront in an angry mob. They were jeering and hissing at the *Ordek* so loudly that it sounded like a storm.

"I think they know we're PIRATES," Captain Bibble observed.

"I told you we should have lowered our flags and docked farther away. They don't know we're not here to steal from them," Oscar said.

George looked for a gap in the crowds. "We don't have time for this. Did you hear those church bells as we sailed past Greenwich? C.R.U.M.P.E.T.S. is probably starting soon. We have to find Don Nadie and stop him before he can get his hands on those scientists."

"They know we're pirates. They think we're the enemy. I'm sure Don NADIE didn't get this kind of welcome. UNACCEPTABLE. A CANNON blast should take care of these ruffians," Captain Bibble roared. "Men, open the GUNPORTS."

George jumped in front of Captain Bibble. "No, stop! I have another idea. Lower the gangplank and let me off."

"They'll tear you APART." To George's utter shock, the pirate captain's single eye filled with anguished tears.

He fixed his watery gaze on his son, who met his stare. "M-m-my crew and I can't help you down there. The MINUTE we touch dry land, we'll lose our sea legs and become U-U-USELESS," he choked out, lip quivering with a barely contained sob. "I'm a TERRIBLE father who can't even PROTECT his SON."

Oscar threw his arms around his father's waist and squeezed. "But you're *my* father. That's enough for me."

George smiled at the sight of his friend with his father. "Captain Bibble, can you and your crew find Don Nadie's ship and destroy it? Then, if he tries to escape, he'll be trapped on land."

Captain Bibble sniffed, eye gleaming. "It would be my PLEASURE. But what will YOU do? You can't face those MAGGOTS alone!"

"It's all right. They won't hurt me," said George, drawing himself up as tall as he could. "Leave it to the world's most feared Truffle Assassin. I have a plan."

Captain Bibble ordered the gangplank be lowered. George grabbed a scrap of canvas and tied its corners together to make a sack. He stuffed a dirty rag inside to give it a lumpy appearance. He tied a black neckerchief around his forehead to look more menacing. Adjusting his hands to make it appear as though he was struggling under the weight of it, George held the improvised bag high above his head and stomped onto the gangplank. The crowd erupted into a new chorus of insults.

Oscar joined him at the top of the gangplank. "I'm coming with you."

"Grab my shirt and stay close to me," George said. "If this works, we'll get through the crowd."

Oscar nodded and clutched the back of George's shirt.

Chin thrust in the air, George took a step toward the crowd, lifting the bag higher over his head with every footfall. "Listen to me or you'll all die!" he shouted.

"Get back on yer ship, pirate scum," a broad-shouldered dockworker yelled back. At the same time, he hurled a fish head at George. It splattered fish juice all over his jacket, but George continued moving forward.

"I'm no pirate. I'm *far* worse than that," George shouted back. "Look at my face. You know who I am."

The dockworker's eyes narrowed, then sprang open in shock as he recognized George from the sketches of him in the newspapers, but George knew he had to keep talking until word spread to everyone in the crowd. Mustering all the oratorical skills his grandfather had taught him,

George projected his voice to address the teeming mass of people that stood between him and the city—more specifically, between him and the Council for Radical Undertakings in Mathematics, Physics, Engineering, Technology, and Science, whose convention would commence any moment.

George pounded his chest with one fist while holding the empty bag aloft with the other. Several onlookers laughed. "I am George Foote, the great Truffle Assassin. I may look like a boy, but make no mistake, I can kill everyone in this crowd with a twitch of my fingers. My deadly poisons have killed so many people. Why then would I not hesitate to kill each one of you? I have returned to England to exact my revenge, not on the King as you have been told, but on the treasonous pirate Don Nadie. He is the real villain of this story, not me. And he is my intended target. Let me pass and I will let you live."

The crowd's energy shifted as if he'd thrown a rock into a pool of water. No one was laughing or jeering at him now. Heads turned to each other, mumbling in hushed voices. Now that he'd made a ripple, he needed to part the sea.

It was time to use a trick he'd learned from Ada: the power of suggestion.

George continued, "In this bag is the deadliest poison known to mankind, the poison apple of the Galápagos. One whiff of its noxious scent and you'll succumb to the toxin immediately. If anyone tries to prevent me from reaching the city, I will not hesitate to use it. Now—stand aside!"

George looked pointedly at the dockworker who had thrown the fish head at him. The man stepped back to make room for George and Oscar to disembark. The other dockworkers around him did the same. Holding the empty canvas bag overhead threateningly, George thrust his foot into the throng. A young sailor shrieked. Like magic, people moved aside to make a space for George and Oscar to pass, then closed in behind them.

"It's working!" Oscar whispered into George's ear.

George felt a thrill of exhilaration as men twice his size backed away from him, fear shining in their eyes. He'd never felt powerful before. But now, when he bared his teeth and growled, he wasn't a puppy; he was a wolf. This must be how Don Nadie felt looking down at everyone from his long legs. For a stomach-turning moment, George was in his long-lost great-uncle's head, looking out at the world. He felt invincible. The feeling was so intoxicating that George himself forgot that he wasn't really a Truffle Assassin and that the bag above his head wasn't really carrying a deadly poison. However, his bad luck certainly didn't forget.

When George and Oscar were nearly through the thickest of the crowd, someone jostled Oscar, who bumped into George, who lost his balance and tripped. They both hurtled forward, arms flailing. George regained his balance before he hit the ground, but not before he had to let go of the bag. A corner fell open, exposing the deadly poison apple.

Or the lack of it.

The crowd gasped and stepped back. They were frozen in their panic, waiting to die. But nothing happened. One man kicked the sack, revealing the dirty swab rag tucked inside. "That's not poison...."

George leapt to the canvas bag, but it was too late. He'd been exposed as a fraud. A new ripple of understanding passed through the people around them as they turned to one another, muttering that the poison wasn't real—

Cut off by a blood-curdling scream of agony. A thin man in a floppy hat stumbled to his knees, falling out of the crowd, reaching a pale hand for George. The man fell to the ground, coughing, choking, and gasping for air. Horrified, George watched the dying man's chest spasm as he drew his last breaths. The man died, facedown on the ground, curled into a ball at George's feet.

Heat rushed into George's cheeks. Panic raced up his spine. Had he accidentally used poison? He didn't think the power of suggestion worked that way.

"The Truffle Assassin is going to kill us all! Run for your lives!" a rosy-cheeked woman shrieked. The crowd became a stampede, pushing and shoving each other to get away from George and his poison until there was no one left on the docks. Ruthie sprinted from the *Ordek* to the dead man and began poking at his side.

George felt a tug on his ankle. He glanced down, and the dead man took off his floppy hat, smiled, and winked.

"Frobisher!" George exclaimed. He helped Frobisher to his feet, and they wrapped their arms around each other. He barely recognized his former manservant. His eyes were clearer, and his skin was no longer gray. His deep wrinkles had smoothed, making him appear twenty years younger. It suddenly occurred to George that he had no idea how old his manservant was.

"We have to hurry," Frobisher said in a deep voice that rang out clear as a bell. "Miss Byron needs us."

"You're back from the spa!" George exclaimed. "And you can talk!"

Frobisher beamed. "I got my land legs back. The spa treatments worked, my dear boy. Now, no time to waste. Off we go."

Frobisher led them to a one-horse cabriolet that George recognized as belonging to Lady Byron, Ada's mother. George, Oscar, and Ruthie clambered into the seats, while Frobisher leapt onto the driver's platform at the back of the sleek carriage. Frobisher slapped the reins over the horse's back, and they took off like a shot.

George twisted around to talk to Frobisher. "Where's Ada? Is she all right? Was Il Naso with her? Have you seen Don Nadie? Do you know who he is? Where are we going?"

"Miss Byron is fine. She sent me to bring you to C.R.U.M.P.E.T.S. if you arrived at the docks," Frobisher said. "I can't explain everything to you now....I hardly understand it myself. I came home from Vienna, and

326

Dorset Square wasn't the same as I left it. The Society was everywhere, but Miss Byron has been evading them with the use of several disguises. Oh—and she has a message for you," he said, pulling a slip of folded paper from his pocket.

While George unfolded and read Ada's note, Frobisher continued. "This Don Nadie character has taken over our house, George. He's turned it into an exhibit hall for C.R.U.M.P.E.T.S. We couldn't stop him."

George shivered at the thought of Don Nadie turning his beloved No. 8 into a trap for scientists, but Ada's scribbled words pierced his fear. Oscar and Ruthie peered over his shoulder as he recited them aloud: "Follow the tube."

Chapter Twenty-Nine

The cabriolet had almost arrived at Dorset Square when a sudden traffic jam slowed the horse to a stop.

Frobisher abandoned the cabriolet in the middle of the road (much to the dismay of the horse), and they went the rest of the way on foot. After some instruction from Oscar, Ruthie walked down the street with stiff arms and legs, as if she were a mechanical creature on her way to be displayed at C.R.U.M.P.E.T.S.

The neighborhood buzzed with activity. The green of Dorset Square had been trampled by eager onlookers. C.R.U.M.P.E.T.S. was about to start. Carriages were depositing the most distinguished minds in the world at the doorstep of No. 8. Or to be more precise, at the doorstep of

No. 8–10. The construction was completed, and No. 10 was now attached like an enormous house-shaped tumor to the side of No. 8 by a new brick hallway. People streamed in and out of the giant house, which was made even larger by big, swooping tents on either end. The monstrous building swallowed half the block.

"Follow me." George pressed forward to join the line of scientists entering No. 8–10. Invitations were being checked by a doorman in a red coat. Frobisher gripped George and Oscar in fear, but George quickly saw there was nothing to be afraid of—yet. The man was clean-shaven with not a mustache hair left, but George would have recognized his singular nose anywhere. The disguised Il Naso gave him a nod, filling him with confidence.

Still, Oscar hung back from the line. "I don't understand. If Ada knows Don Nadie is coming here, why not just find a way to cancel the event? I'll stand here and yell, 'Fire!' Everyone will go home, and no one will get hurt."

"We'll never get a chance like this again," George said. "We know where Don Nadie will be and what he's planning. He's too powerful to let him get away. We can stop him once and for all today."

"But"—Oscar bit his lip—"are you sure, George? What

if something goes wrong and one of you gets hurt? I think we need more help. Maybe my father and his crew are feeling better—"

"There's no time, Oscar. We can do this. Ada needs us. Please, we can't turn back now."

Oscar nodded and swallowed hard. They all marched to the front door of No. 8, where the doorman greeted them with a smile and a wink. Il Naso handed George and Oscar wire-rimmed glasses and formal black frock coats to wear. "Go inside, little rabbit. Miss Byron will be glad to see you."

Winking at the disguised policeman, George slipped inside and tugged Oscar along the wall. Frobisher shielded them from view. George's house had been transformed. Although George was dismayed by how little it resembled its former self, he was surprised at how well it suited its new purpose of hosting a scientific exhibition. Every hallway and room was filled with the latest inventions, some as large as a horse, some as small as a pencil. From behind his glasses, George goggled at the engines and magnets, steam-powered looms, and gas-powered heaters, as well as powders and crystals of every color that might kill or cure—it was impossible to tell by looking. Dozens of bespectacled scientists milled about in the parlor, which now opened onto the hallway that led into the large room of No. 10. Rows and rows of chairs had been set up to turn No. 10 into a lecture hall. Don Nadie was not hard to spot in a crowd, but he was nowhere to be seen.

George crept to the trumpet-shaped mouthpiece that protruded from No. 8's wall. None of the attendees seemed to be paying attention to it. The speaking tube that led between Ada's house and his was too simple for Don Nadie. Running his fingers along the molding, George found the latch that opened a small door in the wall: the entrance to a narrow passageway that Ada had carved out to install the tube in his walls. "Eureka," he breathed.

Oscar and Ruthie on his heels, George eased into the passage and began to climb the ladder that ran parallel to the brass tube. Because he could not fit inside, Frobisher closed the hidden door behind them with a soft *click*. Together, they ascended into darkness, all the way to what used to be George's bedroom directly above the parlor on the first floor. His heart nearly burst with joy when he pushed open a hatch identical to the one downstairs and saw Ada framed in the square of light.

"Ada!" She crouched on the small balcony next to

a huge apparatus. The hulking mass of metal was suspended over a tub of water, with glass pipes and tubes passing between several copper canisters.

Ada shot up when they entered, beaming. She hugged them quickly. Her time in captivity on Don Nadie's ship didn't seem to have affected her physically as far as George could tell, other than a large scrape on her chin, which had scabbed over.

"George! Oscar! Ruthie! I was worried you wouldn't find a way to get here, but I knew I could count on you. Good thing Frobisher is still in touch with a few of his old pirate friends. Really, Oscar, your father should tell his crew to keep quiet about harboring an infamous killer like George, the 3rd Lord of Devonshire. Messenger birds are *very* easily intercepted," she said, patting Ruthie's head. "Escaping from Don Nadie wasn't nearly as much fun without you, but I have to admit it was far less time-consuming. I didn't even have to use all my acid. Disappointing, really. With all those inventions, they didn't think to design a better pair of handcuffs. Anyway, you're just in time to stop him." She said all this while fastening a sausage-shaped leather collar around her neck, as casually as if she'd seen them only yesterday.

"Ada, I have so much to tell you—you won't believe it, but we found the *real* Star of Victory!"

Quickly, George and Oscar began to tell her what had happened after the Society of Nobodies took her away—but as soon as he got to the strange girl named Stella, who was cursed with good luck, Ada gasped and pieced most of it together. "Ha! How wonderful! Where is your great-aunt?"

George's face fell. "She refused to help us."

Ada frowned, then wrapped George in a hug and patted his back. "I'm sorry, George. The good news is that I think we can defeat Don Nadie on our own," she said confidently.

"His name is George," he corrected without thinking. Now that he'd told the story again, it was getting harder to forget Don Nadie's true name—the one his grandfather had taken from his brother.

"Oh—right," Ada said, a curious expression on her face. She handed wadded-up linen sheets to George and Oscar. "Here's the plan. There are two doors and two windows leading into No. 10. Give a sheet to Frobisher and Il Naso, then each of you will wait by a door or window. As soon as Don Nadie or George senior or whoever he is enters and Il Naso gives the signal that all the members of the Society are inside, you'll shut and lock the doors and shutters and stuff these linens underneath. Don't let anyone in or out until you hear me yell for you. Understand?"

"Where will you be?" George asked.

Ada pointed to a glass helmet just like the diving helmets they'd worn to reach the underwater wreck of *La Isla*. "As soon as the doors are closed, I'll turn on this factitious airs machine. In a few minutes, No. 10 will be filled with a nontoxic gaseous compound similar to the sleeping tea—it will make everyone very sleepy and very giddy, the way you might feel the moment just before you fall asleep after an exciting day. Everyone except me will take a pleasant nap or be consumed by a giggle fit for a few minutes. I'll slide down this rope here and tie up Don Nadie and any other members of the Society who are with him." She gestured toward a coil of rope tied to the banister. "See? Easy as pie!"

"Easy as pie," George repeated distractedly. It *was* simple. His trip to the Galápagos didn't seem to matter at all.

Ada led them through a new hallway to a balcony that overlooked the newly constructed lecture hall below. The rows of chairs were nearly full. The light in No. 10

dimmed as Il Naso began closing the shutters from the outside. The noise from the crowd grew louder as everyone assumed the dimmed lights meant the opening lecture was about to start. "Make sure you're each at a door or window before Don Nadie arrives," Ada said.

George lingered on the balcony for a moment. His gut kicked unpleasantly. Which was wrong. Vanquishing Don Nadie was everything he'd wanted. He shouldn't be feeling nervous or guilty. "What happens after we tie up Don Nadie?"

"We can't trust the police here," Ada said. "Vice-Chancellor Shadwell made that very clear. My friend Princess Victoria has offered her assistance, and I trust her completely. After we take care of our villain, we can calmly explain to her uncle, the King, that you did not try to kill him with a batch of fungus." She gave George a gentle shove toward the stairs leading back to his bedroom. "Hurry. This plan won't work unless all the doors are closed."

"All right." Oscar and Ruthie stayed upstairs with Ada while George took up his position behind the door in the parlor leading into the lecture hall, bubbling over with nerves. Ada was so confident in her plan.

It was a good plan. A good plan to defeat an evil person. Don Nadie was evil.

George senior, the 1st Lord of Devonshire, was evil, he corrected himself. But the words sat strangely in his mind.

Why wasn't he happy?

His great-aunt's words floated into his mind. *Sometimes a broken thing cannot be put back together.*

George pushed his doubts away. A steady stream of people passed by him. Young students with eager faces, hoping to gain knowledge, mingled with older men and women who were loudly debating scientific theories. These were the smartest people in the world, and they had no idea what was about to happen. If Ada hadn't been able to escape and stop him, what would Don Nadie have done to these scientists?

Maybe he wouldn't end up doing anything, George thought as he watched a woman walk by with a colorful eruption of bird feathers exploding from her hat. Maybe Don Nadie was all bluster and boast and when the time came for him to finally do the unthinkable, he would realize his plan wasn't going to make him happy. Nothing that hurt others could ever bring him the satisfaction he was seeking.

"Stop it," George mumbled to himself, and pushed the thought away, more forcefully this time.

From the foyer, a rhythmic, familiar *tap tap tap* on the marble floors began faintly but grew louder and louder. George watched as Don Nadie stepped into the parlor. The wooden boards squeaked under his weight. A tendril of fear curled around George—but then went limp. He wasn't watching Don Nadie stride in. He was watching his great-uncle.

On his stilts, Don Nadie stood head and shoulders above everyone else. He had to crouch beneath the doorways as he walked through them. George shrank back. He pulled up the collar of his coat to hide his face as Don Nadie walked by. But he needn't have worried. All of Don Nadie's focus was on the crowd assembled inside No. 10. His gaze swept greedily over the rows and rows of scientists before resting on the portrait of himself and Estelle hanging over the fireplace.

He'll never know she's alive if I don't tell him, George remembered with a pang.

A few red-coated members of the Society, including Roy, his sister Rose, and Shaw, followed Don Nadie inside No. 10 and took up positions around the room.

The assembled scientists quieted as Don Nadie arrived at a very tall podium, which had been built to match his very tall height. No one was left in the parlor. It was time for Ada's plan to be set in motion. Il Naso whistled a tune from his position outside the front door.

George pushed the door closed softly. He turned the key in the lock and stuffed the cloth under the door, just as Ada had told him to—though his mind churned as he stood with his back to the door, standing straight as a toy soldier. George knew the room was filling with sleeping fumes. Peals of laughter sounded through the door. The gas was working.

George removed the key and peeked through the keyhole. In the tiny sliver of room that he could see, Don Nadie swayed back and forth on his stilts, trying to keep his balance. The woman with the feathered hat was nodding off in her chair. Several members of the Society yawned and lay down on the floor to take a nap. A shadow blotted George's vision briefly. It was Ada, sliding down the rope from the balcony. George looked away. He didn't want to see what happened next.

Maybe Ada's plan was so simple because, for once, it was not the right plan.

For the first time since he had unlocked its secret in Spain, George retrieved the butterfly pendant that he'd taken from Patty's neck. He had kept it with the Star of Victory safe as he traveled across the world. His grandfather had left behind so many clues that led to Estelle that George had accidentally stumbled across several of them without knowing it. Arthur had been practically screaming the secret in the only way he could.

But Don Nadie had no one to help him solve Arthur's puzzles. Estelle had never sent him a letter telling him that she wasn't dead. He'd rejected all the clues Arthur had sent out into the world. How could he have known his sister was alive?

If he had, would it have even mattered?

George inhaled sharply. Maybe his grandfather Arthur Foote hadn't meant for George to destroy his great-uncle. Maybe he had something different in mind for him. Maybe he wanted George to be a hero not by saving the world...

...but by saving Don Nadie, the true George Devonshire.

George's stomach lurched. If Don Nadie saw that his sister was alive, maybe his heart could be softened. Estelle had said that some broken things couldn't be put back together—but what if she was wrong? Scraps of broken things could make something new. Ada proved that every day in her workshop, with every new invention she created. Was it possible to put his own family back together again and make it new?

A tidal wave of certainty rushed through him. If George could draw a picture of his future, he knew who would be in it. George couldn't bear to wait any longer—if he didn't act now, he never would.

He ripped the cloth away from the entrance. A *whoosh* of fresh air filled No. 10 as George threw open the door he'd been supposed to keep closed.

Chapter Thirty

Wait!"

Ada was crossing Don Nadie's hands together behind his back when George burst into the room. Most of the men and women in the crowd were slumped over in their chairs. The rest were giggling blissfully.

The plan had succeeded, but George had failed.

"George, what on earth are you doing?" Ada's voice was muffled behind the glass diving mask, but her anger was clearly audible.

"This isn't right," George said, stepping around anesthetized scientists. He was beginning to feel woozy himself.

Ada began to wrap a length of rope around Don Nadie's

wrists. He smiled up at George sleepily. "He's going to hurt people," Ada chided.

George shook his head. He unwound the ropes from his great-uncle's wrists. "There's another way to stop him. I have to tell him about the real Star of Victory. He deserves to know."

Ada took off her helmet and shook out her dark curls. Her lips twitched, but eventually, she said, "What he deserves is to go back to prison."

George stood over Don Nadie, protecting him. "My grandfather ran circles around him. George Devonshire never felt good enough. His brother and sister were always off having adventures that he never quite understood. They played games and solved puzzles that he couldn't understand."

The face of his own father surfaced in his head, sneering, *Brains of porridge! Brains of porridge!*

Hot tears had begun to stream down George's face. "I know exactly how that feels."

"His situation is entirely different. You're not like him at all," Ada said. She moved toward Don Nadie again, but George blocked her while Don Nadie snored peacefully between his feet.

"Only because I was lucky enough to meet you,"

George said passionately. "Don Nadie was lonely. I thought I was lonely, too—but I was wrong. First I had my grandfather, then Frobisher, and then *you* to show me that I *was* good enough. His family was taken away from him. His entire identity. If he knew Estelle was alive, he might not need the Society of Nobodies to be his family anymore."

Fresh air filled the room and George's chest. Ada studied him like an equation she hadn't yet figured out. The effects of the factitious airs weakened. Don Nadie snorted awake at the same time the rest of the audience regained their senses.

"Estelle," Don Nadie said woozily, as if waking from a dream.

Meanwhile, a chaos of giggles and shouts erupted as people awoke to find the organizer of the conference handcuffed along with several of his cohort.

Ada climbed onto a chair and stood with her arms spread wide. "Calm down, everyone. There's no need for alarm. This man was trying to steal your inventions, but he's been stopped. C.R.U.M.P.E.T.S. is safe."

George spread his arms wide, too, like a shield, to protect his great-uncle until his head was cleared of the factitious airs. Behind him, Don Nadie pulled himself up on the podium to stand on his stilts, staggering like a baby giraffe finding its feet. An occasional hiccup caused him to nearly fall over. But with a sudden jerk of his arm, his eyes flashing, the tall man's fingers reached for the walking stick on his hip. A fearful wave of doubt made George recoil—but Don Nadie's hand hesitated. Instead, he only snarled, "Don't listen to this girl. She's a known associate of this boy, the most wanted criminal in the British Empire, the Truffle Assassin."

All sleepy eyes turned to George. Confusion and fear spread through the audience at the mere mention of the Truffle Assassin. The room erupted into a beehive of activity as the audience looked for a way to escape. Scientists crawled to the windows only to find them shuttered and locked.

"Unhand me. No, no, no—"

Someone grabbed George and shoved him toward the door to the parlor. He broke free and dove at Don Nadie's stilts to keep him from walking away. Ada grabbed on to his other stilt. She began to tie his legs together with a rope, but it was like wrestling a praying mantis.

"QUIET, EVERYONE!" A commanding voice caused a hush to fall over the crowd as surely as a blanket.

344

Beaming, Oscar leaned over the balcony. "Go on, George. Continue your speech."

"Thank you, Oscar." George climbed onto a chair so that he was closer to Don Nadie's height. He looked into his great-uncle's eyes, trying to see inside his mind. "Is this what you wanted? Do you hate me so much that you want to see me locked away just like you were? You want to turn me into a Nobody? Well, I'm not a Nobody, and neither are you."

Don Nadie paused, and George saw a flicker of humanity in his eyes. But the words that came out of his mouth were hard and cold. "Don't pretend that you care what happens to me."

"But I do care. If you'll listen, I can explain—"

"ENOUGH! ENOUGH OF THESE GAMES!" Don Nadie snarled. He broke free from Ada's hold long enough to jerk his walking stick backward, pressing it into a hidden panel in the wall. On the other side of the room, an iron gate descended from the ceiling, cutting off the entrance. They were all trapped inside together.

Ada tightened the rope around Don Nadie's stilts to keep him from moving any further. "I told you, George! He's shown you exactly who he is over and over. He's just a brute who wants to take what doesn't belong to him and use it for evil. *Science* shouldn't be a weapon. Trust me, George. I know exactly what kind of man your great-uncle is. Your grandfather knew, too," she snapped, tightening the rope yet more. "Don Nadie doesn't deserve to be free. Now stop this, before you ruin everything!"

George turned to Ada. "You're smart, but you don't know everything, Ada. People can change. *I* changed."

"You were never going to hurt anyone," Ada said stubbornly.

"No, but Don Nadie has been hurt, too." George took a deep breath and let all his feelings spill out of him. "Don Nadie isn't a machine. He's a human being. You solve problems with your brilliant inventions. But Don Nadie isn't a *problem*. Do you remember what Oscar said on the beach? Don Nadie isn't a villain or a hero. He's somewhere in between. He's—he's my family."

Ada cocked her head, mouth pinched in a tight line.

"When my grandfather was a boy, he lost his parents. Instead of turning their backs on him, the Devonshires made him family. Somewhere along the way, that family got broken. They stopped fighting for each other and they stopped forgiving each other. Some families may be too broken to be put back together, but I don't think this one is. There's still hope. I know there is. Maybe that's why my grandfather never gave up on my father, no matter how much of a disappointment he was. He was trying to tell me that family is the most important thing, whether it's a family that you're born into or one you make with friends. It's more important than money, than fame, than power."

George looked at Don Nadie, who was also George Devonshire, who was also once a boy who lost his parents and his sister. He was angry, but that anger was a mask hiding a deeper pain. It was like looking into a mirror, if mirrors reflected what you could become—and what you once were.

Leaning toward his long-lost great-uncle, George said, "All I've ever wanted was my family back. If one of these scientists invented a machine that could reverse time, I'd use it to change how my parents and my grandfather died. But until then, I'm going to do my best to put the family I have left back together. I think you want the same thing."

Don Nadie swallowed. The fog in his eyes cleared, if only slightly.

George took a deep breath. "All this time, you've only wanted to be the 1st Lord of Devonshire. You chased me across the world for a piece of paper that gave you your name back. Well—Don Nadie didn't have a family, but George Devonshire does." George gestured at the childhood portrait of Estelle and George Sr. behind him. "Your sister is alive."

Don Nadie looked at the portrait quickly, then dropped his eyes to the ground. "How dare you speak of my sister," he said, but his voice was no longer booming. "She's been dead for forty years."

"That's not true," George insisted. "She survived the sinking of *La Isla*. She's been living on Chatham Island ever since. My grandfather left clues behind, but you didn't see them." He swallowed back tears. Beside him, Ada grabbed his hand, giving him strength. "But I'm the biggest clue of all."

Don Nadie scoffed. "How so?"

"He gave me your name," George said. "He named me after *you*, not himself. He wanted us to find each other. I'm sure if he were still alive, he'd tell you the same. That he loved you, and that he was sorry for everything that happened."

"I don't believe you. You only want to see me lose," Don Nadie said bitterly.

"Don't you see? There's nothing to win or lose. Do you

want your name? You can have it. Do you want No. 8? It's yours. Do you want your family back? We're right here. All you have to do is ask. Ask me to be your grandson. Ask me to take you to your sister."

George Foote stepped down from the chair and knelt next to George Devonshire. He clasped his hands together like a beggar. He'd never felt so exposed or vulnerable, like one of Mrs. Daly's baby rats, pink and defenseless and hoping not to be eaten by something with sharp teeth. But he'd also never felt so free. No matter what happened next, he'd done his best to save his great-uncle. Warmth climbed up his back—and soon fuzzy orange arms curled around his neck. He smiled. Ruthie always knew just how to comfort him.

Don Nadie looked as though a frog had jumped into his throat. He stared down at George, his forehead wrinkled in confusion. "You want me to be your—your grandfather?"

"I want us to be a family," George said.

"And so do I," said a quiet voice.

Their heads snapped in the direction of the sound.

Estelle.

Chapter Thirty-One

Estelle's younger self looked out serenely from her portrait while her real self stood nervously in the middle of No. 10, wringing her hands. She still wore her faded apron, as if it were armor she couldn't bear to take off. Don Nadie squinted as he looked beyond the wrinkles and creases to recognize the sister he thought had been lost forever.

"Estelle," Don Nadie breathed, collapsing forward onto the podium. He blinked several times. "Is it really . . ." He trailed off breathlessly.

Estelle only smiled in response, which was all it took to answer his question. The 1st Lord of Devonshire's face contorted further while tears began to stream down his cheeks.

Don Nadie, George's great-uncle, was crying.

Out of the corner of his eye, George saw Ada and Oscar rousing the remaining scientists, who had managed to continue napping through the recent excitement. Estelle took a few cautious steps toward her brother until they stood only inches apart. "It's been a long time. You've grown quite tall."

Don Nadie stomped each foot in response. His stilts retracted beneath his shoes, bringing him down to earth. He wrapped his arms around her and rested his chin on her shoulder. "I thought I had lost you."

"I didn't want to be found," Estelle said.

Softly, George asked, "What changed your mind?"

"Don't flatter yourself into thinking it was you," Estelle said to George laughingly. "Well, it was a little bit of you. And some of Stella and my daughter. Mostly, it was time."

Estelle helped her brother, the notorious Don Nadie, into an armchair. He sank backward and gazed up at her. "Am I dreaming? Just yesterday . . . I—I can't believe it."

George watched as Estelle sat next to Don Nadie. They began to speak in hushed tones. For so long his heart had been grieving for his lost family, but now it was *full* in a way he'd never imagined it could be. An immense feeling of pride almost barreled him over. He had brought his family home. No matter what happened next, he knew he'd done what his grandfather wanted.

Estelle wiped a tear from Don Nadie's cheeks with her sleeve. "You have a niece and a grandniece, too. They came with me to England, and they want to meet you."

"Where are they?" Don Nadie asked, looking around the room anxiously.

George was about to ask the same question when two things happened at once:

A loud crash made his head turn. The iron gate rattled as it was beaten from the other side with the hard knock of a battering ram. *Knock. Knock. Knock.*

At the same time, one of the sleeping scientists groggily sat up and bellowed, "ADA BYRON! GET OVER HERE THIS INSTANT!"

"Pardon..." Ada trailed off as the small scientist ripped off his bowler cap to reveal a shower of dark curls done in the same style as Ada's. He—or *she*, George realized—raised a single dark eyebrow. "Augusta Ada Byron, where have you been?"

Ada went completely pale. "Mother! What are you doing here?"

George's jaw dropped. This diminutive woman was Ada's mother. Though he'd heard Ada talk about her, he'd never seen her, and she wasn't at all the way he'd pictured. She was as dainty as a kitten, though Ada had always spoken of her as if she were a tiger.

Another loud noise came from outside. This time it was a crash as a shutter was ripped from its hinges, flooding the dim room with light. "Erm, Ada—"

Lady Byron completely ignored George, crossing her arms. Her high voice was as crisp as a gingersnap. "What am I doing here? What are *you* doing here? According to Mrs. Somerville, you're supposed to be postponing your enrollment in school to spend more time with your mother, but according to the newspapers, you're supposed to be dead."

Ada crossed her arms back. "Well, *you're* supposed to be in Vienna with Frobisher."

A blush flashed across Lady Byron's face, then was gone. She and Ada each drew up to their full heights, their chins jutting out at the same angle, the same stubbornness stamped across their brows. George took a tiny step back. If mother and daughter were about to wage war, he didn't want to be caught in the cross fire.

Another *thud* echoed in the room. Both shutters ripped away from the window, and soldiers in red coats and tall, furry hats peered in through the glass.

"After a day or two of mud treatments, I started to wonder how my only daughter was adjusting to her new school. I think you can guess what happened when I wrote to Mrs. Somerville to inquire after your health. If I didn't know you so well, Ada, I would have been very worried. I knew you wouldn't be able to resist the most prestigious scientific symposium ever assembled if you were indeed in the land of the living. It would have been nice to have heard the truth from you instead of having to spy on you like a busybody eavesdropping from behind a curtain in some silly melodrama," Lady Byron said, waving a C.R.U.M.P.E.T.S. invitation like a lawyer presenting evidence in a courtroom.

Ada put her hands on her hips. "Spying is your favorite pastime. Admit it. You knew I'd never get into the carriage to go to Mrs. Somerville's school. As long as I'm not embarrassing you in front of your friends, you don't care what I do."

"Embarrassing me?" Lady Byron repeated, bringing a

hand to her mouth in dismay. She shook her head. "Ada, I'm prouder of you than anything in the world."

"I—I..." Ada stuttered, all the defiance on her face vanishing into a look of surprise. George had never seen Ada at a loss for words.

Outside, soldiers began to bash the window with their bayonets, sending glass shards crashing to the floor. Ada and her mother shouted, "Be quiet!" at the same time, but George quaked with every *boom* and *clang* of the soldiers' weapons striking the poor façade of No. 8–10. Once again, Ada's plan had worked well. Too well. Not only had Princess Victoria showed up, she'd also brought an army with her.

Lady Byron addressed her daughter. "I only wanted you to get all that silly adventuring out of your system and devote yourself to your studies. But instead of furthering your academic training, you built another one of your slapdash machines to go on a wild-goose chase. And this time you faked your own death! How do you think that makes me feel?"

Ada's curls quivered, though when she spoke, her voice had softened. "When have you ever cared about feelings? You'd turn me into an automaton if you could. Your perfect little daughter with the well-rounded mind and perfect manners who never causes a fuss and never makes a mistake."

Lady Byron's arms dropped to her sides. "Darling, that's not true. You only hear what you want to hear."

"I hear what you say! Nothing I do is ever good enough for you. Just now you insulted my machines. You called them slapdash! You said you'd take them all away if I made any more." Ada pointed her finger at her mother's chest. "And you called my adventures silly."

"In the case of your machines, I was referring to the incredibly dangerous mistakes you made in constructing them. I can't believe you took that whale out into the water. Did you adjust the hull thickness for the increased interior radius of your new design?"

Ada's cheeks glowed pink. "I hadn't considered the pressure differential."

"Then *slapdash* was a generous term, don't you think? Do your friends know you could have killed them?"

Ada turned to George, her eyes regretful. "It was worth it, though. Wasn't it, George?"

George had no clue what Ada and her mother were

arguing about, but he was going to take Ada's side regardless. "Yes, absolutely. If I was going to be killed by anyone, I'd hope to be killed by Ada."

Ada's spirits seemed to lift. She stood on her tiptoes. "And I won't be shipped off to Somer*vile*'s School for Ladies of Substance when my friends still need my help."

Lady Byron eyed the window, and then the entrance, where soldiers were still scurrying to knock down the iron bars. "I'm declaring a temporary cease-fire. We can continue our battle later. Until then, come here." Chin still stuck in the air, Ada folded herself into her mother's chest. Lady Byron kissed the top of her daughter's head and said into her hair, "I'm glad you're all right."

"Open up in the name of the King!" a voice shouted. After another loud thump, the soldiers lowered a wide plank into the open window like a drawbridge lowering over a moat. A squadron of red-coated guards thundered into the lecture hall, carrying another board, which they laid to make a ramp into the lecture hall leading from the window. They formed a blockade in front of the exits and turned their bayonets on everyone in the room.

"No, please," Estelle said, holding up her thin hand

against the weapons. The sight made George dart between her and the bayonets.

Suddenly, Stella skipped into the room through the shattered window. She was holding the hand of another girl about her age who was covered in ruffles and had a doll-like face framed by perfect golden curls. "Granny, I made a friend!"

The little girl smiled. She let go of Stella's hand, pushing her shoulders back to stand tall. A man of enormous girth squeezed through the window behind them. The buttons on his waistcoat strained to remain closed. George had seen those portly jowls before—on his sixpence. It was George IV, the King of England.

The guards saluted and Ada curtsied. George just stared.

"These are your friends, Vicky?" the King asked incredulously.

Blood rushed to George's head. He was in the presence of royalty. He dropped to his knee. "Your Majesties," he murmured.

The King peered down his nose at George. "Good heavens, isn't that boy the Truffle Assassin who's been trying to kill me? Is everyone in this room trying to kill me? Vicky, I'm very displeased you've brought me here. The first rule of being a monarch is to stay alive. If I teach you nothing else before you become queen, I hope I've taught you that."

Princess Victoria shook her golden curls. Although she looked like a doll, she sounded quite grown-up when she spoke in a thin, clear voice. "The boy isn't the one who tried to kill you, Uncle. I have tried to tell you a million times. We're here because of the Society of Nobodies. They were plotting to form an army to take over the government. The vice-chancellor was part of it."

"Ah yes," the King said. "Terrible name for a society. I never liked that Shadwell, either. His eyebrows were too bushy. That's another lesson for you, dear. Never trust someone who doesn't trim their eyebrows."

George's hand flew to his eyebrows.

"Thank you for the advice, Uncle. I'll remember that," Princess Victoria said. She turned to Ada. "Can you confirm that this is the entire Society?"

Ada bit her lip, looking between George and the King. George spotted Roy and Rose in the crowd, exchanging meaningful glances and silent nods. Suddenly, the two of them stood and bolted for the door, only to be bowled over by soldiers with bayonets. "We captured them before they could do any harm," Ada said.

"Well done," Princess Victoria said. "Guards, take them away."

The guards roughly took hold of the prisoners and began marching them one by one out through the window.

George couldn't bear the thought of his new family member spending the rest of his life in a prison cell. "Where are you taking them?" he asked.

"To Newgate Prison," Princess Victoria replied. "We have all the evidence we need to charge them with a number of crimes."

"But this man has just spent forty years in prison—" George began.

His uncle cut him off. "Save your breath, George. I knew what I was doing when I started this venture. I may belong in prison, but the rest of the Society doesn't. I can't be your grandfather, George, until I've done right by *my* family."

Without his stilts, Don Nadie was able to kneel down in front of George without much effort at all. They stared at each other at eye level for the first time since they'd met inside the house with no door. From this distance, George was able to make out the sparks of lightning flashing in his great-uncle's eyes. "You do look like him, you know."

"I know," George whispered, voice strangled with tears. He wished this moment didn't have to end.

"I can tell you about him one day. If you want," the older George said hurriedly.

George nodded. "I'd like that."

Smiling, Don Nadie turned to the King. "Your Majesty, I've taught these thieves how to steal, how to lie, and how to pretend not to care. If anyone deserves the blame for their actions, it's me. They were young and angry, too malleable for their own good. I shaped them into what they are, so how can they be held responsible for what they've done? Send me to prison, but let them go. I am the one— the *only* one—who should be punished for these crimes."

When he had concluded his plea, everyone turned to the King to see if his heart had been softened. George held his breath expectantly. The King patted his hands on his rotund belly. "Was that supposed to impress me? Take them all out of my sight."

The King of England turned to climb through the window as regally as he could, and it wasn't long before Ada was chasing after him. George broke into a smile when he caught the phrases "Now really," and "Let's be reasonable, shall we?"

George and Estelle flanked Don Nadie as he was led into a prison carriage waiting outside. George didn't know if he'd ever see his great-uncle outside prison walls again, but somehow, that was all right. His grandfather had made him believe that it was his duty to protect a priceless treasure for the rest of his life. But that priceless treasure was his family, and now that he'd found them, they had nestled into his heart for him to carry around wherever he went. He didn't have to solve any more mysteries to feel whole. He had a new life to start, one without secrets waiting to surprise him. He could finally stop looking for his grandfather's legacy. Now he could become it.

"I'll see you soon," George promised Don Nadie. "I think we have a lot of stories to tell each other."

Epilogue

The best endings are not happy endings. The best endings are a little bit sad, and they teach you something about how to be a better person. That's what Granny says. She says in the story with the little girl in the red cape and the wolf, it's a little bit sad because the wolf eats the girl but it also teaches you not to talk to strangers or you'll die," Stella explained.

George stopped sanding the wooden podium that had once been made for Don Nadie. Estelle had adjusted it by sawing off several feet from the bottom. She was in the backyard with Frobisher, adjusting more furniture that Don Nadie had made. "That's not how I remember the story," George said. "I thought a brave woodcutter killed the wolf and saved Little Red Riding Hood."

Stella shook her head. "That's not a good ending! It's too happy. What does it teach you?"

"Watch out, Stella!" Ada cried from atop the neck of a mechanical giraffe she was riding so that she could reach the ceiling of No. 10 with her paintbrush.

Stella danced out of the way just before a glop of yellow paint dripped where she had been standing. It splashed onto the marble floor, and a drop hit George squarely on the forehead. Ada had insisted on painting the walls of No. 10 yellow because it was apparently the best color for encouraging learning and stimulating the brain.

"I'll clean it up," Stella said.

While George wiped the paint from his face, Ada touched up the last swipe of yellow near the ceiling. "I heard a different version of the story," Ada said. "Little Red Riding Hood pushes the wolf into the fireplace and saves herself."

George ran his hands along the edges of the podium, which were now as smooth as glass. "Why are we talking about endings, anyway? My speech is going to be about beginnings. Beginnings are the most difficult thing, according to oratory. You have to grab your audience, be sympathetic, give background on your topic, and present your position. That's very tricky to do. Endings are easy. If you run out of time, all you have to do is stop and say 'the end.' It's not the best way to do it, of course, but it works."

Ada slid down the neck of the mechanical giraffe and landed without a sound. "I don't think we should be talking about beginnings *or* endings. We still have a lot of work to do before the greenhouse can open. Oscar doesn't even know about it yet! He said Captain Bibble would be leaving at high tide, which means he should be here within the hour. What else is on the list to do before he gets here?"

The to-do list was sitting on the podium. Naturally, George was the keeper of the list. He read the items that had not yet been crossed off: "Ask Oscar if he wants to stay here and start his school. Make a sign for the school. Hang the sign outside. Get a proper front door. Find students."

"Find students for what?" Oscar asked, suddenly poking his head through the door from the parlor. His gap-toothed grin was sunnier than the yellow paint on the walls. Ruthie's orange head peered from behind his tousled brown hair.

Stella darted over to the doorway and pulled him inside No. 10. "Students for the school," she explained.

365

Oscar turned around in the big, open room. His eyes lit up with wonder at the gleaming marble floors, the butter-yellow walls, the bookcases, and the podium in front of the fireplace. It was bright and inviting, and was starting to feel like part of the new No. 8–10 instead of the terrible nightmare it had been in George's imagination.

"It looks incredible. I was only on the *Ordek* for a few days, and you've done so much work. I hope when I open my greenhouse for the mind, it looks just like this," Oscar said wistfully. He stared up at the portrait of Estelle and Don Nadie as children hanging over the fireplace, right next to the oil painting of George's grandfather.

"It will. I mean, it does. That is, if you still think that's where you belong." George stepped forward. He opened his palm and showed Oscar a freshly cut iron key.

Oscar's eyes darted from George to Ada to Stella in utter confusion. "How—what?"

"Every greenhouse needs a gardener. No. 8–10 seems to have everything you'd need. What do you say? Will you open your School for Somebodies here?"

Oscar gaped, unable to form words.

"We only have a few more things to do and it will be all ready for you," George continued. "Ada is going to be starting at her new school soon, so she won't be around to get you into any more trouble. I've given Frobisher the original key to the house. He's going to be responsible for keeping the members of the Society away from crime when they get out of prison in a few months. I think a school for finding their talents is just the thing they need to help them lead productive lives as law-abiding citizens."

"And his uncle George has agreed to take correspondence lessons from Newgate Prison," Ada said.

George's heart still beat double time at the mention of his great-uncle. Though the villain formerly known as Don Nadie would serve ten years in prison for his crimes, the King had agreed to give George and Estelle special visitation rights. On Sunday, George and his family had luncheon in the prison yard, which was surprisingly lovely. The brother and sister had agreed to write each other often and to avoid any puzzles in their letters or regrets about the past forty years.

"You're serious? You did all this for me?" Oscar asked, his voice squeaking as he held back tears.

"You can have a place of your own. A place where you can paint and keep your rock collection where it will never sink," George added.

"I've made sure this is the sturdiest house in London," Ada said.

Oscar looked around the room bewildered. "I don't understand. You really did all this for me? But where will you live, George? Aren't you going to stay here? What about your truffles? This is your house. I don't want to take it from you. I've asked my father to take me to the islands of Polynesia when Ruthie goes home to Borneo. Won't you mind if I'm gone?"

"One question at a time!" George laughed. "You're not taking the house, I'm giving it to you and Frobisher. You can do whatever you like with it. I can't stay because I'm going to take a trip with my family. Estelle has asked me to escort her and Stella back to their home in the Galápagos. Our bags are packed and our ship leaves soon."

"And then what are you going to do?" Oscar asked.

George looked at his friends and family, everyone he loved. They were all safe and happy. Being with them made him feel more at home than he'd ever felt. This was where he belonged. Not in a certain house or in a particular place, but with his friends and family. He wished he could freeze time and stay like this forever. In that moment, he felt like the luckiest boy in all of London.

He'd flown over continents, sailed the seas, and lived to tell the tale. The adventures of George, the 3rd Lord of Devonshire, had been wonderful and strange. It was time now for George Foote to find his own way in the world, whatever that might be.

"I don't know exactly where I'm going," George said. "But one day, I'll be able to tell you all about it."

THE END

Author's Note

Dear Reader,

I find myself writing yet another note of apology to you. This book, like the first, contains many lies. There are always lies in fiction; most of them are necessary to entertain you.

Some parts of this book are based on real places, real inventions, and real people—therefore, you might be tempted to think that every detail is correct and historical. Many of them are, and many of them are not. The Alhambra is real, and so are the Galápagos Islands. However, a voyage to the Galápagos like the one described in this book would have taken several months under the very best of conditions, not several weeks. Long sea voyages aren't very exciting, though, so I hope you'll forgive me for this misrepresentation.

Another misrepresentation that I must confess to

making is that the Mrs. Somerville in this story was in no way *vile*, nor did the real Ada Byron avoid the chance to study with her. Mary Somerville was a self-taught mathematician and scientist. Her first husband did not approve of her studies, but after his death, she dove into studying mathematics with full passion. At the relatively advanced age of forty-five, Mrs. Somerville published her first scientific paper and quickly gained a reputation for possessing an extraordinary mind. Soon after, she moved to London, where she met Lady Byron, Ada's mother.

Without Mrs. Somerville, Ada Byron might have remained a footnote in history instead of being recognized as the scientific genius she was. It was Mrs. Somerville who tutored Ada in mathematics, and it was Mrs. Somerville who introduced Ada to Charles Babbage, the inventor of a calculating machine that would change the course of Ada's life. Instead of being obsessed with building flying machines, at eighteen years old, Ada became obsessed with Babbage's invention until the end of her life.

Meanwhile, Mrs. Somerville's own career was far from over. It was just beginning! She became interested in the stars and wrote a textbook explaining the mathematical movements of the solar system. The book was an instant success. She went on to write four more scientific textbooks over the next four decades. She lived to the ripe old age of ninety-one.

Without Mrs. Somerville's textbooks, generations of scientists might never have been inspired to explore the natural world. Planets would have remained undiscovered; electromagnetism might have gone unexplained. Indeed, scientists might not have been called *scientists* at all without Mrs. Somerville. They would have been called *men of science*, but the gender-neutral term *scientist* was coined instead because Mrs. Somerville and other women of science were too talented to be excluded.

I must of course give the final word to the real Ada Byron. She and Mrs. Somerville wrote each other frequently about their shared love of science, as in this letter Ada sent to her on July 8, 1834:

> *I think you must be fond enough of these [machines] to sympathize with my eagerness about them. I am afraid that when a machine, or a lecture, or anything of the kind, comes in my way, I have no regard for time, space, or any ordinary obstacles.*

Acknowledgments

Thank you, dear Reader, for returning to read this second book about Ada, George, Oscar, and Ruthie. As a second child, I have always been keenly aware that firstborn children get all the excitement and fanfare. Therefore, I am grateful that you have given this book the same time and attention as the first.

This book would not exist without the wonderful team at Glasstown Entertainment. For supporting me and giving me the opportunity to tell these characters' story, I do not have adequate words to express my gratitude. Many talented professionals at Glasstown have helped shape this book: Kamilla Benko, Lexa Hillyer, Lauren Oliver, Emily Berge, Diana Sousa, and Stephen Barbara. But my deepest thanks go to Alexa Wejko. She is the genius behind the curtain, and this book is equally hers.

But wait, there is another team to thank! Thank you to Lisa Yoskowitz and Hannah Milton at Little, Brown

Books for Young Readers for their editorial vision. Thank you to everyone at LBYR who has worked on and ever will work on this book: my publicist, Katharine McAnarney, as well as the copyeditors, marketers, and interns who work behind the scenes. Thank you also to Iacopo Bruno for creating another incredible cover illustration.

Thank you to my wonderful community of family, friends, and coworkers who have cheered me on and supported me in big ways and small, especially all my new friends in the Electric Eighteens.

Finally, thank you to my foster daughter for teaching me what it means to be a family. You are the bravest person I have ever known.